TELL NO TALES

ERIK CARTER

Copyright © 2024 by Erik Carter

All rights reserved.

No part of this book may be reproduced in any form or by any electronic or mechanical means, including information storage and retrieval systems, without written permission from the author, except for the use of brief quotations in a book review.

ISBN: 9798321735220

CHAPTER ONE

Noyo, California
The 1990s

THE DIFFERENCE between bravery and foolishness is often just a matter of timing.

But timing had never been Matt Jennings's strong suit.

Matt's boots whispered against the asphalt, a soft *scuff-scuff* in the stillness of the night. Cool air. Misty. 1 in the morning. The Noyo Harbor parking lot was too crowded for that hour, a jumble of cars spread over the dark stretch. Streetlights threw long, unsteady shadows that shifted with each flicker. There was the sound of lapping water. Matt moved carefully, laying each step down as quietly as he could.

He paused, listened. Nothing. Only the soft sound of waves kissing rock and concrete a few yards away. Moving on, he stayed low, weaving through the parked cars, then paused once more, crouching low behind a Chrysler's wheel well.

He tuned his ears to the quiet, listening even more intently. This time, he detected another gentle sound mingling with those peaceful waves—a whisper of movement, several pairs of feet stealthy in their advance, echoing the caution of his own steps taken just moments ago.

Shit!

They were persistent, still on his trail.

He dashed off, angling to the left to avoid one of the harbor's streetlights.

While technically the harbor was in Noyo, hence the name, for all intents and purposes, it was in Fort Bragg—the *California* Fort Bragg, a small city, not the Army post in North Carolina. People frequently confused the city with the military base. Matt was accustomed to it. For his entire life, he'd had to explain away this common mistake.

Fort Bragg, California, was far from the bustling military hub of the same name on the opposite coast. Rather, Matt's Fort Bragg was a quiet place of 6,000 souls—according to the most recent census in 1990—known for its picturesque Pacific views, historic train rides through the redwoods, and the unique Glass Beach.

It was where Matt had grown up.

Now, it could end up being where he died.

He paused again, leaning against the cold metal of a sedan, his breath coming out in controlled bursts. There was a prickle at the back of his neck, a sixth sense honed by years of police work. The men were close, closer than Matt wanted to admit, though he wasn't surprised he'd found himself in this predicament. Things like this'll happen when you unearth something you shouldn't have, something that others would kill to keep buried.

His mind flashed on the investigation, to the documents he'd found, the photos, the connections he'd made. Pieces of a puzzle that someone didn't want completed. At first, Matt hadn't fully understood the scope of what he'd discovered, only that it was big.

But how *could* he have? Things like this didn't happen in lil ol' Fort Bragg, California.

At least, that's what his naïve former self had believed nine months ago.

Matt shook his head, forcing his thoughts back to the present. This wasn't the time for reflection; it was the time for action. He scanned the lot, searching for any sign of movement, any hint of his pursuers. And found one—a slight shifting of shadows to his right.

They were there, closer than he'd thought.

His hand went to the 1911 holstered at his side. He took it out and tightened his grip hard against the handle, squeezing out the shakes, comforted by the weapon's familiar weight.

His eyes narrowed, focusing on the subtle shift in the shadows. There! A figure moved, almost imperceptibly, but enough to notice. Chest thundering, he watched and waited to see if the shadow would move in his direction.

It did.

Oh, shit.

They'd found him.

His heart rate spiked, and he fought to keep his breathing steady. Years of training had taught him to stay calm in the face of danger. Right now, that training was all he had.

Without a sound, he slipped behind a nearby pickup truck. The figure advanced, a dark silhouette against the dim light. It was closer now, looming larger, and the details sharpened—a tall, broad frame, the outline of a hooded sweatshirt, and a hint of metal glinting in its hand.

Matt's own hand was steadier now on his 1911, his senses hyper-aware of every sound, every movement. And when the figure paused...

...Matt took off again.

He darted between cars, a shadow among shadows, moving

with a fluidity born of desperation. His footsteps echoed in the empty lot, as did those of the figure he'd just seen in the darkness—along with several other sets of footsteps.

The parking lot was a maze, a tangled mess of cars and shadowed spaces. But Matt had been here dozens of times. The hometown kid had an advantage over these guys.

Ahead, the path was blocked by one of the men. As the guy shifted into a patch of street light, Matt saw the face and recognized it—Leo Barnes.

Barnes shifted left, right, sweeping his pistol in front of him.

...but he hadn't noticed Matt's presence right behind him.

A second ticked passed.

And another.

Then Barnes moved on. The path ahead was now clear.

Matt grinned as he silently released the breath he'd been holding.

He broke into a sprint. The cold night air bit into his lungs. He was nearing the edge now, the fence that marked the lot's boundary, a final hurdle.

And there it was: the gap he'd spotted earlier.

His exit.

But as he neared the opening...

Crack! Crack!

...the night erupted with gunfire. Bullets sliced the air, slamming into cars and the ground. Matt hurled himself behind a vehicle. The rough asphalt bit into his jacket, scraped his elbows, tore the skin on his palms. He felt the warm trickle of blood on his hands.

Flashes of light. Moving shadows. The men were closing in.

Crack! Crack! Crack!

Matt responded with a blend of training and instinct, firing toward the sporadic muzzle flashes that cut through the darkness. His attackers stayed hidden, approaching cautiously, but their presence was betrayed by the sound of their movements and the occasional muttered curse.

Then ... it stopped. Nothing. Quiet. Whispers. Boots scuffing on concrete.

Matt whipped around, saw the fence, took off.

No time for strategy, just survival. He wove through the vehicles, each movement bringing him closer to that gap in the fence. It was now within reach, just a sprint away...

Then, a jolt to the senses.

CRACK!

A single gunshot, much louder than the previous ones, so powerful that Matt could *feel* it, the raw energy of the thing, knowing instantly what it was: a high-powered rifle round.

He glanced up.

Left.

Right.

There. A sniper.

The man was perched atop a warehouse, just visible in the misty glow of a streetlight, crouched low behind a Barrett M82A1 sniper rifle.

A storied and legendary weapon.

A monster that can punch a hole straight through a wall.

The M82 was mounted on a bipod. A very special bipod. Unlike the famous gun itself, few people would recognize the weapon's bipod.

But Matt did.

Muzzle flash.

CRACK!

A bullet screamed past, nicking the concrete near Matt.

The next was closer—*CRACK!*—thudding into a car inches from his head.

Both shots had been close. But missed. With each shot, Matt had shuffled a few yards farther back from the fence.

The sniper was missing on purpose, using the massive rounds to steer Matt away from any chance of escape. The guy was clearly a pro.

And, of course, the guy had that special bipod.

Matt's heart pounded in his chest, a relentless rhythm of adrenaline and raw fear. A direct dash to the fence was suicide now; the sniper had him boxed in.

Instead, he rushed back into the vehicles, going to the right in a hopeless attempt to skirt the other men scattered throughout the lot. He darted in a wild, erratic path, a desperate attempt at unpredictability.

Each crack of the sniper's rifle shrank his territory, steering him farther from the fence, herding him back into the killing ground.

Two more shots.

CRACK!

CRACK!

The first round struck five yards in front of him. The second hit three yards away, blowing a crater in the asphalt, shutting off the path in front of him. Matt dove behind another car.

A pair of deep breaths.

Then he moved again.

CRACK!

He veered leftward, *had* to veer leftward.

And as he stumbled around a van, he saw the other men emerging—shadow figures moving with tactical precision, weapons raised. Their dark forms seemed to merge into a single threatening entity. His heart raced faster, furiously, as the men closed in on him, their intentions unknown but undoubtedly dangerous.

Matt couldn't go right. Not with the sniper.

Couldn't go backward, either.

Matt was being herded, driven into the arms of his

pursuers. They were closing in, a tightening noose. He heard their footsteps, their hushed, eager whispers as they converged.

CRACK!

Another round from the M82. Debris peppered Matt's pant leg, burning.

Instinct urged Matt to use the 1911 again. But he didn't. Because the other men weren't shooting, only closing in. If they'd wanted to, they could have turned him to mush by now.

He glanced around, assessing his options, finding none. The sniper had him pinned down, and the circle was closing too tight, too fast. No way out.

Only one choice.

He slowly crouched, set his gun down, and lifted his hands.

The sniper's gunfire stopped. The night was suddenly still. Matt's surrender had changed the game. The other men stepped out from their hiding spots, moving with confidence, predators homing in. Each held their pistols steady, aimed directly at Matt. Their faces were all hard lines and cold eyes. They were dressed for the job—tactical gear, urban-style, dark fabrics with copious pockets, blending with the night.

Blank faces. Neither satisfaction nor eager anticipation. Their hardened eyes spoke of lives full of evenings like tonight. Just another job. Professionals, no doubt about it. Hired muscle or professional hitmen.

Matt stood there, arms raised, the cool night air brushing against his skin.

He counted the men closing in around him. Six. And the sniper. Seven of them in total—*at least* seven. They were close enough now that he could see the glisten of sweat on their foreheads, the stubble on their sharp jawlines.

The investigation had led Matt to this awful situation, an investigation that had begun some nine months earlier.

But, really, it had all started with a faded memory—many, many years old.

Seven rough men had Matt surrounded.

Yet he felt oddly detached.

CHAPTER TWO

A WEEK LATER. Mobile, Alabama.

A similar situation. Another man in the darkness, slinking through motionless vehicles.

But this individual wasn't prey; he was a predator.

Vigilante assassin Silence Jones moved through the junkyard, blending with the darkness. Copious shadows made it easy to stay hidden. A place like this didn't want to draw attention to itself with exterior lighting or elaborate security systems or razor-wire-topped fences. A place like this wanted to convince you it was your average, run-of-the-mill salvage lot—not a chop shop.

By all appearances, the interior yard seemed practically defenseless. But Silence knew better. There'd be more guards besides the man Silence had left unconscious at the gate. Plenty of them. That's where Silence's skill set came in. Despite his size—a broad-shouldered six-foot-three—Silence had long ago honed the art of stealth.

The air was thick with the scents of earth and pungent automotive fluids. Rusted cars were piled sky-high, skeletal frames throwing jigsaw-pattern shadows. Tangles of knotted metal frozen in modern-art-worthy death throes. Flat tires, so dry-rotted that their cracked patterns looked like fissured desert earth.

Silence navigated among the teetering steel mounds, scanning for any sign of movement. Above, the night sky was clear, star-speckled, and indifferent to the sprawl of forgotten metal below and its concealed crimes.

He moved with confidence, his earlier reconnaissance paying off. Earlier that day, in the afternoon, wearing a costume of soiled rags, Silence had slipped in with two other men—these guys genuine drifters—and gotten a solid hour of exploration before he and the other two were chased out of Gabe's You-Pull Salvage Yard. Now, each nook and cranny of the place was etched in his memory—potential hideouts, escape routes, danger zones. So as he prowled the darkness, Silence had his bearings and a sense of confidence, following the mental map he knew by heart.

Aside from guards and the man in charge, Silence had one additional thing he was keeping his eyes peeled for: a classic Camaro. This vehicle was his reason for being there. It belonged to a Mobile cop, Detective James Mahoney. Jimmy. An old friend.

Three years ago, in a different side of Mobile, in a different kind of darkness, Mahoney had been Silence's unexpected ally. Silence's mission had been high risk, a human-trafficking ring operating out of Alabama's five largest cities: Huntsville, Birmingham, Montgomery, Mobile, and Tuscaloosa. Being on the coast, Mobile was the center of it all —the ring's importation/exportation hub, all those people in shipping containers coming and going, crossing oceans.

Detective Jimmy Mahoney, a cop with a knack for bending rules when justice demanded it, had provided crucial inside information that had turned the tide. He hadn't expected anything in return from Silence. That kind of trust was rare, almost extinct. Silence and Jimmy hadn't developed a friendship, not in the usual sense, but a bond had formed. Tonight, Silence had a favor to return.

A man named Gabriel "Redline" Oliver had swiped Jimmy's 1969 Chevy Camaro.

You don't mess with a guy's car.

Especially when that guy's chummy with a world-class operator.

Redline was the puppet master, the shadowy figure orchestrating the chaos. Silence had never laid eyes on him, yet he knew the breed—smooth as spilled oil, lethal as the jagged edges of the scrap metal littering the man's salvage yard. At the helm of a parasitic empire infesting Mobile, Redline's game was dismantling stolen vehicles and peddling their parts. But with gems like Jimmy's cherry red Camaro, the vehicles didn't end up in pieces. Instead, they were spirited away intact—aside from filed-off VINs—finding new homes beyond state lines, sometimes even crossing international borders.

Oh, and Redline dabbled in drugs as well, occasionally shipping a little white powder along with a sawn-off catalytic convertor.

Diversification. It's what smart businessmen do.

With so much to pin on Redline, Silence was not only going to bring the Camaro home but also take down the entire chop shop operation. This wasn't a mission his employers, the Watchers, had put upon Silence. It was a self-assigned mission. Personal.

And it had landed Silence in a world of trouble.

Falcon, his boss, had a rule: *No involvement in local matters*. As someone who couldn't just stand by when bad things were happening, Silence loved to break this rule. His activity in Mobile was a particularly egregious affront to Falcon's imperative, as Mobile was only forty-five minutes away from

Silence's home city of Pensacola, Florida, making it particularly "local."

And Falcon knew exactly where Silence was. A GPS dot resided in Silence's right forearm—surgically embedded years ago, a permanent addition—allowing the Watchers to track him in real-time. Zero privacy. Undoubtedly, Falcon was somewhere staring at a computer screen, seething, as he watched the flashing dot representing Silence wink up at him, not from a map of Pensacola but of Mobile.

Oh well.

Right on cue, Silence felt his cellular phone vibrate in his pocket. Cupping his hand over the device to shield the glow of the multiplex screen—lest it betray his position—Silence glanced at the incoming number.

Yep. It was Falcon.

Silence flipped the phone open.

"Sir?" he said, trying to whisper, which was a difficult task, as his voice was distinctively crackly and growly.

"*What the hell do you think you're doing?*" was Falcon's immediate, scathing response.

"Something ... necessary," Silence said, his gaze steady on the murky outlines of forsaken metal.

There was a brief, pregnant pause, then Falcon's voice again. "Are you in a threat zone?"

Silence's eyes swept over the darkened lot, looking for movement, SMGs, sawed-offs. "You could say that."

Another pause from the other end of line.

"Fine," Falcon spat out finally. "You take care of whatever the hell it is you're up to in Mobile. But you'll be sanctioned for this, asshole!"

Beep.

Falcon was gone.

And Silence moved on.

His boots crunched on gravel as he approached a circle of

light cast by a solitary lamp. A guard in a jean jacket was leaning against a car door, cigarette dangling from his lips, smoke twisting languidly upward. He didn't notice Silence until it was too late.

The guy's eyes widened as Silence's hand came down over his mouth, cutting off a screech. He made a move to counter, but Silence stepped inside the strike, swiping the arm aside as he twisted it behind the man's back.

With a second flurry of movement, Silence transferred his hand to the man's neck—while his other hand remained smashed over the guy's face—and applied force. Silence's grip was firm and controlled as he held the guard's writhing, powerful mass in place against the car door. The man's eyes slowly fluttered shut under Silence's sleeper hold. As the man went limp, Silence lowered him to the ground.

Silence moved on.

He slipped from shadow to shadow, his senses alert for any sign of the Camaro, scanning the vehicles. Each car, truck, and motorcycle in the junkyard showed signs of its distinct journey that had led to this final resting place. Once-shiny exteriors were now dulled and chipped. A brown '60-something Ford sat next to a battered '80s Toyota pickup truck, while a Harley, still exuding a sense of pride despite its lack of a headlight or seat cushion, lay dead-center in the aisle ahead of Silence.

For a few drawn-out moments, Silence saw no glimmering candy red paint with oversized metal flake.

But then, there it was.

The Camaro. Even half-covered in tarps—with the other half covered in dust—Redline had no way of hiding that glimmering beauty. The red paint shone out of the filth. For a moment, Silence allowed himself to feel the weight of what the car represented—this was Jimmy's baby, and its illustrious exterior was shining like a distress beacon in the surroundings, calling out to go home.

But the moment passed as quickly as it had come. There was work to be done.

Then, the Camaro could go home.

A sudden clamor of voices. More guards—more oil-stained clothes, more cigarettes dangling from lips, more ugly faces—converged on Silence's location. Three of them, filtering in through the vehicles, coming from different directions, closing in, their steps hurried.

Silence didn't have much time. He positioned himself behind the open door of a gutted sedan, its interior stripped to the bone. He crouched down.

The first guard came into view, swinging a flashlight that sliced through the darkness, a Glock sweeping laterally in his other hand. Silence waited until the beam of light pointed away, then lunged, his hand gripping the tire iron he'd snatched from the sedan's rotted floor pan.

The tool was designed to loosen lug nuts.

But it worked just as well for loosening a man's grip on a pistol.

With a swift, controlled strike to the guard's hand—followed by a piercing metal-to-metal clang—the Glock went flying, making an impressive arch before it fell to the dirt. The man screamed, throwing his face skyward. The tire iron had broken some metacarpals, evidenced by the crack-crack-crack that emitted from the blow.

The man stumbled back before tripping and falling on his ass with a grunt. His flashlight clattered away, doing a dance floor light show on the vehicular shells surrounding them.

The second and third men came together, rushing at Silence with fists drawn, teeth bared. Quickly, Silence assessed their hands. No weapons.

Silence used the sedan's door as a shield, thrusting it into the men's path. As the door gave a cantankerous bellow from its rusty hinges, the collision threw the attackers backward.

Both men fell, landing next to their screaming associate with the broken hand. One struck the ground headfirst, instantly unconscious, and the second barely had time to react before Silence's fist connected with his jaw. He was out before his face hit the dirt.

Silence surveyed the three fallen guards. Groans and ragged breaths briefly filled the otherwise silent night air. He stepped over the men, his eyes set on the makeshift office building in the back—a corrugated steel structure with a waveform-warped roof, scarred with rust and illuminated by a flickering sodium bulb.

Silence approached. The heavy door gave in with a moan as he pushed it open. The place was a graveyard of scattered papers, the hodgepodge office furniture coated in a thick patina of dust. A metal desk stood sentinel at the far end, folders strewn across it. Behind the desk: Redline.

He sat on an old leather chair, the springs sagging under his weight. Dark hair. Greasy beard. A boulder for a head. The guy looked like someone who never expected to be surprised, yet there he was, his eyes widening ever so slightly as they locked with Silence's.

A prideful smile wiped away the shock on Redline's face. He was clad in a leather jacket—maroon and heavily scuffed—and his hands were large, thick-knuckled, resting on the arms of the chair with the tense stillness of dormant power. His face bore the scars of many encounters; they seemed to itch for one more.

"Well," Redline said in a voice reminiscent of one of his reclaimed motors, "I've never had anyone get past my boys before, stranger. But here you are."

He pushed himself up from the chair with a graceful ease that belied his size. The springs squeaked.

"I want..." Silence said and swallowed. "The Camaro."

The swallow was a deliberate pause, one of Silence's techniques for soothing the pain that presented itself in his throat every time he spoke. Years back, a violent encounter had stolen his voice, leaving a mess of torturous scar tissue. Now, each word was a struggle, a reminder of the life-changing incident that not only took his voice but also, more indirectly, led to his dark life as an assassin.

Redline stiffened, his eyes flickering with a hint of unease as they glanced at Silence's throat. Not only was Silence's voice pain-inducing, but it was a guttural sound, harsh and raspy, like gravel tumbling down a metal chute. At that moment, Redline's confidence wavered, his brow creasing slightly. Silence knew that reaction well—the shock, the unspoken questions. Few people could conceal their bewilderment at Silence's voice upon hearing it for the first time.

Gathering himself, Redline said, "The Camaro, huh?" The now-bolstered voice registered a blend of amusement and admiration. "She's a beauty, ain't she? 1969 SS, candy-apple red. Bad news, friend. She's spoken for."

Silence's mind flashed on Jimmy Mahoney. Stubbly. World-weary. Twice divorced. A good cop. A good man.

"You're damn right..." Silence said and swallowed. "She is."

Silence lunged forward, closing the gap between them in an instant.

Redline reacted with that inexplicable speed of his, a flash of movement as his hand reached beneath his jacket. But Silence was quicker, darting to the side just as the knife gleamed in the piss-yellow fluorescent lighting.

The blade sliced through nothing but air, and Redline's momentum carried him forward, unbalanced. Silence capitalized on this, spinning around and using Redline's weight against the man. His leg shot out, connecting with Redline's knee. The joint buckled with a sickening pop, and Redline roared in pain and fury. The knife clattered away.

Redline's burly frame tumbled toward the metal desk. He hit with a meteoric impact, causing the desk to spill its documents into the air. The metal structure shuddered, and a dust cloud blossomed skyward, Los Alamos style.

Silence closed in. He unleashed a barrage of strikes, each one precise and vicious. Even sprawled on the desk, Redline was formidable, his large frame still lending advantages—reach and raw strength—and he swiped at Silence with broad, arcing hooks.

A palm strike to the sternum forced Redline back farther on the desktop. Then came a Muay Khao knee strike, a specific technique from the broader Muay Thai martial arts style, right into the man's ribs. Redline howled.

Silence's hand shot out, fingers finding their way to the pressure point just beneath Redline's ear. It was a precise attack that reduced the marauding bear of a man to a mere puppet, his movements suddenly jerky and uncoordinated as his strings were cut. Redline's eyes rolled back as he slid off the desk, landing with a thunderous crash that shook the flimsy office.

Silence stood over him, chest heaving but otherwise unmoved by the violence he'd wrought. He watched as Redline lay sprawled on the linoleum floor, breathing shallowly.

Turning on his heel, Silence made for the three-foot black metal safe—its door slightly ajar, like an invitation—tucked away behind the battered desk. Stacks of greenbacks were visible in the door's gap. Silence grabbed a plastic garbage bag from the metal shelving on the opposite wall.

He began shoving all the money in. It was piled haphazardly inside the safe, a display of Redline's greed and disorganization. Silence worked quickly.

Redline groaned as he inched his head off the floor and watched through swollen eyes. He lifted a heavy, feeble hand in Silence's direction.

"Come on, man. That'll wipe me out!" he said.

Silence didn't turn to face him. "That's the point."

He grabbed the last stack, put it in the sack, and pulled the plastic drawstrings. He'd done a mental count as he worked: roughly thirty thousand dollars.

All the pain Redline had brought. All the distress.

And only thirty grand in the coffer.

Pathetic. In more ways than one.

With the money bagged, Silence stood up and stepped past Redline, who continued to paw the air feebly. Silence pushed through the heavy, groaning door back into the night. He strolled to the Camaro and carefully pulled back the tarps, mindful of Jimmy's precious paint. The car was already going to need a hell of a detail job after its misadventures with Redline and his ghouls; Silence didn't want to add to the problem.

The door closed with a satisfying thud. The car smelled good—aged leather and well-kept trim—a scent that came from careful preservation in the face of inevitable entropy. This was augmented by remnant smells of Jimmy's high-end car care products; he used them on everything—dash, seats, steering wheel. Jimmy was cheap as the day is long—the kind of guy who ate exclusively off discount menus and only bought clothes with coupons—but not with the Camaro. With the car, Jimmy spared no expense. Silence couldn't wait to give it back to him. He inserted the key, turned it, and the engine growled, a beast shaking awake.

Silence eased the car away, the headlights cutting through the darkness as he maneuvered through the maze of the junkyard. As he hand-cranked the window down, he heard approaching sirens, distant but drawing closer. He gave it some gas.

The gate was already open; Silence had taken care of that upon first arriving less than half an hour ago, right after dealing with the first of Redline's goons, leaving the man incapacitated. Driving past this unconscious man, Silence gunned the Camaro, speeding through the opening, shooting past the black BMW sedan he'd left parked outside.

The BMW had been his ride from Pensacola. It was Silence's vehicle, but he was ditching it. Like Redline's offerings, the BMW was a ghost car, untraceable. However, whereas Redline filed away his vehicles' VIN numbers, Silence's car had a bogus VIN that couldn't be tied back to him. The Watchers provided Silence with automobiles like this, switching them out every six months.

Since the BMW was completely undetectable and Silence needed to return the Camaro to Jimmy, he was abandoning the car. This move was going to piss Falcon off even more.

Oh well.

He was out, the Camaro prowling the streets now, the sirens fading into the background as he put distance between himself and Redline's operation.

Earlier that evening, on his way to the salvage yard, Silence had crossed an overpass and saw a homeless encampment—a tent city—in the muted, amber-colored glow below. The Camaro roared onto that same overpass now, and as Silence looked down, he saw the homeless community once more.

That same amber glow of streetlights he'd noticed earlier covered the place, casting long shadows from concrete pillars across the patchwork of tarps and tin. Life thrived under this cover of relative darkness. Dozens of souls. Steel barrels with fires sent smoke spiraling skyward, and figures gathered close to them. A creek-like mud puddle wound its way through the center of the disorder.

Silence eased off the gas, the Camaro's engine humming as he coasted over the tent city. He cranked the window down farther, all the way. The night's chill kissed his face. He reached over, snatched the garbage bag from the passenger-side floor, loosened the tie, and thrust it into the slipstream. It caught, billowed, and broke open. Cash tumbled into the darkness.

Bills swirled in the air, fluttering down into the encampment. Cries of shock and joy rose up as people emerged from their shelters, hands reaching, snatching at the money raining upon them.

Silence crushed the now-empty plastic bag, wedged it under his thigh, then stomped the gas pedal. The Camaro roared.

He drove on.

CHAPTER THREE

THE FOLLOWING EVENING. Pensacola, Florida.

"I said, your best friend is dead," came the woman's voice from Silence's cellular phone, reiterating her moments-earlier statement. "How do you feel about that?"

Though the woman couldn't see the gesture, Silence shrugged as he said, "Fine."

"Fine," Doc Hazel repeated. "You feel fine after hearing your best friend has died?"

"Not my friend," Silence said, shortening what should have been *He's not my friend any longer*. Broken English was another of Silence's techniques to help with the torment in his painful throat.

He settled back into the ancient sofa, triggering a rush of musty air, which made him wrinkle his nose. He was in the domain of Mrs. Rita Enfield, his next-door neighbor. The house mirrored its owner and the sofa beneath him—all steeped in age. The scent of the past lingered everywhere.

A mildewy scent.

Ugh.

"But he *was* your best friend," Doc Hazel said.

"Haven't even thought..." Silence said and swallowed. "About Matt Jennings..." Another swallow. "In years."

He honestly hadn't. In fact, when Doc Hazel first said the name *Matthew Jennings* a few moments earlier, he hadn't even remembered it. It took him a moment to realize she was talking about a person from his past. A boy. Someone Silence hadn't known since he was eight years old, almost nine, back when Silence went by his original name, Jake Rowe.

The woman on the phone, Doc Hazel, was Silence's Watchers-mandated mental health professional. He had never asked for counseling, but his employers rarely considered his wishes. Despite Silence's reluctance, Doc Hazel's presence had become a constant in his life, one of the few things that remained unchanged and dependable.

She was his designated mental health professional, yes, but more generally speaking, she was a Specialist, one of Silence's innumerable superiors in the Watchers. While the higher-ups made the hard decisions and assassins like Silence conducted the dirty work, Specialists were the organization's backbone. They handled tasks such as providing weapons and money, compiling intel, and covertly navigating the legal system. All the logistical nitty-gritty matters.

Including mental health services.

Doc Hazel was perpetually fixated on discussing Silence's damn feelings, and tonight she'd wasted no time in getting to the heart of it. As soon as Silence had picked up the phone, she informed him that Matt Jennings had passed away and demanded to know how it made Silence feel.

Silence had blinked, thought, tried to remember.

Matt Jennings.

A figure from his distant past, dredged up from the depths of his memory. After reacquainting himself, Silence had waited a beat, seeing if he actually *could* feel something. A pang of grief, perhaps. Or a twinge of nostalgia. But there was only a vague sense of recognition, like passing a faintly familiar face on the street, the face of a child.

"How'd he die?" Silence said finally.

"Car accident," Doc Hazel said. "Driving on Highway 1, north of Fort Bragg, almost to Westport. Lost control on a curve, went over the guardrail, down the rock face, into the Pacific."

"Alcohol?"

"No. Coroner suspects a heart attack."

Heart attack... Damn. The guy had been Silence's age.

In fact, several months younger.

"No wife, no kids," Doc Hazel said. She paused, and Silence could hear the faint rustle of papers in the background. "Suppressor, Matt was your best friend growing up, yes? Surely his passing must mean something to you."

She'd called him *Suppressor,* which was Silence's codename. He also had the numerical title Asset 23 and its shortened form, A-23.

After hearing that Matt Jennings had suffered a heart attack at what seemed to Silence at a relatively young age, Silence certainly did experience a few feelings: unease, apprehension, and a sense of his own mortality.

But these weren't the feelings that Doc Hazel was probing for. She was looking for touchy-feely emotions. She was looking for something more personal.

Silence was about to reiterate that he barely remembered Matt Jennings. But stopped. Because that wasn't entirely true. Even as the words had formed on Silence's lips, a memory surfaced unbidden.

He saw himself at eight years old, young Jake Rowe, tall for his age and big, too, facing down a pack of sneering bullies. And Matt, loyal Matt, standing shoulder to shoulder with Jake, fists clenched at his sides, ready to wade into the fray.

It was the only distinctive memory Silence could find of the boy. A single snapshot, preserved in muted colors, soft focus, and grainy texture.

Just that one moment. Everything else about the childhood friendship was hazy, distant. Unimportant.

So Silence replied with, "Nope."

"I see," Doc Hazel said. Silence could hear her pen scratching on a notebook. Always with her damn notes, her damn analyses. "Well, I'm sure it's at least mildly intriguing to you. Anyway, I'll see you soon, Suppressor."

Silence's brow furrowed.

See you soon? What the hell?

"What does that mean?" he said.

But Doc Hazel had already hung up, leaving him listening to the blunt sound of the dial tone.

Slowly, Silence lowered the phone from his ear, staring at the rubber buttons, which glowed yellow-green with their backlighting. A trickle of unease worked its way through him, cold and slithering. He shook it off, snapped the phone shut, and tucked it back into his pocket.

Banishing the thoughts of Doc Hazel, he turned to the other woman, the one who was with him, sitting a few feet away. Rita Enfield had waited patiently during the phone call, perched on a clawfoot armchair opposite Silence, her feet dangling short of the floor, her milky eyes fixed on him despite being entirely sightless. Mrs. Enfield was small, black, frail, and had hair even whiter than her functionless eyes. She lived next door to Silence, across a gravel drive, in the East Hill neighborhood of Pensacola.

She coughed—a dry, brittle sound, low but with enough punch to fold her in half, squeeze her eyes shut. It wasn't the first time she'd done so since Silence had come over.

They sat in her living room in a Victorian house that had once been beautiful. In the right hands, its antique charm could have shone, but under Mrs. Enfield's watch, it had morphed into something unsettlingly eerie. The place was perpetually shrouded in darkness—a logical choice for a blind resident—and though Mrs. Enfield was meticulous in her cleanliness, a sense of lingering dust somehow pervaded. The aged and peculiar decor tipped the atmosphere into haunted house territory.

Silence eyed the smut romance paperback sitting in his lap. There it was, that damn cheesy cover he was all too familiar with. *Kingdom of Desire*'s title gleamed in gold. Tristan, rugged in his white tunic and boots, held Lady Vivienne, dressed in a beaded golden gown. Their long hair swirled in an ethereal breeze, bodies entwined, lips almost meeting, defiance and longing etched against a castle backdrop.

Silence reached for the water glass on the table in front of him. Another sip would buy him some time, a few more seconds of avoidant delay. He dreaded reading *Kingdom of Desire* almost as much as he dreaded speaking to Doc Hazel.

After so much experience with the book, the *Kingdom of Desire* storyline was imprinted in his mind: a young royal, recklessly in love with a commoner, ensnared in high-stakes drama. He could recite chunks of it verbatim. He'd read the romance novel aloud to Mrs. Enfield countless times over the years. The ritual lasted for months because Mrs. Enfield insisted on keeping the reading sessions to a maximum of fifteen minutes, mindful of Silence's painful throat.

Mrs. Enfield listened to copious audiobooks, mostly on tape but also recently on CD, having been introduced to the wonders of digital discs via her former caretaker, Lola. But *Kingdom of Desire* had long been out of publication and had never received the audiobook treatment. And though it was an obscure title, it was Mrs. Enfield's favorite book and a treasured component of the old woman's life.

That's why Silence had read the novel to her in his awful voice so many times.

Every Thursday afternoon.

That is, every Thursday afternoon when he was home in Pensacola, not out in the field eliminating the scum of the world. It was a small kindness for the elderly, childless widow who lived next door to him. An attempt to bring some color into her sepia-toned life.

Finally, Silence opened the book to the page he'd left off at before he took the phone call. He proceeded.

"'As he took her...'" Silence read and swallowed. "'By her delicate shoulders...'" Another swallow. "'Lady Vivienne felt a shiver more pronounced...'" Another swallow. "'Than her racing heart, which—'"

Tiny, wrinkled, dry fingers reached out and patted his knee.

"That's enough, Silence," Mrs. Enfield said in her withered voice. "Your throat needs a break after all that reading and your phone call."

Hallelujah.

Silence snapped the paperback shut and put it beside his water glass on the table. As he shifted back into his cushion, his companion on the loveseat purred louder.

Baxter.

A massive and perpetually peaceful orange tabby.

Silence looked at the cat, and when their gazes met, Baxter's purring grew even louder, his yellow eyes going dreamy with admiration.

A long trail of drool hung from the side of Baxter's mouth. The cat was a constant drooler, and now a small puddle was forming on an old bath towel that Silence had placed on the antique loveseat to protect it.

Silence turned to find another pair of eyes looking at him, these milky and lifeless. Mrs. Enfield smiled serenely, and her hands were stacked on her lap—a mound of dark, dry skin atop her washed-out lavender dress.

"Thank you, Si," Mrs. Enfield said, her withered voice full of warmth as she settled back into the armchair. She was always overtly appreciative when he read the book to her.

Her eyes closed as a reminiscent smile came to her face. She pointed to a framed photo on the console table—her deceased husband, Rory.

"Rory would sit right where you are and read to me for hours. I do cherish that book."

She told him this almost every time he read to her—how Rory was the first to begin the tradition of reading *Kingdom of Desire* to her when she went blind in her thirties.

Years after Rory's passing, Mrs. Enfield's caretaker, Lola, began reading the beloved book to the old woman. When Lola left for Tennessee, Mrs. Enfield's new next-door neighbor inherited the duty. So Silence continued, dutifully unfolding the tale of *Kingdom of Desire* again and again, year after year.

Mrs. Enfield's eyes were still closed, her lips still upturned in a contented smile. Silence looked to where she'd pointed a moment earlier and saw the familiar black-and-white framed photo: Rory, a bulky African American man with an inviting smile and a mustache, alongside a twenty-something version of Mrs. Enfield, whose eyes were clear and bright, not yet blinded. They were wrapped in each other's embrace in a park setting.

Next to the photo of Mrs. Enfield and Rory was another framed image.

A photo Silence loathed...

Housed in a pewter frame, it was Lola's doing, having snapped the photo at Mrs. Enfield's behest a few years back. Dominating the frame was Silence, rigidly seated in one of those bizarre chairs of Mrs. Enfield's, Baxter sprawled contently on his lap. The cat stared boldly out of the photograph, blissful and drooling on Silence's pants. Baxter's grin far outshone Silence's, which was more a mask of confusion, a grimace because of the bizarre and uncomfortable situation: posing with a cat on a peculiar chair for a photograph meant for a blind individual.

"Couldn't help but overhear your phone call," Mrs. Enfield said, pulling Silence's attention away from the wretched photo. "So sorry to hear about your friend passing away."

Though she couldn't see the gesture, Silence shrugged.

"Like I said…" He swallowed. "Barely remember the guy."

Mrs. Enfield tutted softly and shook her head. "Now, Si, don't be so quick to dismiss it. Even if this man didn't mean much to you, maybe your friendship meant the world to him. Shared experiences can impact people in different ways, you know."

Silence grinned. There was something about Mrs. Enfield, a certain perpetual wisdom that shone from her like a soft light. It was an insight into the human condition, and it reminded Silence of the wise-beyond-her-years discernment C.C., his deceased fiancée, had fostered when she was alive. Mrs. Enfield had the uncanny ability to understand people, their silent battles and unspoken dreams. He suspected this was somehow tied to the woman's blindness, the unrequested dismissal of the visual world, focusing on the other senses, a lifetime of careful observation.

Mrs. Enfield settled back in her armchair, her hands folded primly in her lap. "I'm reminded of my own dear friend, Louisa," she said. "Years and years ago, when my Rory first fell ill, Louisa showed up on my doorstep out of the blue. She gave me a casserole dish and a shoulder to cry on. It was a small gesture, but, oh, it meant the world to me at the time."

Mrs. Enfield sighed.

"I always meant to tell her how much that kindness meant to me, how it had buoyed me during one of the darkest times in my life. But you know how it goes—life has a way of getting away from us. There's always something else that needs tending to. And then one day, I got the news that Louisa had been killed in a car wreck. Just like your friend. Senseless tragedy. I never got the chance to thank her."

Silence shifted in the loveseat, its fossilized frame creaking beneath him.

He didn't respond.

Mrs. Enfield leaned forward and laid a hand on Silence's arm. Her skin was thin as parchment, dry to the touch, threaded with veins and knobby knuckles.

"I suppose what I'm trying to say, dear, is that we never know how much time we have with the people we care for. Best to appreciate them while we can, to make sure they know the impact they've had on us."

Her blind eyes glanced toward the console table behind them, somehow finding the framed picture of her and her late husband. Silence looked, too. Rory smiled out at them from behind the glass, frozen in time. Forever young.

"Do you ever think about that?" she continued, suddenly taking on a philosophical tone. "About never knowing how much or how little people mean to each other. I sometimes wonder if I loved my Rory more than he loved me. That sounds bad, I know, but I also consider that maybe it was the other way around; maybe *his* love outshone mine." She paused and looked away, white eyes dancing side to side in thought. "But in the end, I suppose it doesn't really matter. I loved that man, and he loved me."

Silence frowned. The notion Mrs. Enfield had just put forth struck him as patently absurd. People who are in love do and *should* love each other the same. That was the sort of love he'd shared with C.C. He knew, with a bone-deep certainty, that he and C.C. had loved each other equally. Passionately, fiercely, all-consumingly. And in equal measure. Anything less than that was unthinkable, a pale imitation of the real thing.

Mrs. Enfield turned her head to cough, the sound dry and hacking. It seemed to rattle in her bird-thin chest, shaking her shoulders with the force of it.

Just a cold, Silence knew. Nothing to worry about. But still, at her age, any illness was a cause for concern.

His mind circled back to the story she had just shared about the lost chance to express her gratitude to a dear friend before the friend passed away.

It was just a cold, he reassured himself again. Mrs. Enfield wasn't going anywhere. She'd be around for a long time yet.

But still...

Mrs. Enfiled had done a lot for Silence. While he'd given his gratitude to her whenever it was appropriate, he'd never offered an overarching show of appreciation for *all* she'd done for him.

He felt the words welling up inside him, burning the back of his throat: *Thank you.* He wanted to say it to Mrs. Enfield, to tell her how much her friendship meant to him, how much her quiet wisdom and gentle guidance anchored him in a world that often felt like a turbulent sea.

But he didn't.

His throat was raw and screaming at him after all the *Kingdom of Desire* reading and the phone call with Doc Hazel.

He could tell Mrs. Enfield *thank you* soon enough.

It was only a cold.

She was gonna be okay. She'd still be there tomorrow when his throat felt better.

Silence's phone rang again, shrill and startling. He fished it out of his pocket, glanced at the screen.

Doc Hazel.

Again.

He flipped open the phone.

"Yes, ma'am?" he said.

"Suppressor," Doc Hazel said, something odd in her tone that he couldn't quite place. "I need you to do something for me. Go look out the window."

A cold sensation flashed over Silence, across his entire body, a pissed-off varietal of dread.

A sort of reluctant intuition...

He stood up and approached Mrs. Enfield's large picture window, which looked out over the quiet East Hill street. He pulled back the drape, looked out.

There, a few yards to the left, standing in a pool of streetlight on the sidewalk in front of the adjacent house, *Silence's* house...

...*was Doc Hazel.*

She, too, had a cellular phone pressed to her ear. A coy little grin played on her lips. She raised her free hand and waved, fluttering her fingers at Silence.

CHAPTER FOUR

Curtis Hyer stood under the towering presence of the abandoned factory complex, its crumbling structures throwing indistinct shadows in the faint moonlight. The tangle of rusted steel and shattered windows formed a labyrinth before him. A distant wail of a train echoed through the walls.

Hyer's team—a group of men as tough and unyielding as the environment they navigated, the same men who tracked down Matt Jennings the previous week—fanned out on either side of him. They moved with a fluidity born of countless nights like this. Hyer had handpicked each man, not just for their skill but for their unwavering loyalty. In lower regions of society where allegiance was currency, trust was worth more than gold.

Their target was Leo Barnes—a name that had become a stain on Hyer's operation, a man who'd made a horrible mistake. Barnes had been with the team last week at Noyo Harbor in Fort Bragg. After that operation, Barnes vanished. He'd been gone for several days. But Hyer's other men—the competent ones—had tracked Barnes down to this location on the outskirts of Sacramento. Barnes's mistake had to be accounted for.

So did his fleeing.

Ducking beneath an angled pipe caused a shock of pain to jolt through Hyer's back. He'd pulled a muscle working out the previous night—during his last set of lat pulldowns, he suspected. Gym injuries came with the territory of midde-agedness, but it was worth it, because years of disciplined training had honed Hyers physique into a formidable weapon—broad shoulders, a thick chest, and powerful limbs.

He paused, sensing something amiss. With a subtle hand gesture, he signaled his team to halt. Boots scuffled on concrete as the other men stopped on either side of him. Hyer detected faint sounds—a generator's distant hum, the scurrying of some vermin animal, and wood brushing against metal.

But there had been something else he'd noticed a moment earlier...

He listened.

Listened...

There. There it was. A barely perceptible shift of the night's chorus. Footsteps.

Barnes was close.

Hyer's lips curled into a slight smile. He took off, leading his men deeper into the maze of alleys, their footsteps both muffled and amplified by the thick layer of dust and debris.

They approached an old warehouse at the end of the pathway, and Hyer held up a hand again. The team halted. Hyer carefully peered inside the building, his eyes adjusting to the darkness. The place was filled with rows of crates and crippled machinery. Hyer could make out a faint silhouette crouched behind a crate in the far corner, his back pressed against the wall.

A slight movement from the figure made the man's face

glow in the moonlight before it escaped back into shadow. It had happened in a flash.

But Hyer had seen him in that half second of opportunity. Barnes.

Without hesitation, Hyer signaled for his team to spread out and flank the man. They moved swiftly and silently, weapons at the ready. Hyer didn't match their pace. He advanced slowly, falling behind the others as he went deeper into the warehouse, his eyes never leaving Barnes. As he approached the frightened man, Hyer ran a hand over his clean-shaven head and down his face, calluses catching on his neatly trimmed beard.

"Oh, Barnes," he called out in a calm voice. "Whatcha doin' back there?"

Barnes peeked over the top of the crate. Eyes wide. Lips wet. He struggled to form words, his mouth opening and closing.

"I ... I..."

The other men positioned themselves on either side of Barnes, pointing their pistols at him.

"No one's gonna hurt you," Hyer said with mock kindness. "You made a mistake. But we're a team. We stick together no matter what."

Barnes hesitated for a moment before slowly standing up from behind the crate. He looked around at the others, his former associates, all armed and ready to take him down if necessary.

The air was thick with the scent of rust and decay. Barnes, cornered and shaking with fear, looked nothing like the man who'd been part of Hyer's trusted circle only a few days ago. His usually confident posture was now hunched and trembling with fear. The once clean-shaven and well-dressed man was now disheveled, his clothes torn, and his face contorted with panic. He was pale. Sweat beaded on his forehead.

He looked small and vulnerable.

Hyer stepped forward, his boots echoing through the cavernous space. He stopped when they were twenty feet apart, close enough for Barnes to see his eyes.

"Tell me, bud. Why'd you run last week?"

Barnes licked his lips. He looked around at the other men and their guns, then up at the rusted metal beams straining under the building's weight.

"I ... I had to," he muttered weakly.

"Had to?" Hyer folded his arms. "You're gonna have to do better than that."

All around them, the warehouse seemed to hold its breath, the silence punctuated only by the distant groaning of metal and the soft creaking of old wood. Hyer's men were statuesque in their positions, eyes fixed on Barnes.

"I have a family, Mr. Hyer," Barnes said. "My chick. My two boys. I knew if I failed you ... they'd be dragged into this. I couldn't let that happen. Not to them."

Barnes's hands were raised slightly as though to surrender or ward off an invisible blow.

"You think I'd hurt your family?" Hyer scoffed. "That's an insult." He paused. "And that's your final mistake."

Then, in an ultimate display of disrespect, he turned around entirely, his back now facing Barnes, and let his gaze drift over the other men, one by one. With a casual flick of the wrist, Hyer gave the order to no one in particular, to all of them.

"Finish it."

Without a second glance, he strode away. The sound of Barnes's voice, high-pitched and desperate, was quickly drowned out by the deafening blast of gunshots that echoed through the dark night sky.

Hyer winced slightly at the sheer volume of it, but he continued to walk, otherwise unaffected. He reached into his pocket, pulled out a pack of cigarettes and a lighter, and lit one up. He took a long drag.

As he exhaled, smoke snaked out of his lips, mixing with the sharp tang of gunpowder.

The hole in the operation had been plugged.

But deep down, Hyer recognized this as just the latest in a series of complications. First came the drawn-out saga with Matt Jennings. Direct fallout from that mess led to Barnes, one of Hyer's top guys, dropping the ball. And then Barnes had almost vanished, slipping away like the smoke dancing out of the glowing end of Hyer's cigarette.

It was clear to Hyer that a new strategy was necessary. Time to get ahead of the game, to tighten the procedures to the point where leaks were impossible.

Given the magnitude of the operation, nothing less would suffice.

CHAPTER FIVE

SILENCE'S HOME was a study in monochrome, hues of black, white, and gray dominating the decor. Sleek, modern furniture made of glass and metal occupied the space, their cold, hard surfaces softened only by the occasional oversized houseplant, vibrant greens offering a stark contrast to the otherwise muted palette. The air was still, punctuated only by the soft, rhythmic ticking of a minimalist clock on the wall. It was a space that echoed Silence's nature: efficient, uncluttered, and stylishly subdued.

And with him in this space, seated across from him, was Doc Hazel.

She was in his house.

Enraging, yes.

But oddly complementary. Aesthetically speaking. Doc Hazel's clinical precision and cold attractiveness—with her angular face and sharp skirt suit—subtly echoed the meticulous and structured ambiance of Silence's lair.

This visit differed from their usual meetups in nondescript places around the country. While Doc Hazel had previously come to see him twice in Pensacola—once at the airport and another time at a rental office downtown—this was her first time visiting his actual home.

His home...

She'd commanded him—*commanded* him ... in his own home!—to sit on his sofa, a long, gray, squarish stretch of non-tufted fabric with firm but comfortable cushions. Silence knew why she'd done so. As his mental health professional, she would soon have Silence lie down on the couch before he was commanded to talk to her and reveal more than he was comfortable with. A classic shrink session.

He glanced at Doc Hazel. Her presence was a reminder of the Watchers' ever-present control in his life.

The air between them was charged, crackling with the tension of Silence's controlled rage, but Doc Hazel's demeanor was as calm and clinical as ever. Silence felt her evaluating him, her hazel-colored eyes sharp and discerning. She had a way of looking at him that seemed to strip away layers, probing for the truth beneath. This skill made her excellent at her job.

...or her *supposed* job, rather. Silence had always held the suspicion that she wasn't a genuine mental health professional, that she was simply playing the part for the sake of the Watchers.

Silence shifted, the sofa creaking under his weight. He tried to get comfortable. Couldn't. These mental health counseling sessions were a requirement. And he hated them.

Doc Hazel's expression was as unreadable as always. She was in a gray business suit, tailored like it was painted on her. Her glasses were huge, the kind that said smart but with a twist. Hair pulled back tight, no-nonsense. Her legs were bare, like the last time he saw her, a tradition of sorts. The shoes were Prada black patent leather high heels, glossy.

Doc Hazel's professionally alluring attire during the sessions was undoubtedly another mind game played by the

Watchers. Generally, the organization treated Silence and all the other field agents like tools, like pawns. Indeed, that's why they were called "Assets." Each of them was a criminal, a righteous individual who had committed a heinous act, liberated from their judicially imposed sentence and conscripted into a society of murderous vigilantism until their debt had been paid off. The Watchers instructed their Assets to perform unthinkable acts that had slim chances of survival.

Paradoxically, the Watchers also treated Assets like royalty, with many fringe benefits such as healthy salaries and free vehicles.

The mental health sessions made Silence uncomfortable, not just for the sheer sake that he didn't like being mentally poked and prodded but also because of the always slightly seductive way in which Doc Hazel dressed—those short business skirts, bare legs. The Watchers were well aware of Silence's undying love for his deceased fiancée, C.C., and forcing him into these meetings with an attractive woman—who looked slightly like C.C., a fact that was undoubtedly not coincidental—was another example of their mind game bullshit.

Doc Hazel sat there, patiently waiting, a wordless challenge. Silence knew the drill. He would be told to lie down soon, to begin the session. To talk. To open up.

But Silence wasn't going to fold.

He wasn't going to lose this game of chicken.

Finally, a tiny smirk broke through Doc Hazel's clinical facade

"I'm sure you know why I'm here," she said.

Silence nodded. He could guess...

"I'm your punishment," Doc Hazel said. The tiny smirk persisted. "Falcon wants you to know he's irate about the stunt you pulled last night in Mobile."

Guess confirmed.

Silence's fists clenched on his knees.

He didn't respond.

"We can't have Assets acting on their own accord," Doc Hazel continued. "It goes against everything we stand for."

Silence's jaw tightened as he felt the irony of her words like a punch to the gut. *Everything the Watchers stood for?* His mind filled with resentment as he considered the Watchers' version of justice—cold and calculating, illegal, murderous, meted out from the shadows. Judge, jury, and executioner rolled into one clandestine body, answering to no laws but their own, yet they got pissed off when a member of the organization took matters into their own hands.

Infuriating.

He remained silent, clenching his jaw even tighter.

"Falcon handed me the reins, so I've come up with a suitable punishment for your actions," Doc Hazel said.

Silence leaned forward.

"I thought this meeting..." he said and swallowed. "Was the punishment."

"Yes and no."

Doc Hazel reached into her attaché case and pulled out a photograph. She handed it to Silence.

It was an old photograph, 1960s, faded and worn at the edges with a washed-out palette—not unlike the mental photograph Silence's mind had conjured when Doc Hazel had first called—and Silence started when he saw the face looking back at him.

His face.

But also *not* his face.

It was his former face before the Watchers' facial reconstruction surgery. It was also much younger.

Jake Rowe, eight years old. Standing beside him was Matt Jennings—slightly younger, several inches shorter. Medium brown hair. Piano key pattern of teeth. Both boys wore the carefree expressions of childhood.

The phone call he'd received earlier...

The first of the two calls from Doc Hazel...

...when she'd told him that Matt Jennings had died.

Silence stared at the photograph. He thought again about the incident with the bullies, the memory that had surfaced when Doc Hazel first called, a fleeting moment in a long-forgotten past. But looking at this frozen snapshot in time stirred nothing in him. No sorrow, no nostalgia. Just a distant recognition of a life that once was. Matt Jennings had been a part of that life.

And Silence hardly remembered the guy.

As Silence handed back the photo, Doc Hazel leaned forward to take it, her eyes not leaving his.

"This visit isn't just a checkup, Suppressor." Her voice was steady, but there was an edge to it, a reminder of the authority she wielded. "I know you despise delving into your feelings, so *that* will be your punishment. You're going back to Fort Bragg, California, to reconnect with your roots, reexamine your childhood, come face to face with the death of your former best friend, and report back to me."

Silence looked up from the photograph, met the woman's robotic gaze.

Blinked.

His jaw tightened even more.

The self-assigned mission in Mobile. Jimmy Mahoney's Camaro. Candy apple red. Annihilating Redline's chop shop operation. Raining the ill-gotten money down upon the homeless camp.

Silence had known there would be fallout. But being sent back to Fort Bragg, his own ghost-ridden hometown, was a twist he couldn't have possibly anticipated. He felt a surge of anger, a rare emotional response from a man who prided himself on his control.

"And there's more," Doc Hazel continued. She reached into her bag again and pulled out a brochure, bright pink and garishly cheerful. In bold letters, it proclaimed:

YURA'S YOGA RETREAT

On the cover was a woman whose name was listed as *Yura Turner*. Silence noticed the energy first, exploding out of the still image, the kind that suggested both kindness and confidence. Yura appeared to be of mixed race, Asian and African American. Her broad smile reached her eyes, and her hair was a fireworks display of curls. She had the kind of face you remember.

Beneath Yura's name was a tagline:

It's *YURA TURN* to live your best life!

Clever...

Flipping the brochure open, Silence read the main text:

Discover the Serenity Among the Giants with Yura's Yoga Retreat!

Nestled within the majestic Navarro River Redwoods State Park, Yura Turner, owner of Sacramento's hottest chain of yoga studios, invites you to an unparalleled experience. Step away from the hustle of the city and immerse yourself in tranquility among nature's giants ... *the redwoods!*

This retreat is a haven where traditional yoga harmonizes with innovative approaches. Experience energizing classes suitable for all levels with Yura's expert guidance.

Join us and see why Sacramento is buzzing about Yura Turner. Embark on a rejuvenating journey with Yura's Yoga

Retreat, where every breath aligns with the natural grandeur of the redwoods. *A transformative experience awaits you!*

Slowly, Silence looked up at Doc Hazel.

He blinked.

"This," Doc Hazel said, gesturing to the brochure, "is your chance to dive into those stubborn emotions you keep locked away. Yura's approach is unconventional, but effective. It's time you faced what you've been avoiding."

Silence couldn't find the words to respond. The idea of attending a yoga retreat, especially one hosted by someone as exuberant as this Yura Turner lady, was absurd. It was so far out of his comfort zone that it bordered on the surreal.

He looked at Doc Hazel and found her expression blank, as always.

"The yoga retreat is being held in a state park, only half an hour from Fort Bragg," she said, answering the question he hadn't asked, "After you spend a day reconnecting to your hometown roots, you'll spend the next couple of days in the redwoods realigning yourself. Two birds, one stone."

Silence's mind raced.

A yoga retreat. Fort Bragg. Matt Jennings. His past and now this unexpected, bizarre future colliding in a way he couldn't have predicted.

He set the brochure down on the coffee table, its garish colors clashing with the desaturated tones of his home.

He didn't respond. Instead, he stared into Doc Hazel.

Hard.

It had no effect.

"Your flight's set up for tomorrow morning," Doc Hazel said, her tone matter-of-fact. "Everything's been arranged, as per protocol."

Silence glanced again at the brochure. Yura Turner's smiling face beamed up at him from the coffee table, all teeth and sunshine. He wondered what Ms. Turner would make of him—an assassin who could easily conceal his identity but couldn't hide the shadows in his eyes.

It promised to be quite the encounter, that was for sure.

"Speaking of protocol," Doc Hazel said, "lie down, please."

Here it was.

Finally.

The moment Silence had been dreading.

He hesitated. Exhaled. Then complied.

Lying down, his six-foot-three frame devoured the sofa's length. As he stared at the ceiling, he felt Doc Hazel's eyes on him, probing, analyzing.

"Your friendship with Matt Jennings," she began, her tone methodical, "you've stressed that it was many years ago, during you childhood, and relatively brief."

Silence grunted in affirmation.

"Your relationship with Cecilia was also brief."

She always referred to C.C. by her full name, Cecilia. It made things more clinical. It was yet another way of toying with Silence.

"You were together for less than a year before her death. Only a matters of months," Doc Hazel continued. "And, similar to your friendship with Matt Jennings, the relationship is now years in the past, distant, nothing but an image in your mind's rearview mirror."

Her statement hung in the air like a challenge, a provocation.

Silence's response was immediate and visceral. He shot up onto an elbow and glared at her.

"C.C. and I were engaged!" he snapped, sending a jolt of fiery pain down his throat. He swallowed. "Being engaged..." Another swallow. "Negates the brevity." Another swallow. "It was serious. *Real!*"

Doc Hazel was unshaken, unimpressed. She just looked right back at him. "If you say so."

Silence's fists quivered. He pictured C.C.—*alive, smiling, holding his arm, dead, in a pool of her blood, the blood had been warm, going cold, face destroyed, beaten relentlessly*—and his fury boiled. But he held back his words, clenching his teeth tightly together. He lay down, returned his attention the ceiling, the anger simmering within him.

I can't believe she said that! a female voice said in Silence's head. *The gall! The nerve!* The voice sighed, and then, in a more controlled tone, it continued, *It's good that you said nothing back to her, that you just laid back down. Yes, love, control your anger. Control* all *your emotions. Self-soothe. Good, love.*

It was C.C.

An internalized version of C.C. often spoke to Silence in his mind. In life, she'd been wise well beyond her years, and Silence relied on that wisdom even after her death. She spoke to him during times of high stress, which were frequent in Silence's line of work as a vigilante assassin.

Doc Hazel was still looking at him, still blank-faced. "Calm down."

In Silence's mind, C.C. sighed again.

Yes, I suppose Doc Hazel's right about that, C.C. conceded. *You should relax now. Relax, love.*

After a moment, Doc Hazel's voice cut through the tension, and she was slightly gentler now. "Relax, Suppressor."

Her phrasing was creepily, infuriatingly similar to what C.C. had just said.

"Let's revisit your beach fantasy," Doc Hazel said. "Describe the house to me." Her tone was ever so softer yet, clinically coaxing.

Yes, go with this, love, C.C. added. *This is an excellent exercise to help calm that wild mind of yours.*

When she was alive, C.C. had helped Silence—who C.C.

had known as Jake Rowe—to organize his chaotic mind space. She'd done so with techniques like mind mapping, meditation, breathing exercises, and self-reflection. The spectral version of her now residing in Silence's head continued with the work and sometimes encouraged Doc Hazel's methods.

Silence closed his eyes. Took a deep breath.

And tried to conjure a mental image of the fictional beach hut.

This was a sporadic yet ongoing component of his sessions with Doc Hazel: being asked to describe the beach-life-post-Watchers fantasy she had coaxed out of him years ago. It was a glimpse into what life could be like for Silence in an unknown future when he was no longer an Asset.

He began, his terrible voice sounding remote.

"Small beach house..." he said and swallowed.

With those first words, his mind began painting the mental picture. A simple home. One-bedroom. Right on the beach. Palm trees and undergrowth created a shadowy area past his door. He looked through the window.

Good, love, C.C. said. *Good. See it. Feel it.*

Waves. Gentle waves lapping ahead.

"Very good, Suppressor," Doc Hazel said. "Go on."

Beyond the window, there was bright sunlight.

"Blue sky," Silence said and swallowed. "Clear water, sparkling." Another swallow. "Palm fronds."

Very good, love. C.C said. *Keep going.*

Palm fronds—verdant and bright—rustling ahead of him. And a stretch of sand, glowing in the sun.

"Sand," Silence said. "Sense of..." He swallowed. "Peace. No more killing. Just..." Another swallow. "Sun and palm trees."

Silence's voice had taken on a distant quality, as if he were truly there, in that imagined place of peace and solitude. For a moment, the room, Doc Hazel, the weight of his past, and the uncertainty of his future faded into the background.

Good, love. Very good.

"Very good, Suppressor," Doc Hazel said, her wording once more gratingly similar to that of C.C. "You may sit up."

Silence's eyes flickered open, the images of the serene beach hut flashing out of existence, back into the stark black-and-white-and-houseplant-green reality of his living room.

He sat up, looked at Doc Hazel.

They stared at each other.

Then Doc Hazel stood, her movement gracefully feminine yet still robotic. She glanced at the bright pink brochure on the coffee table.

"Have fun in California," she said with a hint of snark. A brief pause, then with a wry grin that confirmed the snark, she added, "Good luck, Suppressor."

Silence remained still, watching her.

That line, *Good luck, Code Name*, was the standard Watchers line offered to Assets being sent into the field for another life-threatening mission.

But this time, there was no imminent danger, no mission fraught with peril.

This time, he was being sent to his hometown to reconnect with his roots, a form of punishment.

This time, Doc Hazel was just being a smartass.

Doc Hazel snapped her attaché case shut and took off, Prada heels click-clacking on Silence's gray-stained hardwood floor.

Silence watched the door shut behind her.

He was alone.

Fort Bragg. A yoga retreat. Yura Turner. It was a lot to process.

Usually, he enjoyed his downtime between missions.

This time, he'd rather be in the field.

Suddenly, C.C.'s voice—devoid of the standard serenity, returning its earlier rage—erupted in his head.

Bitch! C.C. screamed. *That goddamn bitch! Not only did she question the strength of our bond—AGAIN—but now she's sending you to the other side of the country just to toy with you.*

Silence ran a hand up his cheek, over his forehead, through his hair. Sighed. He closed his eyes, trying to calm both himself and C.C. down. As much as he wanted to agree with her, *he* needed to be the voice of reason for once.

Internally, he replied, *They're punishing me, yes, but I'm sure that ultimately, this has something to do with their efforts to sort out my mental health. Good intentions, I suppose.*

All C.C. could say in response was, *That BITCH!*

Silence let out another sigh. His shoulders drooped.

There was an absurdity to all of this—using his own internal voice to calm down another voice inside his head, that one belonging to his deceased fiancée, someone who'd been dead for years.

Despite how much he hated his mental health sessions with Doc Hazel, maybe it wasn't such a bad idea for a guy like him to receive them...

He returned to the coffee table and picked up the brochure and the old photograph. Yura Turner's positivity screamed at him from the Pepto Bismol-pink page—cavernous smile, manically happy eyes. Next to her, young Jake Rowe and Matt Jennings smiled up at Silence as well.

He held the items in his hands and stared at them for a long moment.

Though C.C. had gone silent in his head, he sensed she was still there, still fuming, still stewing about what a "bitch" Doc Hazel was.

Silence blinked.

Then headed for his refrigerator to grab a Heineken.

CHAPTER SIX

THE NEXT MORNING.

Silence maneuvered the glimmering black BMW—another freebie from the Watchers, a perfect doppelgänger to the one he left behind in Mobile—through the subdued streets of Fort Bragg, California. The car's polished exterior gleamed against the town's understated charm. He took in the painted murals and the quiet dignity of the Victorian storefronts that stood as guardians of the past.

The little kid version of himself never recognized how charming this town was, he realized.

Cruising along, the car hummed a quiet tune over the aged asphalt, passing the weathered signs advertising the famous Skunk Train—a historic ride through the redwoods. The Pacific braced the edges of town, the relentless waves a soundtrack to his trip down memory lane. He observed the tourists mingling with the local fishermen, a dance of the daily catch against the backdrop of a misty early morning. The salt air mingled with the scent of fresh pine. Fort Bragg had polished a few of its edges, but the grit of a working town underpinned its streets, honest and unpretentious.

The place had changed with time, naturally, but the essence of what he remembered lingered in the air—the scent of the redwoods and mom-and-pop restaurants, a fragrance that had seeped into his childhood. On the south side of town, technically in a separate municipality, Noyo Harbor bustled with activity, its docks alive with the clang of metal and the shouts of fishermen. The harbor, a vital artery, pulsed with life even in the early morning, much like Silence suspected it had during the heyday of the logging industry and the railroad boom.

Driving through the streets, Silence was enveloped by a wave of nostalgia ... which made him curse Doc Hazel internally. Fort Bragg had been his home from birth to shortly before his ninth birthday when his family moved cross-country to Florida.

His father, Kirk Rowe, a hotel manager, had been an unassuming man when the family lived in Fort Bragg—not too loud, not too bold, neither mean nor particularly kind, neither smart nor stupid—but when Silence's mother, Angela, died shortly after the family transplanted to Pensacola, things changed. The death shattered the balance of the family.

Silence's father, unable to cope with the loss, had surrendered to his grief and the bottle. With that unremarkable aura of his, Kirk Rowe became a complete but mundane alcoholic. He was never violent with his son Jake, only negligent. He didn't disappear from Jake's life, only became an empty shell, unenthusiastic, uncaring. This left Jake to navigate his adolescence essentially alone.

It was a loss of both mother and father.

Jake suffered loss again years later as an adult.

C.C.

Silence remembered the numbing pain, the abyss of loss so profound that he had sought solace in the same escape his father had—alcohol. It was Mrs. Enfield, his brand-new next-door neighbor, who became a surrogate mother and steered him away from that path. Her gentle yet firm guidance had kept him from spiraling down the same dark road as his father. She'd been his anchor, his spiritual guardian.

As Silence drove through Fort Bragg, memories of Florida and California intertwined in his chaotic mind space.

And C.C.'s voice was unable to help.

Quickly, everything swirled into a mental haze.

The graveyard was filled with neatly arranged headstones, some leaning with age, others freshly placed. The sea breeze tousled the trees, branches swaying gently. Churned brown earth of the newly filled grave in front of Silence contrasted against the lush grass and vibrant flowers surrounding it.

The headstone was marble, the lettering clear, the edges sharp, revealing pale stone beneath—brand new. At the top was *MATTHEW DELVIN JENNINGS*.

Silence held the photograph Doc Hazel had given him. It showed two boys: one, Jake Rowe, a younger version of himself, and the other, Matt Jennings. The picture was faded, the edges worn.

He looked from the photo to the name written in stone above a pair of dates, the latter of the two being just ten days back. *MATTHEW DELVIN JENNINGS*. The name sounded alien to Silence, a distant echo from a life he'd left behind. They'd been friends once, in the innocent days of childhood. But the memories were just shadows now, elusive and intangible.

His most vivid recollection of Matt was not of their friendship but of an incident. The schoolyard incident. The memory his mind had presented the previous day, where he—or Jake, rather—had stood up to some bullies. Matt had been there, but only as a bystander, a peripheral figure in the unfolding drama.

Silence's thoughts were interrupted by a voice calling out another foreign-yet-familiar name.

"Jake!"

The sound cut through the stillness of the cemetery, jolting Silence from his reverie. Silence started.

Jake...

That was the name he'd heard. Surely not Jake, as in Jake Rowe...

The voice called out a second time, a bit louder. "Jake!"

For a moment, Silence thought that someone had somehow recognized the man standing before Matt Jennings's grave as the man's childhood friend. This was fleeting, however, as two more realist realizations quickly banished this nonsense: first, the notion that Silence hadn't stepped foot in Fort Bragg since he was a nine-year-old, not a six-foot-three grown man; and second, that even if someone thought they saw Jake Rowe, that person wouldn't recognize him now, as the Watchers had surgically reconstructed Silence's face upon his conscription into the organization.

Still, when he turned, his senses were heightened. He found the source of the voice: a man walking in his direction, waving a hand...

...and looking directly at Silence as he drew closer.

Somehow, this man recognized Jake Rowe.

CHAPTER SEVEN

BRYAN HOLIFIELD MOVED CAUTIOUSLY across the cemetery, his footsteps muffled by the soft, well-tended grass. He approached the tall figure standing solemnly at Matt's grave, a man he suspected to be Jake Rowe.

This guy *had* to be Jake Rowe.

When Matt had told Bryan about his childhood friend Jake, he described the kid as unusually tall for his age. The man before Bryan stood around six-foot-three, which aligned with that description. Moments earlier, when Bryan called out "Jake" a second time, the man had turned, just slightly, enough to acknowledge the sound. It was a subtle yet telling reaction.

As Bryan drew nearer, the man turned fully in his direction. Bryan scrutinized the guy's appearance. There was a certain exotic and severe quality in his features, a sharp contrast to Jake's boyish face in the photographs Matt had shown him. In fact, the man ahead had such severe facial features that he bore a striking resemblance to the actor who played Gilbert Grape, the teen idol from *21 Jump Street*.

A bigger, broader version of that actor.

Bryan closed the distance between them. "Hey. Jake Rowe, right?"

But before the guy could respond, Bryan's eyes fell on the photograph in the man's hand. It was an old, faded image of two boys. One of the boys he recognized as a young version of Matt—Bryan knew this because Matt had shown Bryan many pictures from Matt's youth—and the other was the tall kid Matt had pointed out in some of the photos: Jake Rowe.

Bryan looked from the photograph and back to the stranger.

"It *is* you!" Bryan said.

The man's reaction was not what Bryan expected. For a brief moment, he seemed taken aback, almost stunned by the recognition. His dark eyes scanned Bryan's face as if searching for answers in an unreadable script. But it also seemed ... like the guy was hesitating for some reason.

Finally, the man nodded slowly and said, "Yes."

Bryan's forward progress came to a sudden halt. His shoes scuffed in the grass, and he sucked in a breath.

That voice!

It was a ruinous, crackling timbre, harsh and unsettling, as if each word scraped against a rough surface before reaching the air. A hideous voice to hear. Bryan had never experienced anything like it.

He realized he'd taken an involuntary step backward, so he put an awkward smile on his face and closed the gap, extending his hand.

There was another moment of strange hesitation before Jake accepted the handshake, just staring for a long, confused beat.

Bizarre...

Jake clasped with a massive, calloused hand that pulsed with strength. Bryan felt like the guy could easily snap his bones if he wanted. Jake must've been a real gym rat.

"I'm Bryan Holifield," he said, his voice steadier now. "I was one of Matt's mentee in the Due North Mentorship Program."

He paused, watching for any flicker of recognition in Jake's eyes. There was none. Due North was a local program akin to Big Brothers Big Sisters of America.

"It's a Mendocino County thing," Bryan said. "An initiative designed to support at-risk youth in the community."

Jake said nothing, only nodded. His face remained so stony and blank that Matt felt the sudden need to take a step back again. But he didn't.

"Matt talked a lot about you," Bryan continued, "and the impact you had on him when he was young. He told me about a time when you stood up for a smaller kid against some bullies. He said he learned about justice that day, and it ultimately inspired him to become a police officer."

Finally, he got a response out of Jake. And it wasn't what Bryan expected from this evidently stoic and brooding man. Instead of a nod of acknowledgment or a word of gratitude, Jake simply looked confused, as if the information didn't quite fit his understanding. His brow furrowed slightly, deepening the lines on his severe fashion model face.

Since this man was such an important part of Matt's life, Bryan felt compelled to tell him the truth.

Yes, Jake needed to know.

Bryan gulped. "I want to tell you something important," he said, leaning in closer and scanning their surroundings for onlookers. None. They were the only ones in the cemetery in the early morning. "Matt didn't die in an accident. He was murdered."

The statement hung heavily in the air between them.

Again, Jake reacted, this time immediately and pronounced. His eyes narrowed, a spark of interest igniting in their depths. The ruinous, gravelly voice finally made another appearance, this time with a command: "Talk."

Bryan swallowed hard. He had just told this man, a near stranger, that the guy's childhood friend had been murdered. The weight of this implication, the potential devastation, was not lost on him.

But Bryan found himself surprised by the unexpected thought that sprang into his mind: maybe Jake Rowe could be the one to help Bryan shed light on Matt's death. After all, though Matt had never known what became of adult Jake Rowe, it was the influence of the kid version of Jake that propelled Matt to become an investigator.

Yes, Jake could help Bryan.

Help him figure out the truth of how Matt was murdered.

It was a strange notion—wildly impulsive—yet Bryan found himself clinging to it. The countless times Matt had spoken highly of Jake over the years echoed in his mind, nudging him toward this sudden conclusion.

Bryan cleared his throat, steadying his voice.

"Do you remember Curtis Hyer?" he said, watching Jake closely.

Jake shook his head.

"He was a year ahead of you and Matt in school," Bryan said. "A bully."

Jake looked away, eyebrows knitting for a moment, before there was a small glimmer of recognition in his eyes, followed by the faintest of grins playing on the sharp edges of his severe face, the sort of smile that comes from reclaimed memories, ones a person thought he'd forgotten forever. He gave a slight nod.

"Well, he never grew out of that stage," Bryan said. "He turned into a real shithead adult. Matt had been looking into him. He thought Hyer was involved in something dark."

"What do you mean..." Jake said and swallowed. "'Looking into him'?"

"Matt was a cop, like I said, but specifically, he was a detective."

For a second time, a smile broke through Jake's surgically cold features, this time unabated. A big smile. And shockingly warm. It looked almost like pride, like Jake was impressed with what Matt had turned into.

Suddenly, the smile vanished.

"What crimes did..." Jake said and swallowed. "Matt suspect of Hyer?"

"Murders," Bryan said.

Jake didn't respond, only shifted slightly closer.

"See, I'm a forensic accountant," Bryan said. "Matt was a big influence on me. I was never gonna make it as a cop, but I'm good with numbers, and I wanted to be like Matt, and..." He trailed off, realizing he'd gone way off track. He shook his head. "Anyway, a week before Matt supposedly drove off the cliff, he left me these records—expenses, I believe."

He fished a pile of papers from his attaché case and thrust them into Jake's hands.

"Take a look. Maybe they'll explain what Matt was onto."

Jake scanned the spreadsheets, eyes dancing down the columns, across the rows, his expression growing more intense. Then, without a word, he reached into his pocket and pulled out a wallet. From it, he produced a card and handed it to Bryan.

At first, Bryan thought it was a swipe card—it was plastic with the right proportions and rounded corners—but as he turned it over, he found no magstripe on the back. The plastic was opaque; he could see his palm through it. A pair of dark blue stripes cut diagonally down the left side, and dark blue, raised lettering gave a message:

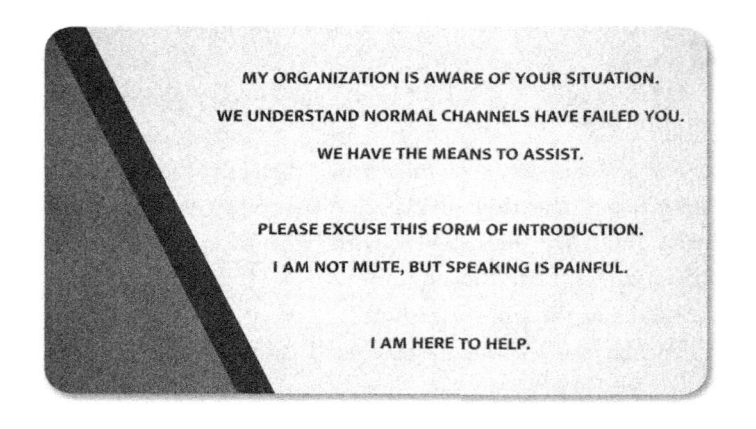

> MY ORGANIZATION IS AWARE OF YOUR SITUATION.
>
> WE UNDERSTAND NORMAL CHANNELS HAVE FAILED YOU.
>
> WE HAVE THE MEANS TO ASSIST.
>
> PLEASE EXCUSE THIS FORM OF INTRODUCTION.
>
> I AM NOT MUTE, BUT SPEAKING IS PAINFUL.
>
> I AM HERE TO HELP.

Bryan stared at the card momentarily before looking back up at Jake.

"I don't understand. It says your organization is aware of my situation, but—"

"Usually I work..." Jake said and swallowed. "Under different circumstances."

"Okay, Jake, but—"

"Don't call..." Jake said and swallowed. "Me that."

"Huh?"

"Call me Drew."

"But your name is—"

"Drew." He gave Bryan a long stare, narrowing his dark eyes slightly. "Only call me Drew."

Bryan stared at the card, still feeling a sense of confusion and unease wash over him. He couldn't quite put his finger on it, but something about this whole situation seemed off. The secretive nature of Jake—or rather Drew now—and this mysterious "organization" he was apparently a part of, it all seemed too good to be true.

A fed.

Jake had to be some kind of fed.

Too good to be true, indeed!

Bryan again felt that rush of optimism he'd experienced moments earlier when he intuitively thought that Jake might be able to help him uncover how Matt was murdered. Now, this feeling was not only bolstered but justified.

If Drew was indeed some sort of secret agent, it aligned with Matt's awe and respect for Jake Rowe. This man, who had once been Matt's childhood hero, was evidently now a mysterious figure embroiled in clandestine activities.

"All right. 'Drew' it is," Bryan said with a shrug. "Can you help me, Drew?"

Bryan held his breath, waiting for Drew's reply. The quietness stretched on until Drew finally broke eye contact and stared into the distance. Bryan furrowed his brow, trying to read the expression on Drew's face but coming up with nothing.

Then Drew turned back to face him.

And gave a firm, decisive nod.

"Let's go," Drew said.

CHAPTER EIGHT

Silence was back in the BMW's driver seat, back in the streets of Fort Bragg. The car's magnificent engine purred, contrasting the tension now bubbling inside Silence, a tension he could never have dreamed would materialize in Fort Bragg.

Matt Jennings. Murdered.

Suddenly, Silence had found himself in a ... situation. Just as suddenly, Silence had an unexpected companion.

Bryan Holifield was in the passenger seat beside him. Mid-thirties, five-ten with a lean build that spoke of regular runs, not heavy weights. Brown hair and eyes. His dark stubble hadn't seen a razor for a couple of days, giving a rugged contrast to the neat light blue shirt.

While Silence drove, Bryan was rifling through the stack of spreadsheets he'd shown Silence earlier, his brow knitted in concentration.

"I'm telling ya, Drew," Bryan said. "I still can't figure out Matt's reasoning for leaving me these numbers."

Drew...

As a security precaution, Silence gave everyone to whom he offered his services an alias. To lower the number of syllables he needed to run through his painful throat, he always chose a one-syllable name. The effect was minuscule but helpful.

Silence looked over at the spreadsheets splayed over Bryan's lap and immediately felt the dopamine rush of investigative intrigue. In domino-effect style, this triggered a second reaction: thinking about Falcon's concept of *No involvement in local matters.*

After the Mobile incident, this would be the second time in three days that Silence disobeyed Falcon's directive. Falcon was already "irate," as Doc Hazel had described, over Silence's actions in Mobile. Given Silence's reason for being in Fort Bragg was punishment for the Mobile affair, getting involved in a local matter in Fort Bragg would send Falcon's anger into the stratosphere.

So Silence would have to be especially careful.

Silence was good at being sneaky.

Bryan began squaring up the papers on his lap. "Even though Matt didn't want me involved, I did some digging," he said, hesitating just a moment before he continued. "These spreadsheets show Matt was looking into Daniel Gray's machine shop during the last two days of his investigation."

Silence turned to Bryan.

"We go there," he said and swallowed. "Where is?"

He was hitting Bryan early with his broken English technique without explanation, but he guessed Bryan would figure it out quickly. The guy seemed sharp enough.

Bryan pointed out the passenger window at the upcoming intersection—"Take a left here"—and Silence pulled the BMW through the turn.

Returning to the spreadsheets, Bryan's fingers traced over the rows and columns.

"Here, look at this," he said. "On the first page, for the second- and third-to-last days of his investigation, Matt listed several items' prices *higher* than their actual cost. That's not usually how someone cheats an expense report, by *over*charging himself. And, besides, Matt would never cheat anyone. So there's something about these amounts. But ... I can't figure out what it is."

As Silence stopped the BMW at a red light, he looked over again at the spreadsheets. Beside the official entries—all computer-printed—Bryan had hand-scrawled a list of numbers along the rightmost column of the spreadsheet. Doing some quick math, Silences saw that these were the overcharged amounts in cents. There were six such of Bryan's notes: *.01, .14, .03, .08, .15, .18.*

The light turned green. Silence pressed the gas pedal.

His mind drifted back to Matt Jennings, not to his childhood memory but to what Bryan had thus far told him about the adult Matt. The details painted a picture of a meticulous, thorough investigator. Silence respected what he'd heard of the methodical nature of Matt's work. Matt must have been a good cop, a man dedicated to uncovering the truth, much like Silence himself in another life—he'd been a Pensacola police officer on the fast track to detective before the series of events that led to his conscription into the Watchers.

The thought of Matt's diligence and his untimely end, the death of a man he knew but didn't know at all, made Silence think...

Something...

But what was it?

That's right, love, C.C. said. *Explore what you feel. That's why you're there in California.*

Obediently, Silence thought of what he knew of Matt Jennings, which naturally made his mind wander back to a different time, a different world. He was no longer in the sleek BMW but in the bustling, chaotic world of an elementary schoolyard during recess. The memory was vivid, dreamlike, yet real.

———

Jake was tossing a baseball back and forth with Matt when a disturbance on the other side of the playground caught his eye. He squinted, making out the figure of Archie, the small second-grader known more for his books than his interpersonal acumen, cornered by the swings. Surrounding him were Curtis Hyer and his usual cronies. Jake had never learned the names of Hyer's sycophants, but he'd assigned them monikers based on their prevailing physical characteristics: Freckles and Dribble-Nose.

Jake couldn't catch their words from this distance, but the scene spoke volumes. Curtis was standing too close to Archie, his body language aggressive, while the younger kid looked like he wanted to disappear into the ground. The two sidekicks were laughing, their actions blurred by distance but unmistakably taunting.

Matt noticed Jake's attention had shifted.

"What's up?" he asked, following Jake's gaze.

Jake felt a familiar knot of anger in his stomach, tightening every second he watched the scene unfold.

"It's Archie. He's in trouble," he said, his voice tense. "Hyer and his idiots are at it again."

Matt shuffled his feet.

"Maybe we should just stay out of it," Matt said.

But Jake was already moving.

His every step toward the confrontation was set with determination, his mind made up. He felt Matt trailing behind him.

Hesitant...

...but following.

Good ol' Matt.

Jake's call to action was clear and urgent, a deep-seated need to stand up for the underdog, especially when that underdog was facing a punk.

And Curtis Hyer was most definitely a punk.

Another red light. Silence brought both the BMW and the memory to a halt.

When Bryan mentioned Curtis Hyer at the cemetery earlier, Silence didn't immediately recognize the name. Bryan's statement about Hyer being a bully jogged Silence's memory, clarifying that Hyer was the antagonist in his single coherent memory featuring Matt Jennings.

Back at the cemetery, Bryan had also said Jake Rowe had significantly impacted Matt Jennings. According to Bryan, Jake's influence seemed to have shaped Matt's decision to become a police officer.

Which was an astounding notion...

Silence's mind fell in a loop, thinking of how he hardly remembered Matt Jennings.

Maybe it was the standing-up-to-Curtis-Hyer incident that Silence remembered, which profoundly impacted Matt. Or maybe there were other similar incidents that Silence had entirely forgotten, other moments of Jake Rowe's youthful nobility, that were also critical to Matt's development.

Either way, young Jake had affected Matt enough to lead him down the path of law enforcement.

And Matt, in turn, had influenced Bryan enough that the latter became a forensic accountant.

Astounding.

Silence remembered his conversation with Mrs. Enfield the previous evening. She'd contended that it didn't matter whether people cared about each other equally. Silence was put off by this, thinking that people should care the same or not at all.

But given his unknown impact on Matt Jennings, perhaps Mrs. Enfield was onto something about the triviality of unequal appreciation.

Mrs. Enfield had also mentioned that she regretted never expressing her gratitude to a friend for an act of kindness before that friend passed away.

Matt had never told Jake Rowe how much he meant to him.

Maybe if Jake Rowe hadn't vanished out of Matt's life for decades, Matt would have been able to do so...

...before he died.

"Turn left here," Bryan said.

Silence took the BMW through the lefthand turn.

"This is it," Bryan said.

The sign ahead was bleached by years, barely announcing *Gray's Machine Shop,* like it was hanging onto the past by a thread. One-story. Unassuming. Drab. The structure stood defiant, an industrial-age ghost, its skin a mix of old brick and worn metal. Grimy windows hid its secrets. It was a place that swallowed the surroundings, exuding a tired kind of permanence.

Silence parked in the weed-filled lot among a half dozen vehicles. A moment later, he pushed through the heavy metal door, and he and Bryan stepped inside. A strong odor of oil and metal permeated the air. The floor was a mosaic of old concrete and scattered metal filings. Workbenches cluttered with tools and machine parts lined the walls. A handful of men in stained blue coveralls milled about the place, shooting looks in Silence's direction.

Bryan took a step ahead of Silence, leading them toward a man at the far end of the shop, his back to them as he worked at a lathe. He turned as they approached, wiping his hands on a greasy rag. Daniel Gray was a burly figure, his face weathered and etched. White beard, tinged yellow at the edges. His eyes were sharp and assessing, framed by heavy brows. There was an air of rugged competence about him.

There was also an air of immediate hostility.

"You're Sam's boy, ain't ya?" Gray said to Bryan. "Bryan Holifield."

"Yes, sir."

Gray's eyes flashed to Silence, back to Bryan. "Who's your buddy?"

"This is ... Drew. He's a ... private investigator."

In the course of Silence's work, people often thought he was a police officer or a federal agent or a private eye or hired muscle working for some criminal outfit. Frequently, it was in Silence's best interests to let the assumption ride. Bryan had mentioned in the car that he thought Silence was a fed. Silence had neither confirmed nor denied. Here, Bryan was going with a lie, saying "Drew" was a private eye. It made logical sense, given the situation.

Silence would roll with this untruth.

Gray grunted, a sound that sank into the depths of the shop. His gaze lingered on Silence, evaluating and perhaps finding him not entirely to his liking.

"What do you want?" Gray said.

"It's about Matt," Bryan said. "He—"

"Matt Jennings?"

Bryan nodded.

"Shit, son, that wound's a little fresh in this town, don't ya think?" He paused, his grizzled defiance softening ever so slightly before he added, "Especially for you. I know you two were close."

This shook Bryan. "I ... Well, I—"

Silence cut in. "Did Matt come here..." he said, swallowed. "Asking questions?"

Gray inched back, eyes widening. "Hell of a voice you got on you, boy." He paused. "Yeah. Yeah, Matt was here."

"What was..." Silence said and swallowed. "He looking for?"

Gray shrugged. "He didn't give specifics. He just said there'd been some bad money moving through Fort Bragg, thought it mighta moved through my shop."

"And what did you tell him?" Bryan said.

Gray bristled. "I told him absolutely not!" His chest puffed, and his tone quickly turned even more confrontational as he added, "Look, kid, you know as well as I do where you need to be looking. If there's anything bad going on in this town, it has one name attached to it."

He left that open-ended for Bryan, who took the cue.

"Lloyd Thorhill," Bryan said.

"Yes! Thornhill!" Gray said, throwing up his hands. "That's where you need to go, not here interrupting my daily operations. I have a quota to fill today, and these dumbasses," he said, motioning toward the men in the coveralls, "are behind." He paused to let his eyes move over both Bryan and Silence. "Now get out of my shop."

Silence stared back at Gray. The exchange had been odd. And not just because of his hostility. It felt funky, off, and it triggered Silence's intuition. C.C. had always told him to listen to his intuition. And she still did, the non-corporeal version of her in his head.

He turned to Bryan.

"Time to go," he said.

CHAPTER NINE

Bryan rode shotgun as Drew guided the BMW toward the Fort Bragg police station. It stood out like a shard of the future dropped into the past, all sleek lines and reflective glass, an architectural statement that felt more Silicon Valley than small-town seafront. Its modernity contrasted with the quaint downtown storefronts—a beacon of advancement amid the town's sleepy backdrop.

Drew parked the BMW and leaned down to peer through the windshield at the building. His raised eyebrow showed confusion.

"Yeah, it's something else, isn't it?" Bryan said. "City built it only about a year ago. That gorgeous old building they used on the south side for years is totally abandoned and about to be torn down. It's a damn shame. People even tried to get it on the National Historic Register to save it. Didn't work."

Bryan watched as Drew continued to stare at the new building for a moment. Then, wordlessly, Drew opened the door and stepped out. Bryan followed suit.

As they approached the entrance, Bryan brought up a topic he'd been dreading.

"So, I mentioned Due North, the mentorship program, back at the cemetery..."

He turned to Drew.

Drew nodded.

"Well..." Bryan said. Paused. "So Matt hadn't mentored anyone for a few years. I know the last kid he mentored was older, high school age. Matt told me about him. But I don't remember the kid's name." Another pause. "But I know someone who volunteers with Due North who might be able to help."

Drew looked at him again, and though he said nothing aloud, his non-verbal said, *And?*

"I ... um..." Bryan stammered. "Well, this person has refused to talk to me. But I ... I'll try to contact her."

Drew looked at him. The stare was heavy, incredulous.

Bryan turned away. He felt pathetic. Which was understandable. He'd just offered Drew a pathetic statement.

But it had been the best he could do.

Even *mentioning* his contact at Due North had made Bryan's heart thunder. He had to take some deep breaths—still feeling Drew's stare on the side of his face—to calm down.

The automatic doors opened for them. Stepping inside, they entered a lobby filled with sleek expanses of polished concrete and glass. Oversized screens displayed community events, and smaller monitors cycled through images of local heroes and notable arrests. The lighting was recessed and even, giving off a clinical luminescence that reflected off the minimalist furniture and the latest in ergonomic design.

Bryan knew the place well. He turned to Drew as he led them toward the back hallway. "We're meeting with Detective Faron Rasnick," he said. "Good dude. He was friends with Matt. I know him, too. In a small place like Fort Bragg, a forensic accountant and a detective cross paths more than you'd think."

Making their way past a water dispenser, they arrived at an open doorway. Behind a desk, a man glanced up from his paperwork, nodded at Bryan, and stood up to greet their visitors.

Faron Rasnick's look was in line with the seriousness of his job. His distinguished appearance was accentuated by his peppered gray hair and the wrinkles on his face, which hinted at years spent scrutinizing crime scenes or rifling through case files.

His suit was well-fitted but not flashy, the kind that spoke of a man who took his job seriously but had no interest in the frills of fashion. His posture was straight, his shoulders squared.

The detective's gaze lingered on Drew with a mix of curiosity and a touch of suspicion before he turned back to Bryan.

"Bryan, it's been a while. How ya holding up?" he said. "Who's this?"

They shook hands.

"This is Drew," Bryan said. Then, remembering his earlier lie, he added, "He's a private investigator."

It wouldn't do to tell Rasnick that he was unleashing a federal shadow man upon Fort Bragg...

Rasnick looked at Drew again. The moment stretched. Rasnick's eyes narrowed slightly, not in hostility but in calculation. A private investigator in Fort Bragg wasn't a regular occurrence. Rasnick's stance shifted subtly, clearly indicating his guard was up.

"A private investigator?" he said, returning his attention to Bryan. "Does this have to do with Matt?"

Bryan nodded.

"Shit, Bryan, we don't need outsiders interfering! This is a sensitive case." He pointed to the open doorway, indicating the busy police station beyond. "And Matt was one of our own. Fort Bragg can handle this."

Drew took a step closer.

"We're well within our rights..." he said and swallowed. "To investigate."

Like Daniel Gray back at the machine shop, Rasnick also had a noticeable response to Drew's unusual voice at the machine shop—cocking his head to the side, narrowing his eyes. Bryan watched Drew and Rasnick assess each other.

Finally, Rasnick said, "So let me guess—you want to see Matt's files?"

"Diplomacy..." Drew said and swallowed. "Works wonders, Detective."

Bryan nodded in agreement, trying to bolster Drew's attempt at "diplomacy," as he'd put it, despite the tightness in his chest.

"You're sure as hell not getting the files," Rasnick snapped. His jaw worked as if he were chewing on an idea. A reluctant sigh, then continued in a calmer tone with, "But I can tell you this much: Matt was digging into some of the local businesses. Seems he found a pattern in the string of recent 'accidents' around town. He thinks they were murders."

Bryan and Drew exchanged a look.

"Any businesses..." Drew said and swallowed. "In particular?"

Rasnick paused, his gaze narrowing as if weighing the risks of disclosing more information. But finally, duty or perhaps the desire to unburden his thoughts won over.

"Matt mentioned Gray's Machine Shop more than once," he said.

"We were just there," Bryan said.

Rasnick nodded, smirked, impressed. "Yeah, we've thoroughly vetted Daniel Gray—*I* vetted him—and he's clean. But there's also Lloyd Thornhill to consider."

The mention of Daniel Gray's same suspicion—Thornhill—made Drew stand slightly taller.

"Thornhill? Gray pointed..." Drew said and swallowed. "Us that way too."

Abruptly, Rasnick pushed off his desktop and turned away from them, leaning over to pull open a desk drawer.

"Thornhill's throwing one of his fancy parties tonight," Rasnick said, reaching into the drawer. He pulled out a sleek, black invitation card and tossed it across the desk to Drew. "Saving a handful of the redwoods, or some such shit. This was my ticket in, but it's yours now. Maybe you'll see something I can't. Consider that my act of 'diplomacy.'"

The invitation had landed with a soft thud in front of Drew. The gesture was oddly powerful, a reluctant extension of trust—or perhaps a dismissal.

Rasnick's eyes were hard, and his message was clear without being said: he didn't like working with a private investigator in any capacity, but it seemed he had little choice in the matter.

Drew gave a tiny grin. "Thanks."

There'd been an ever-so-slight hint of mirth to Drew's single word. Despite his stony professionalism, Bryan detected a bit of pride there, like Drew felt he'd won a minor pissing match.

"Now get out of my station," Rasnick said. "Immediately."

Drew pocketed the invitation.

They turned and left.

CHAPTER TEN

Hyer hated this place.

But it was a good spot to meet.

...when addressing matters of a certain type.

The abandoned foundry loomed over on a forgotten edge of Fort Bragg—far from the idyllic downtown and the magnificent coastline— its skeletal frame etched against the morning sky, still gray but gaining a bit of color as it brightened. Hyer stood in the building's cavernous shell, the quietness around him a contrast to the clatter and roar that must have once filled the air. The smell of rust and dirt hung heavy, clinging to the cool morning breeze that whispered through the broken panes above.

A few yards before him, Daniel Gray's figure was tiny against the vast backdrop of discarded machinery and shadows. Hyer watched the older man, a predator assessing his prey.

"Bryan Holifield, huh? So what did he ask you?" Hyer said, his voice echoing off the metal that surrounded them.

Gray shifted uneasily, his eyes darting around the dimly lit expanse as if seeking an avenue of escape. But there was none.

"He ... he came asking about Matt Jennings," Gray stammered, his words tumbling out in a rush. "He had a private investigator with him. Drew, his name was. Big guy. Didn't say much."

A 'big guy'...

Recent memories presented themselves to Hyer.

Gray nodded and flashed a shaky smile, misreading Hyer's calm for satisfaction. But beneath the surface, Hyer's professional instincts were churning. He had seen the man known as Drew move, his gait, his awareness—it was all wrong. This was no ordinary private investigator; this was someone trained, someone lethal.

"*A private investigator, Gray?!*" Hyer shouted so loudly and so suddenly that the other man jumped back. His voice echoed off the high ceiling. "I saw the security tape. Private eyes don't look like that. Don't be so naive, shithead. This Drew is something else. Something more dangerous."

His words reverberated away—smaller, smaller, gone—then the foundry stood silent around them, the massive presses and conveyor belts dormant, yet crackling with tension.

Then he continued. "So that's why you didn't tell us sooner?"

Gray nodded, quick bobs of the head, like he could will Hyer's mercy. "Right! I thought he was just, you know ... some guy, some private detective."

"Foolish of you," Hyer said, turning away, not wanting to see the moron's face any longer.

As Hyer processed everything Gray had said, his mind raced through the possibilities, the dangers. This new force, Drew, wasn't just another thread in the tapestry—he was a rope, one that could untangle the entire thing and wrap itself tightly around everyone's collective neck.

A noose.

Hyer knew the stakes. And with an operator now in the mix, every move from here on out had to be calculated with precision.

He gave one more look at Gray. Stared for a long moment. And turned to leave, fishing his cellular phone from his pocket as he walked away.

There was someone important he needed to call.

CHAPTER ELEVEN

SINCE THE WATCHERS conducted their illegal and clandestine work by slipping in and out of U.S. government channels, they had access to ahead-of-the-curve technology that wouldn't be revealed to the general public until the twenty-first century. More often than not, this was ridiculously helpful to Silence.

Sometimes, however, it was just a tease. Because cutting-edge technology is frequently useless without an accompanying infrastructure. As a Watcher, Silence knew that someday, in the not-so-distant future, the Internet would be wireless and portable.

For now, Silence was tethered to a wired 1990s lifestyle like everyone else. Which meant that when he was in the field, he spent a lot of time in Internet cafes.

This one in Fort Bragg was called Screens 'n Sips. The place was small but inviting, the smell of coffee wafting through the air, mixing with the faint scent of aging books. Striking artwork from talented locals—all different media—lined the walls and hung from the ceiling. An antique clock quietly kept time in the corner, its pendulum swinging in sync with the soft whirring of dial-up modems.

Silence sat at one of the computer stations. His cellular phone was pressed to his ear, waiting for an answer, and his eyes were fixed across the room on Bryan.

Bryan lounged at a small table, leaned back in his chair with his legs stretched out and crossed at the ankles. One hand lazily toyed with an oversized mug of mocha while the other held a portable CD player, its headphones settled over his ears. His eyes were closed, his face tilted back, perfectly still as he listened.

A woman's voice crackled through the phone line. Moments earlier, Silence had held down his phone's 2 button—the speed dial setting that linked him to a Specialist. The setting was designed to roulette-spin his call through a network, linking him to a different Specialist each time he used it.

"Specialist," the woman said.

Silence proceeded with protocol, issuing the standard Asset introduction: code name and number. "Suppressor, A-23."

"Confirmed. State your business."

"Information retrieval," Silence said and swallowed.

There was the sound of keyboard typing, a pause, then, "Um, Suppressor, it says here that you're on standby, not active, that you've been sent to your hometown to..." A longer pause. "Er, 'connect with your roots,' it says here." Another pause, shorter this time. "Interesting. Seems you've been commanded to pay respects to your recently deceased childhood friend, Matthew Jennings."

"Yes, ma'am," Silence said and swallowed, prepping himself to do something he hated—to lie. "Trying to see..." Another swallow. "What Matt's life was like." Another swallow. "Lloyd Thornill was an associate of his."

It wasn't much of a lie, really. By all accounts, Lloyd Thornhill was a major player in town and, it seemed, a nefarious one. Chances were, Matt, as a Fort Bragg resident and a detective, had had contact with the man.

No, not much of a lie at all.

Silence grinned triumphantly.

But the grin faded quickly. Because the Specialist didn't reply.

After a long pause, she finally said, "Okay, I suppose. Hold, please."

"Yes, ma'am."

Hmm...

Silence didn't like how she'd sounded.

Panic flushed through him.

He thought about Falcon, the man's wrath from Silence's actions just two days earlier in Mobile...

Keeping the phone to his ear, Silence shifted back into his chair, shaking off his paranoia. His eyes found Bryan again, and he scrutinized the younger man's body language.

The headphones were still on, and Bryan's eyes were still closed, his head still tilted skyward. He seemed wholly removed from the situation at hand, engrossed in his music without a care in the world. It was peculiar because he and Silence were investigating *a death*—the death of Bryan's former mentor, no less. Bryan should have been invested, attentive.

Instead, he was checked out, lost in his tunes.

Silence checked his watch. It had been over a minute since the Specialist placed him on hold—longer than usual. Another paranoid notion drifted through his mind: the idea that the Specialist was taking an extra few moments to alert Falcon.

It was paranoid, yes. But what Silence had just done—his information retrieval request while not on a sanctioned mission, while being on a Watchers-mandated mental health trip—would definitely be brought to Falcon's attention.

This was troubling.

But Silence forced the idea out of his mind. He would deal with the inevitable fallout when it happened.

Finally, the woman returned. "Full profile of Lloyd Thornhill inbound. The email is on its way. Anything else?"

"No, ma'am."

Beep.

The Specialist was gone.

Silence sat back, drumming his fingers on the counter as he stared at the empty inbox on the screen. He took a sip from his mug. He'd ordered a coffee, but they were sold out.

Sold out.

Of coffee.

At a coffee shop.

Bryan had suggested chai latte, and Silence had agreed with a shrug. As he tried the beverage now, his nose scrunched. It tasted like a spice rack.

When she was alive, C.C. had, as lovingly as possible, said Silence had an "unrefined palate," evidenced by his preference for cheap pizza and cheaper burgers.

The modern-day C.C., the one who resided in his head, chided him as he smacked his lips and scraped his tongue clean with his front teeth.

Oh, stop it, C.C. said. *Everyone loves chai. Expand your damn horizons, love. Jeez.*

Silence frowned.

A ping from the computer indicated an arrival in his inbox. Grateful for the distraction, Silence pushed the offending mug away and clicked open the message. He scanned the detailed profile the Watchers had quickly compiled on Lloyd Thornhill.

Despite arriving so quickly, the profile was extensive, as

this was undoubtedly the work of several Specialists working simultaneously to comb digital databases and compile the information. There were two solid pages of text and a collection of digitized photographs.

Lloyd Thornhill. Forty-eight years old. Caucasian. Lifelong California resident, the last thirty-one years in Fort Bragg. He was a man with a reputation, both deserved and undeserved. A child of old money and privilege, Thornhill exuded the refinement and entitlement that came with his upper-crust upbringing. He had the polished look of someone accustomed to getting what he wanted—Italian leather shoes, tailored suits, five-figure wristwatches. More striking than his cultivated appearance was his sheer magnetism. Thornhill had powerful charisma and an ability to captivate, which opened doors throughout high society.

But beneath the veneer of sophistication lurked rumors of impropriety. In his college years, Thornhill had been linked to an investment scandal that bilked prominent families out of millions. Though never formally accused, the association tainted his name—and that of his family—at a young age. Afterward, he'd reinvented himself through real estate, developing luxury properties and hobnobbing with the elite.

Of greater interest to Silence was Thornhill's more recent obsession with art collecting. He trafficked in rare finds of dubious origin, acquired through private dealers, and discretely transported to his estates. This pastime took Thornhill around the globe and brought him into contact with unsavory characters.

Art collecting...

This was often a front for money laundering.

Silence leaned back in his chair, fingers steepled before his face. Lloyd Thornhill was certainly an intriguing figure, one whose refined exterior concealed darker leanings. But how might he connect to Matt's investigation, one centered on suspicious deaths labeled as 'accidents'?

For now, Silence rose from the computer station and walked over to Bryan's table. The man was still ensconced in his music, eyes closed. Silence poked his shoulder.

Bryan's eyes snapped open, and he slid the headphones down to rest around his neck as he looked up at Silence. "Did you dig up some useful info?"

Silence nodded. "But we need more," he said and swallowed. "Time for you..." Another swallow. "To make that call."

Earlier, Bryan had hinted at a contact inside the Due North organization, a link he was clearly reluctant to revisit. To Silence, it sounded like an old flame, the kind that leaves scars.

It was time for Bryan to get over the past.

"I guess you're right," Bryan said on a sigh. "You drive a hard bargain, Drew."

CHAPTER TWELVE

ARIA FOSTER PACED BACK and forth, pulse thrumming, staring at her phone—a retro-chic rotary number, bright red —on the accent table by her window.

"Son of a *bitch!*" she said through her teeth.

But her anger wasn't directed at the phone. Not really. It had only done what phones do: ring.

The device next to the phone was the true offender—the answering machine. Its LCD had shown Bryan's phone number, and its digital storage had recorded the voicemail when she refused to answer the call.

Aria paced another full circle through her living room, her bare feet digging into the dense fibers of the Persian rug before stepping off onto the hardwood. She stomped past the tall rubber plant in the corner, crashing through its glossy leaves. Every inch of the space, from the plush furniture to the local art hanging asymmetrically on the walls, reflected Aria's taste for bright colors and visual optimism. But in that moment, her house felt as unsettled as her thoughts, charged with the same tension that hummed in the air before a thunderclap.

All because of that damn message.

...that damn *Bryan*.

Another full loop through the room, and she ended up back at the answering machine. She stabbed a finger into the *PLAY* button.

The message began again. This would be the third time she'd listened to it.

Hey Aria. Uh, good morning. I know it's... um ... I know it's been a while, but I'm in the middle of an investigation, and ... Well, this is a different sort of investigation. It's related to Matt. Matt Jennings. I have a question about his involvement in Due North. His latest mentee, a few years back—I can't remember the kid's name. Due North is never gonna give out the name—privacy laws and all that. But ... um, since you volunteer there, you could share the name. If you don't mind.

A long pause in which she could hear Bryan's breathing.

Listen, Matt told me the kid's name years ago. I just can't remember it. So it's not like you'd really *be giving out confidential information. I got a private investigator working with me on this. Drew. We ... don't think Matt's death was an accident. And we need this info. Please, Aria.*

Another pause.

Call me back. Uh, please. 707-555-8302. Thanks.

A shuffling sound. And the message ended.

She shook her head, irritation simmering in her gut.

Of course Bryan would conjure up a so-called mystery just to worm his way back into her life.

And to use Matt *freaking* Jennings as emotional bait?!

A man who'd just died, someone the whole town had loved...

Unbelievable.

Yet, so like Bryan.

So manipulative.

The piece of shit.

Aria paused by the window overlooking the backyard. It was a view she'd come to appreciate over the few years living in Fort Bragg. The openness of it—trees swaying in the ocean breeze, sunlight dancing on the cove's water in the distance—reminded her of the expansive freedom that had drawn her to her previous career. Out here, though, in her new life with her new career, she didn't feel hemmed in by smog and traffic the way she had down in Los Angeles.

She'd been moving off frustration-fueled adrenaline, but now she realized that all the pacing had agitated her knee. She turned from the window and sank into the office chair, wincing at the twinge of pain. The injury still flared occasionally.

And that bit of discomfort made her think of her old life, just a few years ago, before Bryan, before Fort Bragg. She flexed her hand, imagining how the steering wheel used to feel beneath her grip. The effortless power of it, surging and poised between her fingertips. Aria missed that sense of boldness, of knowing precisely who she was and what she was capable of. These days, certainty came only in small moments—quiet mornings with a cup of coffee, the satisfaction of untangling complicated tax codes, the peace of a dark bedroom and dreamless sleep.

Certainty *did not* come from Bryan Holifield barging back into her world after months of nothing, demanding confidential information and spouting off about a private eye named Drew and some important investigation. Nothing gave him the right to disrupt her equilibrium.

By the tone of his voice, it had seemed like Bryan's investigation was ultimately an attempt at closure regarding Matt Jennings. But tones can be affected. Manipulative people excelled at this talent.

Really, Bryan was looking for closure with *her*.

He wasn't going to get it.

Whether the closure concerned Matt Jennings or her, Aria, what did she care if Bryan received his sense of peace? Some people didn't get neat, tidy endings in life. God knows she hadn't. Her time in L.A. had taught her that.

Aria nodded firmly, decision made. She would ignore Bryan's plea for help.

Let Bryan chase his ghosts alone.

Maybe one day he would learn to stop chasing what was already lost.

CHAPTER THIRTEEN

Silence's BMW slowed and veered off California State Route 128, tires crunching on the gravel road. Yura's Yoga Retreat was only a temporary event, lasting two days, but it was held at a permanent facility.

This facility was surrounded by the largest trees in the world.

Nature's giants.

The redwoods.

The meeting space was nestled within a clearing in Navarro River Redwoods State Park, surrounded by colossal trees that reached endlessly skyward. The sun's rays filtered through the branches, creating a peaceful atmosphere over the small presentation area at the front of the clearing. Other than this designated spot, there were only two rustic buildings and a few log benches to hint at human intervention in the natural surroundings.

Silence stepped out of the BMW—his Allen Edmonds derbies crunching in thick gravel of the parking area, one of two lots flanking the clearing—and was greeted by the earthy scent of the forest. He immediately felt the presence of the redwoods, as if they each had a gravitational pull. Sounds drifted in the air—murmurs, laughter, quiet conversations.

As he approached the clearing, he saw the small group gathered there. He scanned the area, taking in the scattering of yoga mats and the people dressed in sweatpants and tie-dye. Some were clustered together while others sought solace alone near the massive tree trunks—cross-legged, eyes closed, some of them chanting.

Silence groaned.

The redwoods loomed over everything. Silence had grown up around the giants, and though he'd never been back to his hometown until yesterday, he'd seen the godlike trees several more times since childhood. So he was accustomed to them.

But they still took his breath away.

John Steinbeck had coined them "ambassadors from another time." And they truly were. Some of them were 2,000 years old. They had witnessed the rise and fall of empires and eras, including the Romans and the Middle Ages. They had been around long before the establishment of the United States. In comparison, Silence's current predicament —being forced into a yoga retreat while simultaneously getting caught up in the dark happenings in Fort Bragg— seemed small and unimportant.

The redwoods were humbling like that.

Nonetheless, Silence had no desire to do this yoga shit.

Stop it! C.C. chided. *It'll be good for you.*

Sure it will...

Not only was this frustrating, but it was also a distraction. The self-imposed mission back in Fort Bragg was beckoning him to return. There were wildly loose ends in the investigation that needed to be tied together. Time was slipping away, and every moment spent here was one less moment spent trying to uncover the truth behind Matt Jennings's death.

But with a heavy heart, Silence's eyes found the scar on

the inside of his right forearm. Beneath that scar was his GPS dot. Somewhere out there, someone was monitoring his every move. He couldn't just leave the yoga retreat; it was his official reason for lingering in California. To continue his mission in Fort Bragg, he had to participate in the yoga sessions and maintain the facade.

He ran his finger along the scar.

Then groaned again.

Silence made his way over to the group of yoga practitioners, observing the scene. Yura Turner had completely taken over the presentation area, adorning it with her trademark neon pink signs and a sleek podium at its center.

Silence had done his research the previous evening. Yura Turner, it seemed, was more than just a vivacious face. Daughter to an African American father and a Japanese first-generation immigrant, her mixed heritage was a point of pride, and she incorporated this into the open-natured philosophy of her business. Aside from her wildly successful chain of Sacramento-area studios, Yura had also branched out into the burgeoning field of the Internet, posting inventive yoga challenges on her webpage.

Silence stopped at the edge of the clearing, his eyes scanning the crowd until they landed on the woman herself—Yura Turner. She was just as vibrant as described in the brochure, her energy radiating even from a distance. He recognized her signature spiral hair from the photo he had seen back in Pensacola, along with her bright smile and obsessively happy eyes. Yura was deeply conversing with some of her clients, but she suddenly lifted her head to meet Silence's stare, seemingly sensing his presence. Their eyes locked.

He watched as she excused herself from the others with a graceful ease. She floated toward him, her movements quick and airy, closing the gap between them with that wild smile of hers. She halted just a few feet before him and did a little hop on her toes.

She greeted him with a loud "Hey there!", her voice surprisingly high-pitched. "You must be the one who missed the sunrise session!" Her tone was playful, yet her words had an underlying sense of curiosity.

Silence offered a brief, apologetic smile. "Sorry about that."

As soon as Silence spoke, Yura's beaming grin faltered slightly. She glanced at his throat before meeting his gaze again.

Recovering quickly, she brushed off Silence's apology with a flick of her hand. "Don't worry about it. Life happens, dude! I'm just happy you're here now. Remember, we have four sessions each day: sunrise, daytime, dusk, and evening. That's only eight sessions altogether, and I *really* want you to make the most out of your time here!"

Before he could respond, she'd spun back around, hopping off to return to the group she'd left. Silence watched her go. Her energy left a noticeable void in its wake.

Silence just stood there for a moment longer, processing the brief encounter.

Continuing on, he stepped into the clearing. He maneuvered around a group of women in deep meditation and noticed an unlikely pair ahead: an eighty-something white woman and a black guy barely past drinking age. They were more than friends...

...evidenced by the hand-holding and kissing.

The two sat cross-legged on their yoga mats, facing each other. The woman was draped in a soft grey cardigan, radiating grace and timeless sophistication. Her white hair framed her face, and she wore glasses atop her nose. The lines on her weathered face hinted at a life full of experiences—a loooong life—and her poise suggested she held many untold secrets.

Her companion exuded the aura of a nomad, possessing a lean and agile physique. His watchful eyes were alert and keen. A quasi-military jacket hung loosely from his broad shoulders, unbuttoned, shirtless beneath, revealing a chiseled chest of copper-brown skin without an ounce of excess fat. He couldn't have been older than twenty-four.

As Silence approached the camp, the woman's gaze shifted from her companion to Silence, and she greeted him with a warm smile. Standing up, she walked over, her partner following behind her.

"You must be the new arrival!" the woman exclaimed with a thick New York accent—Brooklyn, to be exact, Silence guessed.

She enveloped him in a hug.

Silence flinched, and as he did so, he inhaled something pungently sweet—prehistoric perfume, no doubt, pre-war sort of stuff. He gave the woman a couple of pats on the back. She released him.

"I'm Doris Feldman," the woman said. "And this is Kofi."

The lean man shoved a hand in Silence's direction, smiling wide. Silence returned the handshake.

"Welcome, brother," Kofi said, his smile growing even larger.

There was a genuine warmth emanating from Kofi, evident in the constant sway of his shoulders. Accordingly, his hairstyle was untamed—much like Yura's, actually—a wild mane of natural curls that spoke to a spirit unrestrained by societal norms.

Silence nodded. "Thanks."

Doris and Kofi exchanged a quick look at the sound of Silence's awful voice, but neither of them stopped smiling.

"So you're the one who missed the sunrise session," Doris

said. "Been wondering who'd come to join us. It's been like a mystery game, hasn't it, dear?"

Kofi nodded enthusiastically.

It was remarkable that Doris had noted the exact comings and goings of the yoga retreat members, doing so with as much interest as Yura Turner herself. The lady sure was nosy. But she didn't seem malicious about it, only watchful. As Silence towered over her—she was barely scraping five feet one—she looked up at him with a little wink, showing no ill intent in the least.

Doris inched closer to Kofi, who then wrapped his arm around her. "I can tell we must be quite the enigma to you," she said. "We often are to people at first glance. But love knows no boundaries, young man. And two years back—this was before I moved to Bradenton, you see, when I was still living in Brooklyn—I happened to walk by Kofi on the street as I was leaving my synagogue, and ... that was it. Sometimes, a person's essence just captures your heart. Have you ever encountered someone with a spirit like this man here?"

Silence glanced over at Kofi.

The splayed-open faux-military jacket. The shredded abs. The shoulder-bobbing.

No, Silence couldn't say he'd ever encountered anyone quite like Kofi.

Silence pondered the strange contrast of their relationship, considering the chasm of an age gap. It was evident that Kofi was not deluded into thinking he would have a long future with Doris. And she, in turn, must have known this as well. Silence found it difficult to believe they could have equal love toward one another.

The simple fact was they literally *could not* have much time together.

Much time together...

During his most recent mental health session, Doc Hazel

had attempted to provoke a reaction from Silence by highlighting the limited time he and C.C. had spent together before her passing. And, truthfully, dispassionately, he had to admit that she'd spoken the truth. Silence and C.C. had only been together for a matter of months.

But they'd been engaged.

Engaged!

That's what mattered most—the *depth* of their love. The engagement meant they loved each other in equal measure.

Even though their time together was limited.

...like Doris and Kofi's *necessarily* was.

Suddenly, Silence found that his chaotic mind space was swirling.

Steady, love, C.C. said. *Remember your mindfulness.*

Taking her advice, he closed his eyes, let his body slacken, and felt his touch points—his feet on the ground, shoes pressing into the forest floor; hands in his pockets, fabric brushing his skin. The smell of the trees. The murmur of the yogis.

He opened his eyes.

A five-second meditation. One of the techniques C.C. had ingrained in him.

Refocused on the present moment, his eyes found Doris below him, still wearing that half smile of a grandmother mixed with a yoga-lover. She reminded him strangely of Mrs. Enfield, which sparked a flood of memories: sitting together quietly on his neighbor's porch; *Kingdom of Desire* reading sessions; trials and tribulations with Baxter, the drooling tabby; and the sense of household warmth that came when Lola, Mrs. Enfield's former caretaker, visited from out of state and they all became a makeshift family for a short while, the three of them.

...well, the *four* of them, when including that damn Baxter.

And, of course, he thought of one of the earliest memories he had of Mrs. Enfield—how she took it upon herself, having only just met Silence, to ensure that after C.C.'s death Silence didn't succumb to alcoholism like his father had.

At that time, she'd only known Silence for a couple of weeks...

Back in Pensacola, before Silence left for Fort Bragg, he had wanted to thank her for all she'd done, especially the stopping-him-from-turning-into-a-rotten-drunk thing.

But he hadn't.

He'd come up with excuses, telling himself that his throat was too sore, that he would thank her later.

He recalled Mrs. Enfield's heartbreaking story of being unable to express her gratitude to a friend who had done something wonderful for her before the friend tragically passed away. The opportunity for Mrs. Enfield to express her gratitude was lost forever.

Silence also remembered the persistent cough that Mrs. Enfield had in Pensacola...

...and how old she was.

It's just a cold, he promised himself. *She has nothing more than a head cold.*

As Silence's gaze drifted to the side, deep in thought on these matters, his attention was suddenly yanked back to the present moment yet again.

He'd noticed someone.

A figure standing alone, away from the rest of the retreat, next to one of the behemoth tree trunks. A woman. Late twenties or early thirties. White. Shoulders turned in, arms wrapped around herself. Her hair, a curtain of amber and chestnut, seemed less a style than a shield. A half-smile graced her lips, but it didn't extinguish the wariness in her expression.

It was difficult to be sure from a distance, but Silence thought he noticed a mark on her cheek...

…something like a wound.

Their gazes met briefly, sharing a silent exchange. The woman's eyes held a wary stillness, a woodland creature, minuscule among the giants, on the lookout for danger.

She looked away.

Silence turned to Doris and Kofi.

"Who's that?" he said, nodding in the woman's direction.

They both looked.

"Oh, man, that's Juliette," Kofi said, his energy less-than-exuberant for the first time since Silence met him.

Doris shook her head. "She's a sad-looking thing, isn't she? Well, don't you judge her. She has reason to be like that."

Silence stared back at Doris, waiting for elaboration.

"Vinnie," Doris continued. "Her man friend. A real putz. He was here with her a few times at last year's retreat. Awful man. Always screaming at her. He was here today, too, this morning. Dropped her off. They had another big fight out in the parking lot." She pointed behind her accordingly. "No one knows for sure, but…"

She paused and glanced at Kofi, then returned her gaze to Silence.

"But many of us suspect he's violent with her."

Silence's mind flashed on the mark he thought he saw on Juliette's cheek.

He turned to confirm his suspicion.

But Juliette was gone.

CHAPTER FOURTEEN

SILENCE'S WORK often led him to the seedier areas of civilization, the absolute pits of depravity.

But sometimes, it led him in the opposite direction, to society's summit, all the way to the upper crust.

Perched on a slight incline, the Lloyd Thornhill estate boasted impressive columns and intricate details that glimmered in the moonlight. The Tri-Tree Preservation Gala was in full swing, with guests meandering on the impeccably kept lawn adorned with dainty string lights. A sea of well-dressed individuals mingled, their designer dresses and tailored suits glinting with precious gems and luxurious fabrics.

Silence stood in a short queue at the door. He wore an all-black Zegna suit that hugged his tall frame perfectly, accentuating his broad shoulders and trim waist. No tie. Gunmetal box chain necklace. On his feet, a pair of derbies, Allen Edmonds. The night air was crisp, carrying the faint buzz of high society gathered around him.

The *night* air...

Night.

A realization struck him.

Oh, shit.

Instinctively, he checked his watch but already knew it was too late. The sun had gone down an hour ago; with its departure, he'd missed the dusk yoga meeting in Navarro River Redwoods State Park. Not only would Yura notice his absence again—and, apparently, so would Doris Feldman—but missing another session would surely be a red flag for the Watchers.

Again, his eyes moved instinctively, this time to his right forearm. Though the scar was covered by his black suit jacket, he sensed the presence of his GPS dot, knowing that the Watchers were now undoubtedly wondering what the hell Silence was doing in Fort Bragg. He'd been told to spend time in Fort Bragg on the first day of his excursion to California, but still being there in the evening—having missed one of the yoga sessions, no less—would draw some attention.

Oh well.

When it was his turn at the door, Silence presented Detective Rasnick's invitation to a bruiser who looked more like a security guard than a doorman. He was a homely son of a bitch in an ill-fitting tux with a gaudy lapel pin—a silver eagle with faux sapphire eyes. The man gave the invitation a thorough once-over and looked up with skepticism in his eyes.

"This is Detective Rasnick's invitation."

Silence nodded. "And he gave it…" He swallowed. "To me."

The man looked down at the invitation, took a breath, looked past Silence at the long line behind him, and conceded with a nod, allowing Silence entrance.

But as Silence passed, the man maintained a watchful gaze, narrowing his eyelids.

Silence made note of this, filing it away.

Stepping into the mansion, Silence was immediately

enveloped by opulence, dripping from every corner. Crystal chandeliers hung like frozen raindrops, sparkling over the guests. The attendees were a mix of the wealthy and the influential, their conversations a symphony of polite laughter and hushed negotiations. Women in gowns that whispered elegance and men in suits that spoke of power and wealth mingled with an air of casual sophistication.

As Silence continued through the foyer, his cellular phone buzzed in his pocket. He glanced at the multiplex and saw Falcon's number.

Shit.

He flipped open the phone.

"Sir?"

"Why the hell are you still in Fort Bragg?" Falcon barked. "You missed another session at the retreat. And what's this about an information retrieval on Lloyd Thornhill?"

"Still not done…" Silence said and swallowed. "Connecting to my roots." Another swallow. "I'm studying Fort Bragg…" Another swallow. "To see what Matt's life was like."

"And you're doing so by attending a 500-dollar-a-plate soirée?"

"Yes."

"Bullshit!"

Silence didn't respond.

"You're up to something."

Silence didn't respond.

There was a long, painful delay, then, "Look at your right arm."

Silence wouldn't have complied, but, reflexes being what they are, his eyes went to his right forearm as they had a few minutes earlier, standing in line outside the building. He saw the sleeve of his suit jacket again.

"I'm watching you, shithead," Falcon said.

Beep.

Falcon was gone.

Silence pocketed the phone.

He wandered through the crowd, absently observing the majestic hall, finely adorned with stately women in evening gowns and men in sharp suits. He thought about Falcon's words, annoyed that his superior could track him so easily.

Damn it.

He had to tread carefully if he wanted to carry out this mission without further Watchers intervention. But then again, he had never been good at staying out of trouble.

Trouble didn't just find him, as the saying goes. For Silence, trouble was a seasoned tracker, a manhunter.

He recalled his past rogue missions, his violations of Falcon's *No involvement in local matters* imperative, how exhilarating it felt to operate outside of the strict rules of the Watchers. His latest self-imposed mission in Fort Bragg was no different—it was a chance for him to do the right thing without waiting for the sanctimoniously hypocritical clearance of the Watchers brass.

But now, it seemed his actions might just get him in more trouble than ever before.

He moved through the crowd, his eyes taking in the nuances of interactions around him. Each gesture, each smile, each exchange was a calculated move in the intricate game of high society. It was a world where appearances were paramount, where the façade often masked the true nature of intentions and desires.

As he scanned the faces, he wondered if there was any truth to what he'd just told Falcon about a potential connection between Matt and Lloyd Thornhill. Since Thornhill was a shadowy presence in peaceful Fort Bragg, there was a good chance Matt had investigated the man in connection to the suspicious murders. Silence wondered if Matt had attended a Thornhill function like the one he was currently attending, looking over the faces like Silence was doing.

And for a moment, Silence was living in the shadow of Matt's memory. Following—perhaps literally—in the footsteps of his ghost. Mirror reflections of each other. Two investigators.

Two boys in a schoolyard, ready to confront a trio of bullies.

Silence weaved through the crowd of high-flyers, homing in on Lloyd Thornhill. He had the face memorized from the materials the Specialist had provided. The guy was parked by a bunch of twisted metal that must have been a modern art piece, standing in that relaxed, showy way that screamed old wealth and a lifetime free from money worries. Silence closed the distance, and Thornhill gave him a sharp once-over, hidden behind a smile that looked like it had been polished in boardrooms and ballrooms alike.

There was that face from the photographs. In person, it looked even more smugly wicked. His hair, dark with strands of gray, was combed back in a disciplined wave. Square jaw. A classic, perfectly tailored suit clung to his frame—sinewy, not gym-swollen, but made tough by real-world experience.

Thornhill raised his glass in a half salute, the crystal catching the light. "You must be Detective Rasnick's replacement?" He tapped a miniature walkie-talkie sitting on the table beside him. "My man at the door told me he'd allowed you in."

Silence's mind flashed on the big, ugly doorman with the big, ugly lapel pin.

"I don't believe we've met. Lloyd Thornhill." His voice had the richness of old brandy.

He offered his hand. Silence took it. The hand was lotion-soft but quite strong, and the nails were manicured.

"Drew," Silence said.

Thornhill took a moment with Silence's strange voice.

"So, Drew, you came here with Detective Rasnick's invitation. Does that mean you're a detective as well?"

Silence nodded, rolling with the by-now-well-established Fort Bragg lie. "That's right." He swallowed. "A private one."

"And what might your purpose be at this gathering tonight? Surely not merely for the caviar and champagne."

"For a good cause."

Thornhill wasn't buying it. "The good cause, yes. Saving a trio of our beloved redwoods." He snickered. "And why else are you here?"

Silence leaned in slightly, lowering his voice. "Matt Jennings."

Thornhill's expression remained composed, but there was a flicker in his eyes. "Matt Jennings," he echoed with a sly grin. "*Another* detective." He was still for a beat as he stared into Silence with that grin, then, "A tragedy, his passing. Jennings was well loved in Fort Bragg."

"There are questions..." Silence said. "About his death."

"You detectives always have questions. Jennings had a way of digging up the inconvenient ones."

Silence bristled.

There was something about Thornhill's tone...

"Inconvenient questions..." Silence said and swallowed. "About you?"

"In my position in a town this small, a lot of people come after me," Thornhill said. "But my conscience is as clear as my record." He looked away, his eyes roaming over the party. "Have fun tonight. Welcome to my home. Enjoy the caviar. It wasn't cheap. If you'll excuse me."

Thornhill pulled a cellular phone from his pocket, then pivoted on his heel and strolled away.

Silence, too, moved on, going to a quieter corner. He discreetly activated a listening device—one of the Watchers' many pieces of advanced tech—that he'd stowed in his pocket. This device could pick up fragments of conversations, digitally extracting them from surrounding noise. He plugged in his earbud.

It wasn't long before he caught Thornhill's voice. The words were clipped, tinged with annoyance.

"Matt Jennings's investigation? I have no idea what that was about." A pause, then, "Rasnick! Yes, Rasnick. I know. We're keeping an eye on him. In the event of…"

There was a pulse of static as Thornhill's voice faded away. Across the room, his footsteps clacked on the floor as he turned a corner and disappeared. In Silence's ear, the digital noise-filtering switched off, and the sound of the crowd returned. He powered down the listening device, removed the earbud.

He'd gained no new intel, but from the antagonistic charge of the conversation he held with Thornhill and the slightly agitated sound of Thornhill's phone call, Silence felt bolstered.

He made his way through the mansion, each step taking him further from the gala's epicenter and closer to where the private quarters must be. Thornhill's study, he knew, would be a trove of personal insights. After turning into an empty hallway of wood and plush green carpet, he found the appropriate door ajar and slipped inside unnoticed.

The study was a reflection of Thornhill—opulent yet organized. Shelves lined with books on finance and art, a desk cluttered with papers, yet everything in its place. Silence rifled through the documents, searching for anything that could tie Thornhill to the mission.

But the search yielded nothing incriminating. Instead, Silence found indications of Thornhill's business dealings, his passion for art, and a lifestyle funded by shrewd investments. It painted a picture of a man engrossed in his world of wealth and influence—and, perhaps, some indications of dirty money—but not murder.

During his search, Silence's eyes caught on a series of travel itineraries. He noted that Thornhill had been out of town for a week—the same week Matt Jennings died.

It would seem Thornhill was clean.

Yet the itinerary detail, while intriguing, didn't serve as *conclusive* evidence of Thornhill's innocence. The timing could be coincidental.

Still, Silence couldn't shake off the weight of the conversation he'd overheard through his listening device.

Thornhill had been so agitated…

…but not in a commanding sort of way. He'd sounded … supplicant. Almost subservient.

Thornhill was supposed to be Fort Bragg's Boogeyman. Who the hell could make a guy like that sound like a lackey?

Silence's instincts, honed from years of unraveling complex plots, aligned with the detail he'd found in the itinerary—Thornhill was most likely *not* his man.

But he could lead Silence in the right direction.

As Silence slipped out of the study, his exit was less seamless than he'd hoped. The doorman/security guard—the homely guy with the distinctive silver eagle lapel pin, stood a few paces away—his eyes narrowing as they fixed on Silence. The recognition was instant.

And so was the man's reaction.

"You!" the man shouted as he bolted toward Silence, fist pulled back.

Silence responded instantly, dodging the initial grasp and using the guard's momentum against him.

Then, a swift, precise strike to the ribs.

Then, a calculated elbow to the solar plexus.

Silence's movements were a blend of combat skills honed in far harsher environments than Lloyd Thornhill's mansion.

The guard was tough, his size and strength formidable, and he absorbed Silence's blows well. But Silence's technique and speed were superior. The guard threw a left, missing badly. A right, nearly connecting, but again missing.

Then Silence finally landed a decisive blow—a jab to the jaw right as the man was lunging forward—that sent the guard staggering back, winded and dazed. He tried to stay on his feet. Couldn't. Collapsed.

The man's eyes shut.

And Silence slipped away.

CHAPTER FIFTEEN

THE VOICE in Bryan's ear said, *End of Disc 4. Please change discs.*

He pressed the *STOP* button on his portable CD player and took the headphones from his ears, leaning back in his chair, his thoughts drifting. The creak of a door down the hallway pulled his attention, and he looked up to see Drew emerging from the restroom, rubbing his hands together.

As Drew approached, Bryan gestured for him to come and join him in the living room. This was Bryan's personal space, where he spent most of his evenings. The overall aesthetic was a mix of modernity and comfort, with abstract paintings and black-and-white photography adorning the walls. On the far side of the room was a big-screen TV. The glass coffee table held books on history and a chess set with an unfinished game. The focal point of the room was the plush, beige sectional sofa. Bryan had worked hard to achieve a stylish yet inviting aesthetic—cool meets cozy.

When Drew had entered with Bryan a few minutes earlier and taken in the space for the first time, he'd given an impressed nod. There'd been a subtle lifting of the lips as well. Bryan could tell Drew appreciated the vibe of the place.

It had been clear from the beginning that the big guy had his own sense of style.

Drew emerged from the hallway and walked toward the table, taking a seat. The printouts of the spreadsheet that Matt had given to Bryan before his death were scattered across the surface, detailing Matt's expenditures in neat columns. Alongside them were Bryan's handwritten annotations. Bryan stood from the accent chair and sat with Drew at the table. They both leaned in closer to study the pages.

"Any more ideas?" Bryan asked, pointing to his handwritten listing of the overcharged amounts: *.01, .14, .03, .08, .15, .18*. Beneath this, in different handwriting, was *.59*. Drew had added this a few minutes after they'd arrived and begun delving into the spreadsheet, before his restroom break. It was the total of the seemingly innocuous amounts, barely over half a dollar.

Drew's brow creased with concentration as he analyzed the numbers. "It's a code," he said and swallowed. "Must be." He looked away. "Fifty-nine, hmm..."

Bryan sighed, leaning back. "I guess it makes sense, it being a code. That's why Matt gave it to me, a forensic accountant, to handle the situation if anything were to happen to him. He couldn't risk getting me involved prematurely, but he couldn't risk the information falling into the wrong hands either. But what doesn't make sense is ... why me? Of all the people he knew, of all his connections, why'd he leave this puzzle with me?"

Drew looked up, met his gaze. "He trusted you."

Then, Drew immediately went back to the spreadsheet.

After the impact of Drew's simple statement, however, Bryan needed a moment.

They continued staring at the pages, the room silent except for the occasional rustle of paper. The numbers were a puzzle, each one a piece of a larger picture that remained frustratingly out of reach. The minutes slipped away as they dissected each row, each column, searching for a pattern, a clue, anything.

Suddenly, there was a shift in Drew's demeanor. His eyes, which had been scanning the pages with a mix of concentration and frustration, instantly brightened.

And then, just as instantly, they darkened.

"Dammit!" he said.

Bryan leaned close. "What is it?"

"I suck."

"Huh?"

"I should've seen this..." he said and swallowed. "Earlier."

"You've figured it out?"

Drew nodded. "It's a cipher. We've been looking..." He swallowed. "At it wrong." He stabbed a finger at Bryan's notes —*.01, .14, .03, .08, .15, .18.* "Not fractions of a dollar." He swallowed. "Whole cents."

Bryan shook his head, confused. "Oh ... okay ... Then one, fourteen, three, eight, fifteen, and eighteen cents. I don't see how—"

"*A cipher*," Drew repeated, louder this time, giving it some emphasis. He swallowed. "The most basic cipher of all. Look."

He took a pencil and scratched out a quick note. Two columns. Numerals on the left, letters on the right.

1 A
2 B
3 C
4 D

He stopped at 4, tapping the list with one of his beefy fingers as he looked at Bryan and said, "Get it?"

Yes!

Bryan did get it.

He looked back at the overcharged amounts, now seeing them as whole numbers: 1, 14, 3, 8, 15, and 18.

"Okay, so one is A," Bryan began. "Fourteen is, um..."

Drew waved it off. "I have this cypher..." He swallowed. "Memorized."

He scratched out another note below the one he'd just written.

ANCHOR.

Bryan leaned in, his mind racing to keep pace. "*Anchor?* But what does it mean? Why would Matt—"

Drew cut in again. "An anchor. On a ship." He swallowed. "Noyo Harbor!"

Bryan paused, the gears in his mind turning.

Noyo Harbor, a Fort Bragg landmark. It made sense. A ship's anchor—a cryptic way nod to something local, something both Matt and Bryan would know well. Bryan's mind churned with the implications, the puzzle pieces beginning to align.

"You're right," Bryan said, rising from his chair. "We need to check it out, see what's there."

But Drew was already shaking his head, a determined look on his face.

"No. I got this." His tone left no room for argument.

Bryan opened his mouth to protest, to insist on being part of whatever came next, but Drew was already moving. He stood up abruptly.

"Drew, wait!" Bryan said.

But Drew was already out the door, his figure quickly disappearing into the night.

CHAPTER SIXTEEN

Silence arrived at Noyo Harbor. The port was dimly lit, shadows stretching across the docks and ships. A chill wind blew in off the sea, carrying the scent of brine. Silence buttoned his pea coat and scanned the area.

Some fishing boats bobbed in their slips, rigging clanking in the breeze. A few larger vessels were moored farther out in deeper water. But no recreation or tourism here—Noyo was strictly business.

He thought about the deciphered code word *ANCHOR*. After momentarily cursing himself again for not figuring it out earlier, he realigned his thoughts on the notion of the certainty of it. If there was anywhere anchor-related in Fort Bragg, it would be the harbor.

This was it.

Silence was certain.

As to what the "it" was ... he hadn't a clue.

But he knew he was in the right place.

Silence headed toward an old building ahead to find a vantage point. The corrugated metal structure creaked and groaned as he slipped inside. He chose a stack of crates near a window overlooking the main pier. Settling in, he raised his binoculars and started surveillance.

Most of the boats showed no signs of activity at this hour. But Silence's focus settled on a nondescript thirty-footer at the far end of the pier. Men moved on and off it with purpose, in contrast to the stillness surrounding them.

Watching their furtive body language, Silence felt the first tingles of anticipation. Something about their movements seemed hurried. And secretive. Heavy boxes and containers were being loaded on board, handled with care. The men worked almost silently, with no light or conversation to attract attention.

Silence's instincts told him he could be witnessing smuggling in action. Drugs? Guns? Something lucrative and illegal was going down.

He suspected drugs.

Often, it was drugs. People liked drugs.

Time to get a closer look.

Time...

A realization struck him.

Oh, no. Shit.

He checked his watch . The nighttime yoga session was happening right at that moment. He'd missed another session.

The Watchers would notice this.

Falcon would notice this.

Silence checked his phone. No missed calls. So far so good, he supposed.

For now, he had to put it out of his mind.

He slipped from his cover and skirted the edge of the building, keeping to deeper shadows. He silently traversed a maze of crates and fishing gear until he was within fifty feet of the target boat. Crouching behind stacks of wooden crates, he observed the scene just outside the pool of a security light.

Two men stood near the gangway, conversing in low tones. Silence strained to overhear. The guttural language was unfamiliar, likely some sort of code.

N-17 to row 8.

We done filled row 8 already, idiot!

He studied the pair—both were rough-looking, dressed in dark clothes suited for messy work. Tattoos marked their necks and hands. One revealed a handgun tucked into his waistband as he adjusted his jacket. Silence's pulse quickened. Clearly, these were not fishermen discussing the day's catch.

Edging nearer, Silence found his way blocked by a wall of empty fish totes. He moved to go around them and heard the scuff of a shoe. He spun toward the sound as a silhouette lunged from the darkness. Silence reacted on instinct, sidestepping the attack. The man stumbled past, then whirled with a snarl. Glints of light revealed a knife clutched in his fist.

The man was long and gangly, dressed in tattered cargo pants and, like Silence, a pea coat. Silence settled into a fighting stance, balling his fists. His attacker glared with menace etched on his face. He lunged again, slashing viciously with the blade.

Silence pivoted, feeling the breeze as it narrowly missed him. The man was quick but reckless. Easy work.

Timing his next move against the man's attack, Silence captured the knife arm mid-swing. He delivered an elbow to the temple that sent the man crashing to the ground, unconscious.

Silence stood over him, listening—no reaction from the men in the boat yet. He bent to retrieve the fallen knife, then dragged the unconscious man deeper into the shadows. The whole confrontation had been silent, lasting less than a minute. Silence needed to act while he still held this temporary advantage.

Keeping to the darker edges, he approached the gangway. He heard those same muted, guttural voices of the crew still working. He ducked behind cover and surveyed for his next move.

Then he saw something...

...a glimpse of an open storage compartment at the boat's stern.

Yes!

Now was his chance. He sprinted from his hiding spot and vaulted aboard and through a doorway, pressing himself flat beside the opening. The space inside smelled like cat piss and was stacked with plastic-wrapped bundles. Anticipation wriggled through Silence in an adrenaline rush as he tore at the wrapping. But as he carefully peeled back a section, he found no drugs or weapons...

...but tapes.

VHS tapes.

Videocassettes, packaged like surplus store merchandise. He reached into his pocket and risked a penlight's glow, finding titles like *Top Gun*, *E.T.*, and *Rocky III*. The paper sleeves were all the same—white and plain, with the titles printed in crude, off-center, mismatched letters. Some of them were even *handwritten*.

Pirated movies destined for street sales.

Son of a bitch...

This wasn't it.

This was a rinky-dink, bullshit operation, not something Matt Jennings—nor anyone else—would have died over.

Silence felt both frustration and relief wash over him. The smuggling operation was small-time, unrelated to the heavier criminal influence he was tracking. The *ANCHOR* clue had thrown him off course.

And he'd been so damn *certain* it meant Noyo Harbor...

He took one final glance at the bootleg VHS tapes, then ghosted back onto the pier as quietly as he'd arrived.

Sheltered in the shadows, Silence watched the boat crew continue their offload, unaware of his presence. He would leave them to their petty scheme. They weren't the big catch he was after.

He slipped into the darkness and retraced his steps through the maze of the harbor. As he reached the street, he breathed deeply, clearing the needless adrenaline from his system. His instincts had been right about illegal activity but wrong about the location.

He was no closer to discovering what happened to Matt than when he began.

Shit.

Back to square one.

CHAPTER SEVENTEEN

BRYAN STUDIED DREW, who sat brooding on the beige sectional. Despite the dim lighting in the living room, Bryan could still see the clear signs of frustration etched on the man's face.

Drew had just returned from following yet another dead-end lead. Noyo Harbor, it turned out, had no connection to *ANCHOR*. Drew had found nothing more than a small-time VHS piracy ring, no connection to their larger case.

Bryan knew these false starts were taking a toll, wearing down even Drew's stoic persistence.

It was eating at Bryan, too...

Lloyd Thornhill and his smug old-money privilege. And a wild goose chase at the harbor. Two strikes, and they were no closer to the shadowy forces hinted at by the *ANCHOR* clue.

Drew pulled himself up, moved to the table, and dropped back down. He had a distant look in his eyes, as if he was staring not just *at* the pages of the spreadsheet but *through* them. His fingers rhythmically tapped the tabletop. His typically stony facade was pulled even more taut into a tight-lipped grimace.

Hoping to lighten the mood, Bryan said, "You know, Matt talked about you all the time. I mean, all the time. *Jake Rowe was such a good kid.* Or, *Jake Rowe would kick this guy's ass.*" He chuckled. "In his eyes, you were the epitome of justice. He held you in such high esteem, and not being able to reconnect with you as adults really bothered him."

Drew looked up. There was something there for a moment, in the backs of his dark eyes. Then he nodded absently and turned his attention back to the papers.

Yes, Matt had idolized Drew—or Jake Rowe, rather—but Bryan doubted it was ever an equal respect. Drew was a leader, and it was the sort of leadership that was inherent, not learned at a school or academy. It had undoubtedly been there all along, even when he and Matt were both eight-year-olds.

Bryan pressed on, changing topics. "It's a shame Aria refused to help. But, I get it, after everything that happened between us." He paused. "I hurt her, Drew. Hurt her bad. We were close, man. Until I messed up big time."

Drew looked up at him. Though he neither said anything nor offered any non-verbals, he maintained his attention, not turning back to the papers.

Bryan supposed that was something.

Bryan's mind skirted around the edges of the memory, the details of what he'd done to fracture Aria's trust—and with it, their relationship—keeping it murky, just out of sharp focus. Maybe this was deliberate, this partial amnesia, leaving him numb to the guilt with which he'd tormented himself for so long.

He sighed. "I guess I had it coming, her leaving me. I mean, we were inseparable, and then I just ... I blew it all. It's no wonder she wants nothing to do with this investigation." He paused. "Or me."

The thoughts trailed off, leaving a sense of unresolved regret hanging in his mind.

He couldn't live in the past...

There was a very deadly present to deal with.

He shook it off and leaned forward. "Without Aria's help, that means our only option—"

Drew nodded, cutting in to finish the thought. "Is to go back.." he said and swallowed. "To Daniel Gray."

Despite being at a standstill, their minds were still in sync. That was encouraging.

But before they could strategize the next move, Drew's cellular phone rang. The sharp noise cut through the quiet that had gathered in Bryan's living room.

Drew checked the multiplex, then turned back to Bryan and said, "It's Detective Rasnick."

He flipped open the phone.

"Yes. Mmm-hmm," Drew said and swallowed. "I see. Okay."

As Drew collapsed the phone and put it back in his jacket pocket, his eyes locked onto Bryan's.

"What was that about?" Bryan said.

"We can't talk to Daniel Gray," Drew said and swallowed. "Gray is dead."

CHAPTER EIGHTEEN

As morning unfurled over the clearing where Yura's Yoga Retreat was taking place, the sky blushed with pink, casting a glow that gently nudged away the remnants of night.

The sunrise session was about to begin.

And, for once, Silence was in attendance.

The redwoods were bathed in a gentle light. Silence stood in line, waiting to receive his yoga mat, his broad physique contrasting against the delicate morning glow. Also at odds with the serene atmosphere, his mind swirled with chaotic thoughts.

His distant gaze wasn't on the redwoods nor the rest of the natural majesty. Instead, his mind was miles away, entrenched in the complexities of the case he'd left behind in Fort Bragg.

Daniel Gray was dead.

Another "accident."

Just like the "accidental" death of Matt Jennings.

Just like the "accidental" deaths Matt had been investigating.

Silence's world was one where accidents were scrutinized

until their true nature was revealed—usually something more sinister. He didn't believe in the fairytale called "coincidences." Fort Bragg was hiding something dark beneath its small-town charm, and Silence could feel it in his bones. C.C. had always told him to listen to his intuition. This intuition of his that had kept him alive in countless covert operations was now whispering to him that a deadly pattern was stitched into the fabric of his coastal hometown.

He shifted on his feet as he considered another Fort Bragg notion—his partner, Bryan, what the man had said about "messing up bad" with his ex-girlfriend, Aria. Bryan's confession had been cryptic, shards of truth that hinted at a troubling picture.

Due to the deep regret in Bryan's ambiguous confession, due to the fact he wouldn't give specifics...

...Silence suspected domestic violence.

Which was a damn shame. Because he'd been taking a shine to Bryan Holifield.

Bryan and Aria's intense relationship had lasted mere months, but Silence wondered how deep the scars went and whether alcohol had stoked the fire of Bryan's anger. He knew the type, men who swam in liquor until they drowned all reason.

Like his father.

Not violent.

But alcoholic.

Still, Silence couldn't condemn Bryan on a hunch. Instead, he filed the notion away in his mind.

Silence's eyes then drifted across the clearing. Among the patrons finding spots to unfurl their mats on the soft, forgiving earth was Juliette, the woman he'd seen the previous day, the one who, he'd been told, was a victim of an abusive boyfriend, Vinnie.

Juliette moved with a guarded grace, a fragility that

seemed out of place among the behemoth redwoods. In the growing daylight, Silence got a better view than he had the previous day, and he saw bruises on her forearms.

He bristled.

Yesterday, he'd *thought* he saw a mark on her face.

But now, those bruises were undeniable.

Maybe Silence's subconscious had been so filled with thoughts of the violence in Juliette and Vinnie's relationship that Silence had subconsciously thrust that concept upon Bryan, conjuring a scenario in which Bryan had been a violent alcoholic toward his ex-girlfriend Aria.

Hopefully, that was the case.

As Silence finally reached the front of the line and took a mat—getting a playfully scolding wave of a finger from Yura Turner along with a "Stop missing so many sessions, mister!"—Silence's mind wasn't on the sunrise session or the poses he would hold. It was on justice, on the invisible threads that connected him to these people, to Bryan and Aria, to Juliette, and the dark undercurrents that seemed to be running through the core of this tranquil region of California.

He tucked the mat under his arm, the texture grippy and firm, and made his way to a spot in the clearing. The mat slapped the ground, and he rolled it out with practiced ease. He'd been through quite a few yoga sessions with his borderline-hippie fiancée while she was still alive.

With C.C. on his mind now, the memory of Doc Hazel's words in Pensacola came back to him and stung like a slap: the insinuation that brevity could render a relationship insignificant. Silence's heart clenched—a brief, visceral reaction he immediately quashed.

They'd been engaged.

Engaged!

It wasn't the length of time that defined the depth of

their bond but the intensity and promise that had been snuffed out too soon.

Something dawned on him then...

Bryan and Aria's relationship had only lasted a matter of months as well.

Silence's mind nearly fell into a loop with this revelation.

But he stopped it.

Unlike Bryan and Aria, unlike Juliette and Vinnie, he and C.C. had seen a future together—*They'd been engaged!*—however short that vision had lasted.

C.C.'s voice came to him then.

That's right. We were engaged. That's all that matters.

Silence exhaled, relieved.

Juliette's figure, small and hunched over her mat, brought his thoughts back to the present. She was closer now, only a few yards away. The bruises were stark.

Silence's mind explored a familiar path—alcohol, the likely fuel to Vinnie's violent tendencies.

Alcohol.

Vinnie.

Bryan, possibly.

Silence's father, Kirk Rowe.

And Silence himself. For a brief period. Before someone had intervened.

Mrs. Enfield. More family than neighbor. She'd kept a watchful eye on Silence. She'd been his guardian against an alcoholic heritage from his father.

She'd kept him safe.

Love, C.C. said. *You're tumbling. Hone these thoughts. Make them useful to your current situation.*

C.C. was right.

She always was.

Silence's father had been a melancholic drunk, his sorrows drowning in the bottle, his anger turned inward. Vinnie, it seemed, was the other kind: a storm of a man who cast his fury outward, leaving bruises on skin and soul.

Silence's eyes remained on Juliette.

But a voice pulled them away.

"Morning, Drew."

Silence turned.

It was Kofi. He and Doris were headed his way. Doris wore another grandma sweater; Kofi wore a tie-dyed T-shirt, skin-tight. They took their place beside him and began unrolling their mats.

"You missed two more sessions," Doris said. There was playfulness in her tone, like there had been the previous day, but this time there was also a bit of rebuke.

"Sorry, ma'am," Silence said and swallowed. "I have a question."

Doris smiled. "Yes, dear?"

How she said "dear" reminded him of Mrs. Enfield, once more drawing a parallel between the two elderly women.

Silence pointed. "Juliette," he said and swallowed. "You said her boyfriend is trouble?"

Doris's expression clouded for a moment. "Yes. Vinnie. He's... not a good man. An abusive drunk, I'm afraid. We've tried to help her, but it's complicated."

Doris had said yesterday that she suspected Vinnie was violent toward Juliette.

But she hadn't insinuated that he was an alcoholic.

The confirmation of Silence's earlier suspicion settled in his stomach like a weight.

CHAPTER NINETEEN

ARIA SETTLED into the luxurious leather chair and swirled her glass of merlot. It always had a calming effect on her. Which was a good thing but also a very bad thing. She took another sip, feeling the warmth soothe her restlessness as the afternoon sun slanted through the windows.

Despite the mild sedative effect, her mind continued churning with indecision. Bryan's unexpected call the previous morning had shattered her hard-won peace. His voice dredged up memories and heartache she thought she'd firmly left in the past.

After a year of rebuilding her life, the last thing Aria needed was Bryan blundering back in, especially with wild theories about his deceased mentor and insinuations of murder. She knew how Bryan operated—always chasing the next grand mystery, never facing his own unresolved wounds.

Yet ... something in his voice had given her pause. There was a vulnerability she'd never heard, a desperate longing for answers. Maybe this time, his obsessive quest held real meaning.

Aria sighed, shifting in the buttery leather. She understood the need for closure too well. It was what drove her to walk away from everything in L.A. Only by breaking from her old life had she been able to heal.

Spiritually, anyway. The physical wound persisted.

With this thought, she rubbed her knee, which coaxed out a bit of ache.

But Bryan never had Aria's talent for moving forward. He remained tethered to the past like a boat clinging to a dock. First, his refusal to accept Matt's car accident. Now, this fanciful pursuit of justice from beyond the grave.

Despite herself, she couldn't deny the hints of a deeper mystery that had caught her interest. Bryan was many things but rarely wrong in his instincts. And the way he'd said that he and his private investigator, Drew, didn't think Matt's death had been an accident struck an odd chord of familiarity with Aria.

She wracked her memory, trying to pinpoint the elusive connection, and realized it was a feeling, a sensation. Since she'd moved to Fort Bragg three years ago, something had always felt ... off about the place. Like an indistinguishable undercurrent. Like a devilish inside joke.

Pissed off by her own curiosity, Aria paced to the window overlooking the cove. The water glinted in the morning light. Like so many times at this window, she found peace in the timeless rhythm of the waves.

And somehow, paradoxically, this peacefulness always made her think of the old career she had to leave behind in L.A. after the injury.

Stunt driving.

At times, she missed the adrenaline of it, the heady thrill of cheating death and the laws of physics. But she didn't miss what it required of her. The all-consuming drive that gradually edged out room for anything else in her life. No space left for trust or vulnerability.

In that sense, the injury had been a blessing. It made her appreciate the quieter things, forcing her to return to her backup career of accountancy.

Bryan was an accountant, too. Except he was a forensic accountant.

Looking back, her attraction to Bryan was inevitable. A man who understood her spirit and shared ample portions of it. Together, they'd burned white-hot, a pair of stars.

Until they collapsed like a dying supernova.

The injustice still simmered. Bryan's reckless action had ripped away her last scraps of dignity when she needed them most. She turned from the window, throat tight. Some wounds sank too deep to fully heal.

Like her damn knee.

Except worse.

Yet now Bryan had come to her asking for help, not with flattery or grand gestures, but simple sincerity. However flawed, she knew his desire for truth was genuine. She saw herself in that tireless seeking of his.

Weeks ago, she would have rejected his request outright. And, actually, she had done so yesterday. But solitude had granted perspective, and time softened even the most jagged edges. Perhaps she owed Bryan the chance to do right by Matt Jennings's memory.

Aria moved to her desk and rested her fingers on the phone. Whatever Bryan had stirred up, he was undoubtedly in over his head. That's how the guy was. If she refused him, how long would it be before his perseverance led him into true danger?

A breeze stirred the trees outside, breaking the quiet.

Before she could reconsider...

...Aria lifted the receiver and dialed Bryan's number from memory.

CHAPTER TWENTY

BRYAN'S HEARTBEAT accelerated at the mere sound of Aria's voice on the other end of the line.

After months of silence between them, almost a year, hearing her now sent a swell of emotions crashing through him. Guilt, shame, longing—feelings as raw and real now as the day she had walked out, her faith in him shattered by his actions.

"Aria, thank you," he managed, gripping the phone tightly. "I wasn't sure if you would—"

"I'm only doing this for Matt," she interjected, tone clipped. "You're looking for the name of his latest mentee?"

Bryan nodded, though she couldn't see it. He knew Aria's anger still simmered beneath the surface. He couldn't blame her. His thoughtless assumption had cost them everything.

"That's right," he said. "I need his name and address."

There was shuffling from the other end of the line.

While he waited, Bryan turned around from his position seated at the table and found Drew, who'd been completely silent the whole time. The big man was settled on the sectional, watching Bryan's phone conversation with the now-familiar stoic expression on his face.

"Shawn Corzo," Aria said after the pause. "He lives over on Oakdale. 1422. Apartment 130."

Bryan's hand moved quickly, scribbling down the details. This could be the key to solving the puzzle of Matt's death.

"Thank you, Aria. Truly. I know I don't deserve your help but—"

"You're right, you don't," she cut in sharply. "I'm not doing this for you."

Bryan flinched at her tone, the old wound stinging anew. "I know," he said. "What I did ... there are no words. I shouldn't have ... um..."

There was nothing but white noise on the line. Bryan braced himself for her to hang up, to sever this fragile connection forever. His fingers tightened on the phone.

"It doesn't matter now," Aria finally said, her voice heavy. "Just do right by Matt. Get the answers you need."

"I will," Bryan said. "With your help, I'm closer than ever."

He heard Aria sigh softly. When she spoke again, her tone had lost some of its hard edges. "Oh, Bryan." A pause. "Don't contact me again after this."

"Aria, wait—"

But the line was already dead. She'd slipped through his grasp once more.

Bryan's living room was terribly quiet then.

He turned to see Drew's steady stare still directed toward him. But he discerned a subtle shift in the usually impassive countenance—a slight hint of empathy breaking through the mask.

Bryan slowly set down the receiver. Hearing Aria's voice had sparked an irrational flare of hope that they could patch things up. That this could be a second chance if he just found the right words.

But some wounds never fully mended. The best he could hope for now was to honor Aria's request—get closure for Matt, then walk away for good.

It was better than he deserved.

He stood, crossed the room, and extended the note to Drew.

"I got the name and address," he said quietly.

Drew nodded, that fraction of empathy still showing on his severe face.

"Yeah, buddy," he said and swallowed. "I heard."

———

From the passenger seat, Bryan double-checked the address scrawled in his notebook as Drew's BMW rolled to a stop.

"Yep, this is it," he confirmed, looking up at the dilapidated apartment building. "1422 Oakdale."

The building had definitely seen better days. Its once pristine white exterior was now marred by peeling and cracking paint, like a bad sunburn. The railings and window frames were also tainted with rust stains. Two stories. Maybe forty units.

Bryan sensed the moment's pull, a feeling that harkened back to Matt. This must have been what Matt's life was like as a seasoned detective: going out in the world, finding seedy places, knocking on doors not knowing who—or, perhaps more fittingly, what—might answer.

Bryan was familiar with adrenaline as a forensic accountant, but he always experienced it from a safe distance: through numbers and not physical action. Matt would have been proud to see Bryan step out of his comfort zone and into the field.

Drew and Bryan exited the BMW, with Bryan looking at the building doubtfully.

"What a shithole," he muttered. "Let's hope this kid can actually help us."

Drew didn't reply, face impassive as he approached the building. Bryan hurried to catch up with Drew's long strides as they sought out the unit number.

Finding the apartment, Drew pounded his fist on the door. It drifted open under the force, clearly unlatched. As Bryan leaned around for a glimpse inside, Drew suddenly yelled, "Wait!"

But it was too late.

No sooner had Bryan realized the danger he was in than a pair of strong hands clamped down on his shoulders. In one fluid motion, he was yanked backward through the doorway and plunged into the darkness of the apartment beyond.

Panic surged through him. He twisted and turned, desperately trying to break free from the grip, but his assailant's hold was like a vice.

It was so dark that Bryan could barely see, his eyes struggling to adjust. He could sense more than see the looming shadow of his attacker.

And another!

Another form in the shadows.

Suddenly, an onslaught of punches came raining down on him. Each blow was a sharp burst of pain that coursed through his body. He desperately tried to defend himself, raising his arms in a feeble effort to block the attack, but the sheer force knocked him to the floor.

His knees hit first with a jarring thud, the impact shooting ache up his legs. Bryan gasped, air knocked from his lungs, his mind reeling from the onslaught. He braced for another blow, tensed for more pain...

...but then, as suddenly as the attack had begun, it ceased. The blows stopped, and he heard a heavy thud beside him.

And then another heavy thud.

Bryan's disoriented senses barely registered the sounds of two bodies slamming against the floor. He remained on his knees for a moment, disbelieving, his chest heaving, surrounded by the sudden stillness of the shadows.

The lights flashed on, and Bryan saw Drew at the light switch. Bryan's eyes adjusted to take in the crummy bachelor apartment: ratty furniture, stale air, and walls decorated with tattered movie posters. Breathing hard, he turned to see Drew standing over two crumpled forms.

Drew handled both attackers.

Handily.

Two young men were on the floor. One was a tall Hispanic youth in a sweatshirt and baggy jeans. The other was shorter and heavyset, African American, wearing a T-shirt emblazoned with the *Raiders of the Lost Ark* movie poster. Both were barely out of their teens.

Drew stared down at the tall one. "Shawn Corzo?"

The kid gave a shaky nod, eyes wide with fear.

Bryan rose slowly, dusting himself off, and glanced at both young men. He grimaced from his fresh wounds.

"Take it easy. We're not here to hurt you," Bryan said and shot a pointed look at Drew. "At least, not without reason."

Drew glanced at him, blinked.

Shawn's eyes narrowed in confusion. "Then who the hell are you?"

"I was a friend of Matt's," Bryan said. "We're trying to figure out what happened to him."

Understanding flashed across Shawn's face. "Wait, Matt like … Matt Jennings? From Due North?"

Bryan gave him a nod. "That's right. I'm Bryan. Matt was also my mentor, but that was many years ago."

He gestured to the heavyset teen now slumped against the couch. "Who's your friend? He's got a hell of grip on him."

"My roommate Malik," Shawn said.

Painting, Malik struggled to sit up, but he was too exhausted to do so. He gave up and rested his head against the wall, shooting an irritated look at Bryan. "*Me* with the grip? Man, you damn near tore a hole in my favorite T!"

His gaze shifted downwards, causing fat rolls to appear on his neck as he glanced at his Indiana Jones shirt. At that moment, Bryan made the connection between the shirt and the movie posters adorning the walls. Malik was definitely the cinephile in this apartment.

"Yeah, we might've overreacted," Shawn said. "But Matt warned me someone might show up. So when that door popped open just now, we were ready. *Pow!*"

Bryan's pulse quickened. "Matt thought he was in danger?"

Shawn shrugged. "He just said to be real careful who I trusted for awhile. That he was onto something big."

Frustrated, Bryan looked to Drew. "Matt told me the same thing. But he wouldn't give me details."

Drew's expression remained unreadable. Then he turned to Shawn. "Did Matt explain..." he said and swallowed. "What he discovered? Or who..." Another swallow. "Might be after him?"

Shawn shook his head, glancing away. "Nah man. I figured it was just Matt being dramatic. Typical cop, ya know?" He snickered—part youthful defiance, part reminiscent. "I never thought..." His voice trailed off.

Drew's visage hardened as he assessed the situation. He then turned to Bryan with a barely perceptible shrug. "We've hit..." he said and swallowed. "Another dead end." He turned back to Shawn. "Sorry for the trouble."

Drew then stepped over Malik's still-groaning form and

made for the door. Bryan hesitated, hating to leave this place so empty-handed. But one look at Drew's stony face told him arguing was pointless.

With a frustrated sigh, Bryan followed Drew out.

CHAPTER TWENTY-ONE

Gray's Machine Shop was silent and still in the afternoon light that filtered in through the grimy windows. It was Saturday; the place was closed. Having bested the ludicrously simple lock a few moments earlier with a few swipes of a rake pick, Silence was inside, moving quickly but stealthily through the dormant equipment. Even though it appeared Daniel Gray had a prehistoric set of security measures, Silence would never put it over a gruff guy like him to have some hired muscle sitting around.

Or, perhaps more fittingly, maybe Gray's murderers had a man installed at the shop.

In the police report, Gray's death had been ruled an accident—crushed by machinery while working alone after hours.

But there was no way in hell that was true.

Matt Jennings had also died in a supposed accident two weeks earlier.

Silence didn't believe in coincidences.

He came to the industrial lathe identified as the fatal device. It was circled by plastic police tape, which Silence lifted and ducked under. Squatting down, Silence inspected the machine's heavy chuck, still flecked with traces of dried blood. He slid open the access panel, examining the drive gears and belts. All appeared to be in order.

Yet some nagging sense told him to keep looking. Rising, he circled the lathe, searching for anything amiss. As he reached the back, he spotted it—a safety guard unbolted and lying on the floor nearby.

Stooping to examine it, Silence saw the screw holes showed no signs of being forcibly removed. They had been carefully extracted to *appear* undisturbed.

Accident, indeed.

He felt a tingle at the base of his neck, signaling that intuition of his that C.C. had been so proud of.

Whoever took off this safety guard wanted this "accident" to happen. They'd wanted it to look like Gray had been working on something—a massive turbine, perhaps—and put too much of his weight against the machine, falling into the works.

But this safety guard had not failed.

Which meant Gray's death was likely premeditated murder.

Of course.

Silence was replacing the panel when he caught a faint scuff behind him. He spun just as a steel rod arced toward his skull. Ducking reflexively, he drove forward and slammed into his attacker's midsection. They crashed to the floor in a tangle of limbs.

So...

Here was the bit of hired muscle Silence had halfheartedly prepared for.

The man was powerfully built, with prison tattoos snaking down his thick arms. But his size made him slow. Silence delivered a precise elbow strike to his temple as they grappled. The man's grip loosened enough for Silence to wrench away the steel rod and fling it clattering across the shop floor.

Both Silence and the other man scrambled to their feet.

With a wicked grin, the man lurched forward, attempting to pin Silence with his bulk. But Silence was ready. He stepped into the charge, using the man's momentum to pivot him face-first into the grating.

Before the thug could react, Silence had his arm brutally torqued behind his back. He dropped to one knee, inches from dislocating it. Keeping the thug's wrist locked, he quickly rifled through the man's pockets until he found a wallet. Flipping it open revealed a New Mexico driver's license for one Cal Jameson.

Hired out-of-state muscle.

Silence pocketed the wallet and released Jameson's arm. The man slumped forward, cradling it, glaring hatred even as fear lurked in his eyes. Silence knew this punk was only muscle, not whoever masterminded Gray's murder.

Silence stood up and delivered a calculated strike to Jameson's temple, rendering him unconscious. After brushing off his hands, Silence did one last check to ensure he didn't leave any evidence behind.

He walked toward the secluded office in the back. Quietly, he began his search, sifting through the papers and files cluttering Gray's desk.

Gray sure had been a disorganized shit.

Silence's hands moved methodically, flipping through files and skimming over pages. He was looking for something specific, the word *ANCHOR*, something that would unlock the secrets.

And he found it.

Side by side with another word.

ANCHOR and *EXECUTOR*.

They were together at the top of the paper, each heading

a column of numbers, indecipherable to Silence. They appeared to be serial numbers of some sort.

Both words, he noted, concluded with the same suffix: OR. This intriguing connection tugged at the edges of his mind, prompting him to delve deeper into its potential significance.

He realized then that he had been approaching this all wrong. His previous attempt to decipher the meaning of *ANCHOR* had been too literal, leading him to Noyo Harbor. Perhaps the key lay not in what the *ANCHOR* and *EXECUTOR* meant individually but in their shared etymology.

He stuffed several sheets of paper in his pockets and left.

CHAPTER TWENTY-TWO

Ten minutes later.

Hyer pulled his sedan to a stop outside the machine shop, gravel crunching under the tires. Killing the engine, he stepped out and surveyed the empty lot. No apparent signs of intruders.

But appearances could be deceiving.

Especially with an elite operator moving through town.

Entering the shop, Hyer was met by the familiar smells of oil and iron. He wound through silent machinery until a faint groan caught his attention. In the shadow of a hydraulic press, he found one of the out-of-state contractors—Jameson, he believed this one's name was— hauling himself unsteadily to his feet.

Unbelievable.

These guys hadn't cost much, but their reputation had been strong.

Hyer grabbed a fistful of Jameson's shirt and slammed him back against the machine. "What the hell happened here?"

Jameson's eyes rolled drunkenly. "Some ... guy was nosing around. Tall dude, military-looking. Didn't get a name."

Shit.

It *was* the operator.

Hyer tightened his grip, fingers twisting in the greasy fabric. "And you didn't stop him?"

"Hey, I tried, dude," Jameson said. "Came at him from behind. He was slippery though. Knocked me out cold."

With a disgusted snort, Hyer released him. Sloppy idiots like this one from New Mexico were what happened when you hired cheap street muscle.

But the elite cost *real* money, and this was supposed to be a quick, quiet cleanup job at the machine shop with a negligible money trail and equally negligible paper trail.

"Where was he nosing around?" Hyer said.

Jameson pointed to the lathe—the place of Gray's supposed accident, circled with yellow police.

Shit.

"And when I started to come to," Jameson said, "I saw him leaving there."

He moved his finger, pointing slightly more to his right.

Toward the office in the back.

Shit!

Hyer paced away, mind racing over implications. Undoubtedly, the operator had sniffed out that Gray's death was no accident. That meant scrutiny, deeper digging, going through Gray's paperwork, looking for clues.

As Hyer stomped off for the office, leaving the idiot Jameson swaying behind him, he pulled out his cellular phone and jabbed at the buttons. The line rang twice before a deep voice answered.

But not just deep.

It sounded artificial, borderline comical, like one of those identity-hiding effects used on true crime television shows.

Clearly, the purpose was the same as that television effect: to conceal the man's identity.

"Yes?" the voice said. "What'd you screw up this time?"

Hyer kept his tone low and even. "We have trouble. The professional is putting the pieces together."

CHAPTER TWENTY-THREE

Silence hunched over the table in Bryan's living room, scrutinizing the documents he'd nabbed from Gray's machine shop. Most were invoices for metal parts and machining services, opaque in their legalese but hinting at custom fabrication work. One scrap of paper caught his attention—another document bearing the word *EXECUTOR*, this time scrawled in Gray's clumsy hand. Beneath that, Gray had written *BLACK THORN*.

This was a name Silence knew well—Black Thorn. And seeing in the handwriting of a humble machine shop owner from Fort Bragg, California, was enough to make Silence's pulse jump.

But for now, he put aside the notion, focusing on the first puzzle piece: *ANCHOR* and *EXECUTOR*.

One thing at a time.

Bryan stood in the doorway with his arms crossed, observing Silence's work with a mix of curiosity and investigative impatience. The quiet between them was heavy, broken only by the faint sound of paper shuffling as Silence sifted through the materials. Bryan's anxiety radiated behind him, adding to the tension in the room.

At the shop, Silence had realized there must be an etymological tie between *ANCHOR* and *EXECUTOR*. Now, Silence's instincts told him these weren't names of concepts but of *people*. All clues were showing that there was some sort of shadowy network in Fort Bragg, individuals behind all the deaths: Matt's, Gray's, and the deaths Matt had been investigating. Work like that took a team.

And a team needs a leader.

Silence looked up from the papers and waved Bryan over. Bryan obliged, joining Silence at the table.

Silence pointed to Gray's note.

"If I had to bet..." Silence said and swallowed. "Executor is a person. The leader."

He lowered his face, locking eyes with Bryan to prompt him toward the conclusion Silence had already reached.

"A leader..." Bryan said. "As in, the person Matt was investigating?"

Silence nodded.

"Curtis Hyer!" Bryan said.

"Right."

Hyer had been a person of interest from the very beginning, before Silence arrived at Fort Bragg, starting with the investigative work of his deceased friend, Detective Jennings. Silence considered the implications—Hyer as an enforcer for powerful criminal elements, using his local connections to enable their stateside enterprises for Black Thorn. It was a troubling thought.

As if reading his thoughts, Bryan frowned at the note on the table. "But what's Black Thorn?"

"Illegal arms..." Silence said, swallowed. "Manufacturer out of..." Another swallow. "Romania."

"*Romania?* What are they doing in Fort Bragg?"

Silence sifted through the papers, finding the one he'd seen earlier. "This." He handed the sheet to Bryan. "Serial numbers..." He swallowed. "For boutique parts."

"So ... Gray was making parts for Black Thorn?"

"Under duress."

"From whom?"

"The Executor is my guess," Silence said and swallowed. "Curtis Hyer."

"Okay, so, then Gray shipped those parts overseas to Black Thorn?"

Silence nodded. "Through Noyo Harbor."

"But ... why here? Why would Black Thorn go to Fort Bragg, California? There have to be hundreds, hell, maybe *thousands* of small machine shops in the country."

Silence shook his head. "Can't figure that part out." He swallowed. "But I will. *We* will."

Yes, Silence was truly stumped by the absurdity of an operation like Black Thorn utilizing a guy like Daniel Gray, even if it was through an intermediary.

Stumped ... for now.

Silence pulled out his PenPal notebook. When he had a lot to say, he wrote it out. This wasn't something he did often, but it was helpful.

NedNotes brand PenPal notebooks were compact but thick with plastic covers that came in a variety of bold colors. This one featured rows of turquoise and gold circles. Silence took a mechanical pencil from its position stored in the spiral binding, jotted out a note, and then handed the PenPal to Bryan.

My organization has been watching Black Thorn for the last two years, as have the FBI and NSA. Black Thorn has been consolidating power in the States, and custom weapons are key to this expansion. Word is, they're making a big move very soon. That move could be here in Fort Bragg, and Hyer could be their inside man. Chances are, he twisted Gray's arm, and when Gray got out of line, he broke it.

Suddenly, Bryan was overwhelmed. He threw up his hands, and as he did so, he knocked his portable CD player off the table.

"Shit."

He picked it up.

"You sure like music," Silence said.

Bryan shook his head. "Actually, it's not music. It's an audiobook. An anger-management program. *Tame the Beast.* It's helping me get control of my emotions. You know ... after Aria."

Silence studied Bryan's guarded expression, reading shame and regret in the tight set of his jaw. Whatever happened with Aria had cut deep, fueled by more than careless words in the heat of the moment.

As he thought about it, Silence hadn't noticed Bryan act particularly angry at any point during their investigation. The audiobook must've been working.

Silence thought about Juliette back at the yoga retreat, the fact that she's been physically abused by her boyfriend, Vinnie. He then flashed on the secretive, almost shameful way Bryan had gone about sort-of-but-not-entirely telling Silence he'd been awful to his ex-girlfriend, leading to their breakup.

"This anger. Does it..." Silence said and swallowed. "Ever get violent?"

Bryan bristled, shoulders tensing. "No! You're implying something, aren't you? I would never lay a hand on Aria." He looked away, unable to meet Silence's scrutinizing gaze. "It wasn't *that* kind of problem."

"Alcohol involved?"

"*No!* Alcohol wasn't part of the equation either. Shit, man!"

Bryan was flushed in the face. *Now* Silence was getting some of that anger from him.

Silence nodded slowly. He had misjudged the situation—Bryan's pain came from something less sinister but still destructive. Loss of control didn't have to mean physical violence. Words could wound deeper than any fist.

He fixed a heavy stare on Bryan, urging wordlessly for him to continue. Bryan's shame was substantial in the room, a weight that bowed his shoulders. Letting go was never easy, even when change was necessary.

But it was time.

The heft of this secret was weighing down their investigation.

Bryan just shook his head, eyes fixed on the floor. "I was pissed at her. Okay? Really pissed." His voice was thick with emotion. "' But ... I never meant to..." He exhaled hard. "I have anger control issues. That's why I'm listening to the damn book." He pointed to the CD player. "But it's so difficult. I just ... I..."

He trailed off, looking up at Silence as though he wanted to say something else to end this awful moment of remembrance, to wrap things up, but coming up short.

Damn.

The guy was *still* being guarded.

Silence didn't respond.

Not immediately, anyway.

He looked away from Bryan, mulling over an idea that had just formed.

After a moment, he turned back to Bryan and said, "I know someone..." He swallowed. "Who can help you."

CHAPTER TWENTY-FOUR

AN HOUR LATER, Silence was back at Navarro River Redwoods State Park at the edge of the clearing, which was filling up, only minutes away from the daytime session. There was the rustling of yoga mats being spread out; soft murmurs and gentle laughter from the yogis; the sound of deep, intentional breaths being taken as people focused on their bodies and surroundings.

Silence had made it on time to another session. But this time, he hadn't come alone.

Bryan stood beside him.

Silence watched as Yura approached, her stride radiating the same calm and control she taught in her classes, her face beaming, of course.

"This is Bryan," Silence said as Yura stepped up to them. "He has..." He swallowed. "Anger issues."

Yura's smile didn't waver, her eyes warm and accepting. "Welcome, Bryan! Oh, Drew, this is wonderful of you! You're growing; I can see it. Good on ya, boy. Now, Bryan, don't you sweat this anger-control issue of yours. We all have our issues, and this is a no-judgment zone. Oh, yeah, you got that right!

Now, let's find you a space where you can find some peace. You thirsty? Need something to eat?"

She threw an arm around Bryan's shoulder so quickly and enthusiastically that it made him stumble. She pulled him away—keeping her arm around him, chatting animatedly—and guided him through the maze of mats and meditating bodies. As Bryan grew smaller in the distance, he glanced over his shoulder at Silence with a perplexed expression that gave a silent plea of, *What the hell have you gotten me into?*

Alone now, Silence exhaled. His mind shifted gears, back to Fort Bragg, sorting through the fragments of information he had on the Black Thorn Society. Untraceable firearms were their signature—no serial numbers, no distinct parts, nothing that bureaucracies or forensics could sink their teeth into. With its small-town charm, Fort Bragg seemed a world away from such darkness. But Silence now knew that the threads of the syndicate's web were somehow woven through the town's fabric, invisible but omniscient.

His gaze wandered, drawn to a burst of laughter that sounded too bright against his hush of introspection.

Doris and Kofi.

They were wrapped in each other's arms, their laughter ringing clear. He watched them. Doris, with her elegant bob of white hair; Kofi, lean and lithe and energetic beside her. Fossil and young buck. Bone white and glowing bronze. Jewish and ... Rastafarian? New Age?

They were an odd couple, sure, but there was a rightness about them. Kofi, in his flowing linen shirt—worn wide open, of course, his washboard abs glistening—stood in contrast to Doris's understated elegance. Together, they were like contrasting notes in a melody, yet somehow they harmonized.

Feeling Silence's stare, Doris looked over, her keen eyes locking onto his. She nudged Kofi, and together they turned to him, their faces alight with unabashed joy. They raised their hands, waving not just in greeting but as if to say, *Come join us!*

Silence lifted a hand and started toward them...

...but stopped.

A shout ripped through the air, tearing the veil of calm that had settled over Yura's Yoga Retreat. A voice laced with venom, spitting out poison.

"Yeah, just run away! Run away, bitch. That's what you always do."

The words echoed, bouncing off the massive redwood trunks, and Silence felt every muscle in his body tense. The crowd turned as one, all eyes on the disturbance.

Through the sea of shifting bodies, Silence saw her.

Juliette.

She was at the edge of the eastern parking area, her arms wrapped around herself like they'd been the first time Silence saw her. She moved quickly, her head lowered, leaving the cars and heading for the clearing.

Silence spun around.

He shouldered his way through the onlookers. His gaze cut through the foliage to the parking area, glimpsing a man standing behind the open driver-side door of a sleek blue Mercedes sedan.

This would be Vinnie.

Even at this distance, Silence could see rage rolling off the guy. Coiled tight. Cheeks flushed. His hair was a tangle of dark curls. A shadow of stubble darkened his jawline. He wore a pale blue dress shirt, sleeves rolled up to the elbows.

Silence was still several yards away, so he could only watch as Vinnie dropped back into the Mercedes and slammed the door shut. The sound cracked through the ancient trees, reaching the yogis in the clearing, eliciting murmurs and gasps.

The Mercedes's engine roared, and it took off, stirring up

a dust cloud. The temptation to give chase was there, igniting in Silence's chest. But he was too far away.

His gaze shifted toward Juliette as he hurriedly closed the distance between them, mindful of not appearing menacing. Juliette halted, her eyes lifting to meet his for a brief, heartrending second.

Silence saw it then—the pink mark on her cheek.

It stood out, bold and bright against her pale skin

Fresh.

Adrenaline flushed through him, a dark, bitter anger usually reserved for enemies in the field.

"Juliette?" he said.

Her eyes fixed on him, displaying a blend of confusion, pain, and a bit of fear. She seemed as perplexed by Silence's familiarity with her name as by his unusual voice.

Her own voice was barely audible when she replied, "Yes?"

Silence watched her—the tremor in her shoulders, the way her arms tightened around her torso. "Was that Vinnie?"

Again, her confusion at Silence's knowledge of the situation was evident on her face, but she simply nodded, the movement slight, a tremble. "Yes."

"Did he do..." Silence said and swallowed. "This to you?" He used his eyes to indicate her face.

Juliette's gaze fell to the ground. She nodded.

"Alcohol?" Silence said.

Again, a tiny nod. "Yes."

Silence's anger took on a new form with the confirmation.

Alcohol.

He remembered his father, the smell of spiced rum, the hollow eyes, the quitting on life. A degradation of existence. And Mrs. Enfield, years later, the neighbor who had become a sentinel, her voice gentle but firm as it pulled Silence from the brink of a hereditary abyss. She'd helped him, might have even saved him; who knows how dark the pit might have become.

Mrs. Enfield had helped him.

And he could help Juliette.

Always pay it forward.

"I'm Drew," he said. "I can help you." He swallowed. "Will you let me?"

She finally lifted her gaze, looked at him, her eyes searching his. There was a wariness there, the instinctual caution of someone who had trusted and been hurt.

Hurt badly.

But beneath it, there was a flicker of something else. Hope. Or the beginnings of hope, anyway.

Juliette's lips parted, closed.

Then, a nod.

"All right," she breathed out.

Silence took his phone from his pocket and displayed it to her.

"Do you have..." he said and swallowed. "A cell?"

She nodded and fished in her purse, retrieved her cellular phone.

Silence took the phone from her and flipped it open. He entered his phone number, pressed *SEND* and then *END*. He handed the phone back.

"My number," he said and swallowed. "Call me anytime."

Juliette nodded, her eyes holding his for a moment longer than necessary. "Okay."

She stepped past him, wrapping her arms around herself again.

He watched her walk away.

CHAPTER TWENTY-FIVE

WELL, that had definitely been an experience.

Bryan had never thought he'd attend a yoga class, but back there in the quiet of the state park, he had felt a shift. Those towering trees and Yura Turner's straight talk had an unexpected effect. Turner, with her calm words and understanding eyes, seemed to get under his skin in a good way. Her approach had been a surprising balm to his anger-control problem. Maybe, even, she'd chipped away at something deep inside him.

Bryan was back in the BMW's passenger seat as Drew drove them away from Yura's Yoga Retreat. They were somewhere between the park and Fort Bragg, and Drew had just taken a turn off SR 128. Now, they were on a narrow, winding road that cut through the endless forest. It was a tight path with trees pushing in on either side. Branches intertwined to create a natural tunnel that blocked most of the sunlight.

On Brian's lap was the stack of papers Drew had taken from Gray's machine shop, and on top was the page that Drew had told him to examine. Drew had circled an address, a remote spot in the trees. That's where they were going.

Brian glanced at the address again. Beneath it, Gray had written *JENNINGS*. "So, what is this place?"

Drew didn't turn, just kept his stony face on the road ahead as he pulled the BMW off the paved road and onto a dirt one, which led down a long curve into a gully. "Matt's name is written..." Drew said and swallowed. "With address. He might've..." Another swallow. "Investigated the place." Another swallow. "It's a long shot."

Bryan shrugged. "Fair enough."

He supposed this was what it was like in a real-world, non-forensic-accounting investigation; apparently, one must capitalize on any kernel of possibility. He imagined Matt had been just as dogged at pursuing small clues as Drew.

This address was a slender thread in Drew's investigation, a thread that now tied back to Curtis Hyer. Everything pointed to Hyer as the elusive "Executor"—the shadowy puppet master pulling strings for the Black Thorn Society's operations in California.

A wave of surrealism came crashing in.

Bryan's partnership with Drew had happened on a whim, a decision that came in a fleeting moment at the cemetery, right there in front of Matt's grave, hitting him like a speeding train. At first, the sudden pairing had thrown Bryan off balance. Drew's methods were unorthodox, his demeanor a cold enigma.

But as the investigation unfolded, a sense of comfort had crept in, seeping through the cracks of Bryan's initial resistance. Something about Drew, in the way he moved, the slight tilt of his head when he was deep in thought, reminded Bryan of Matt. It wasn't a physical resemblance—giant, gothic Drew looked nothing like Matt—but something more profound, a familiarity in their approach, a shared unspoken language. In a way, it was like having Matt back again. If only for a little while.

The dusty road abruptly stopped at a sagging chain-link gate, its edges laced with sharp razor wire. Beyond the gate stood a desolate metal structure, possibly an abandoned warehouse or workshop. Time had worn down the corrugated metal siding to a dull, ashen color, and graffiti marred the walls and roofs. The sound of chains rattling was carried by the wind as it gusted through the surrounding trees and undergrowth slowly reclaiming the site.

Drew parked. They got out and made their way through the gate toward the dilapidated building. The main door was slightly ajar, scraping against the dirt as they pushed it open further. Inside, the space was dark and vast, with a floor made of raw earth and steel pillars supporting the roof. Spiderwebs hung from the ceiling, while pools of darkness lurked in the corners atop piles of wooden crates. The air smelled musty, damp.

No sign of recent human habitation. But the thread had led here for a reason.

Bryan's palms were slick with sweat, and his stomach churned. But as Drew stood beside him, radiating calm and assurance, Bryan felt a glimmer of confidence grow within himself. He followed Drew's lead.

Drew moved quietly, senses alert, catlike. Ten yards in, a flurry of motion exploded out of the murk. Figures lunged at them, men wielding knives and lengths of pipe, their eyes wild. Four of them.

Not a situation to walk into unprepared.

But Drew was prepared.

Go figure.

As the first attacker lunged, Drew's reaction was a fluid surge of motion. He pivoted on the balls of his feet, and his arm shot out, fingers stiff, striking a throat. The man stumbled back, clawing at his neck, gasping for air.

Caught up in the chaos, Bryan avoided a wild punch from

one of the attackers—a behemoth in a red flannel and faded Wranglers—and countered with a swift jab to the ribs. For a moment, Bryan felt pretty badass...

...until the man caught Bryan's wrist and threw him into the wall. Pain rocketed up Bryan's ribs, and he shouted out.

Meanwhile, Drew gracefully moved through the swarm of attackers, each strike calculated and forceful. A powerful elbow collided with a nose, producing a loud crunch, while a palm struck a solar plexus with a whooshing impact. His leg moved in a blur as it connected with a knee.

...which happened to belong to the man holding Bryan.

The man released Bryan as he fell to the dirt floor.

The fight unfolded with a brutal rhythm, and Drew was at its center. Men fell one by one around him, their cries echoing off steel walls.

Quickly, the room stilled. Drew stood tall, his chest rising and falling, winded but not breathless, while the four attackers moaned and whimpered in the dirt.

The biggest of the men—the one in the red flannel, the one who'd attacked Bryan—blinked up at Drew and managed to grind out, "You with that other guy? The one who was here before?"

Drew started to answer, but Bryan cut him off, stomping toward the man. "You mean Matt Jennings? The cop? He's *dead*, asshole."

The man's eyes went wide. "Dead?"

Bryan's temper spiked. He tried to calm his anger and remember the audiobook and his recent teachings from Yura Turner.

...but it all got lost in the fog of his rage.

"Yeah, *dead!* So you'd better tell us what the hell he asked you about when he was here. Now!"

Bryan heard footsteps behind him and turned to see Drew approaching. He expected a rebuking for losing control of his anger, but instead, Drew went with the flow of it, grabbing a handful of the man's flannel and yanking him off the floor. He slammed the man into the wall.

Bang!

"*Talk!*" Drew growled in his face.

"Okay, okay!" the man cried. "Take it easy!" He gulped, then words came out in a tumbling rush. "Curtis Hyer has been using this place as storage. That's it, man! Just storage. He's working for this ... group. Out of Europe. All we do is hide the shit in those boxes for him!" He pointed with his chin toward the crates.

While Drew kept the squirming man pinned against the wall, Bryan stomped over to the crates and pulled back one of the tops. The lid fell off and clattered in the dirt, throwing up a dust cloud.

Empty.

Bryan whipped around, throwing a look at the man.

"We ain't got anything now!" the man said. "Hyer and his guys came and took the stuff last week, for ... whatever it is they're doing tonight."

With that last word, "tonight," Bryan and Drew exchanged a glance.

Bryan bolted back across the room. "You said 'Hyer and his guys.' Who were those other guys?"

The man shook his head. "The only person we know by name is Hyer. He told us about the bait, but I don't who the kid is, only his name."

"What bait?" Drew barked, gripping the man's shirt tighter. "What name? Talk!"

He slammed the man into the wall again, rattling metal.

Bang!

"Shawn Something-or-other. I don't know. Some Hispanic last name. I don't remember."

Bryan and Shawn exchanged another look, then Drew turned back to the man and said, "Shawn Corzo?"

The man nodded fervently, cooperatively. "Yeah! Corzo. That was it."

Bryan's heart raced. "Shawn? How's he involved?"

"He was gonna be used as a trap." the man said. "Hyer wanted to draw Matt Jennings out by using Shawn as leverage. But you just said Jennings is dead, so ... I guess Shawn's safe now."

For a third time, Bryan and Drew looked at each other. The non-verbal communication was becoming natural, and Bryan again felt Matt's ghostlike presence.

"Or he's in more danger than ever," Bryan said. And in another moment of realization, he added, "And Aria could be, too! She's the one who got us Shawn's name. Hyer and Black Thorn have surely hacked the Due North servers. Shit, I gotta call her!"

Drew released his grip on the guy's shirt. The man sagged back against the wall. Teetered. And fell back to the floor.

Bryan pulled out his phone, flipped it open.

"Oh, shit!" he said to Drew. "No signal.

Drew checked his cellular phone. Shook his head. Showed the multiplex to Bryan.

No signal.

No way to warn either Aria or Shawn.

Bryan was about to say *Let's go!*, but Drew was already sprinting out of the building.

CHAPTER TWENTY-SIX

YES, Hyer truly hated this place.

It was the air. Not simply the smell of it—which was bad enough—but the fact that with every breath he took, he could practically *feel* himself getting sick, ingesting mildew and mold and God knows what else.

He was back at the abandoned foundry.

This time, he was in a room in the back that had once been an office, sitting in a dry-rotted chair behind and equally decrepit desk. A landline phone was on the litter-strewn surface before him, and he had the receiver to his ear. The man running the show—who had chosen the foundry as their safe house of sorts—had used his connections to install a secure and untraceable phone line in the rotten complex.

Light came in through the half-boarded-up-half-shattered-glass window behind Hyer, illuminating dust particles—mold particles?—which danced languidly before him. While he spoke into the phone, he used a finger to trace shapes in the murk covering the desktop.

"I had a couple of my guys tail them after they left the yoga shit," Hyer said. "But they lost them at some point.

Looks like Holifield and the professional must've turned off the highway. No cell service out there in the trees. Our guys lost communication and lost track of each other. Never found Holifield and the professional. Turns out, they roughed up the guys at Storage Facility 2."

The voice on the other end of the line—though distorted and deep—registered an unbothered reaction. "Unfortunate, but expected. This newcomer is clearly quite capable."

Hyer's jaw bunched. "Doesn't matter how capable if I'd had more men. But resources are stretched thin."

It was a bit of double-speak, what he'd just said. A veiled demand. All along, Hyer had felt a lack of manpower. And the men he'd received—like the doofuses from New Mexico—were below-grade

"Which is precisely why we must use them strategically," the other man said. "Scattered efforts will only weaken results."

The statement brooked no argument. And, like Hyer's comment a moment earlier, it had a hidden meaning, implying poor leadership on Hyer's part.

Hyer bristled but said only, "So how do I proceed?"

"The professional is concerning. If we don't do something, he's going to blow the operation," the voice said. "A change in approach may is needed. Shift focus to the other person of interest."

Hyer's brows rose slightly. "You mean—"

"Yes, *that* person."

Hyer considered this, then nodded. "I'll take care of it."

"If an opportunity arises, you have sanction, but use discretion." The warning was clear.

"Discretion is my expertise."

"Indeed. I chose you for operational skill and initiative. Both are needed now. But patience is paramount. We're almost to the end of this thing. If the professional get the best of us, Hyer, you'll be the one held accountable."

Hyer swallowed. "I understand."

"I hope so." A slight pause. "For your sake, Mr. Hyer."

Jaw clenched, Hyer ground out, "I'll handle this. You have my word, Executor."

CHAPTER TWENTY-SEVEN

As the BMW roared through the trees, Bryan was in the passenger seat, eyes glued to his cellular phone's multiplex screen. Still no signal. The lack of bars mocked him, ratcheting up his anxiety. He and Drew were racing blind. Anything could be happening back in Fort Bragg.

He willed the signal to appear. And as if responding to his desperation, a single bar flickered onto the display.

Yes!

Bryan immediately dialed Aria's number. Drew shot a glance in his direction, assessing the situation, as he kept the car barreling ahead, trees whipping past.

The call rang.

And rang.

And rang...

Then, the answering machine: *Hey, you've reached Aria Foster. I'm not in, but if you'll leave me a—*

Bryan growled and stabbed the *END* button, then the *REDIAL* button.

The call rang.

And rang.

And—

"What, Bryan?" came Aria's irritated voice. "I told you I'm done talking to you."

"Aria, listen—"

"Save it! I already helped you once. I got you the name and address. I'm done here."

"No! That's not—" Bryan stopped, feeling his anger rise with the urgency of the moment. That wouldn't do. Not at all. Channeling the work he'd been doing, he took a breath before he continued. "You and Shawn Corzo are in danger."

A puzzled pause. "What the hell are you talking about?"

"People are coming for you, Aria. You need to leave."

He waited. For a moment, he thought the reception had cut out again. He checked. There was still one bar.

Then Aria said, "Shit."

Bryan ran a hand through his hair. "I know, I'm sorry to call like this, but—"

"No," Aria said. "I mean, shit, you're right! Someone's outside my house right now."

Bryan's chest clutched. "*What?* Who?"

"I don't..." She trailed off. He could sense the tension in her voice as she tried to figure out who was outside her front door.

"Aria, talk to me. What's going on?"

"There's a black sedan parked at the corner of my driveway. No one ever parks there." After a long pause, she added, "I gotta get out of here."

"How? Can you sneak out the back?"

Even as he'd said it, Bryan knew it was pointless. Whoever was staking her out would have the place surrounded.

"Too late for that. I'll figure something—" Aria's words cut off abruptly.

"*Aria!*" Bryan strained to hear anything from her end. "Aria, are you there?"

Only a quiet hum.

Then the line went dead.

Bryan pulled the phone away from his ear and looked at the display.

The bars were gone.

No signal.

CHAPTER TWENTY-EIGHT

Aria peered through the blinds. The black sedan sat idling at the corner of her driveway.

"Holy shit," she cursed under her breath.

Bryan's warning had come just in time.

Once again, she found herself thinking positively about the guy. This was becoming a habit lately.

He'd come through when it counted.

She studied the sedan, mind racing through options. Its windows were tinted, obscuring the occupant.

Aria pressed her fingers against the window frame and breathed deeply. Panic threatened to surge, but she pushed it down. She'd been in plenty of tight spots before, especially during her career in L.A. Stunt school had taught her to remain calm under pressure.

There was only one way to handle this.

Leave the house.

Simply leave.

So that's what she did. She casually stepped out the front door, keys in hand, trying to appear oblivious.

A breeze tossed her hair. The sun was bright. Chirping birds. Rustling leaves. Blue sky.

She threw on her sunglasses, locked the door, and headed down the sidewalk, putting a frown on her face as she looked at the car, one that said *What's this person doing parked so close to my driveway like a creeper?*, not giving away the fact that she knew someone potentially murderous was after her.

She walked toward the Jag, feigning an ease she didn't feel, her gaze flicking to the tinted windows of the sedan, seeking a telltale glint or movement. None came. The car sat there, silent and still.

Her Jaguar XJ-S—a 1978 model that had seen better days—sat waiting for her. It was a classic, which she'd gotten for a steal, and she knew the guy who ran the best restoration shop in Fort Bragg. Its work-in-progress condition left the Jag's lines looking less sleek than in its heyday, but no less elegant. The olive paintwork was mostly original and in decent shape, minus one panel that was marred by patches of primer and rust scars.

Aria approached the Jag, unlocked it, stole another glance at the motionless sedan. As she slipped into the driver's seat, she took in a whiff of old leather mixed with oil and metal, a scent she loved. She turned the key, and the V12 engine came to life with a throaty growl that settled into a contented purr.

She looked at the rearview mirror, to the inert menace of the sedan. Although the situation was potentially deadly, she understood that keeping her cool was crucial if she hoped to escape unscathed. She pressed the clutch, put the stick into reverse, and started to back up. Slowly. Casually. Just a woman leaving her house for an afternoon chore.

She cracked the window and heard a slight *thunk* from the black sedan—the driver had just put the car into gear. The sedan rolled forward in pursuit as Aria turned onto the street. *Easy does it*, she coached herself, scanning for other vehicles.

Not many out here on the rural roads on the edge of Fort Bragg. She'd have to play this just right.

She drove the speed limit for now, edging steadily farther from the more populated areas. She checked the rearview mirror. The other car hung back, not concerned with remaining inconspicuous anymore.

Fine by her. Fewer witnesses for what came next.

Aria's hands were steady on the wheel. When she'd been a stunt car driver, she'd been a different woman, one chasing the Hollywood dream, ambitious and hungry, back before the injury. She'd earned a pretty penny with her skill behind the wheel.

Right now, she needed to draw upon that skill set again.

The road curved ahead.

Time to make her move.

She accelerated into the curve, the Jag's tires biting the asphalt. The sedan hurried to follow.

As Aria came out of the turn, she stomped the gas, engine roaring up to sixty mph. The sedan gave chase but couldn't match her head start.

Aria grinned. *Let's see how you like someone who knows what she's doing.*

She tore along the ribbon of road, trees whipping by in a green blur. The sedan fell steadily behind despite its powerful engine. Aria had the advantage of skill and nerve.

Up ahead, a side road branched off. Aria waited until the last instant, then cranked the wheel sharply left, fishtailing onto the narrower road, tires screeching. The smell of burnt rubber filled the cab.

She used the slide to her advantage, expertly regaining control, feeling the forces through the wheel. Risky, but it gained her precious seconds as the sedan scrambled to follow.

She pushed the Jag faster, coaxing every ounce of speed from it. The V12 growled. Houses flashed by in intermittent clusters as she plunged deeper inland. The landscape grew hilly, the road more serpentine. She attacked each curve, cutting apexes with razor precision.

Glancing at the rearview again, she saw the sedan round a tight bend dangerously late. It skidded off the shoulder in a spray of dirt.

But that driver had some skill, too. He wrestled the big car back on course and kept coming.

Aria's mouth set in a determined line. She wasn't about to make it easy.

An old bridge spanned a creek ahead. Beyond it, the road split. As Aria shot onto the bridge, she wrenched the wheel right. The tires screamed as she held the slide, fishtailing onto the fork. The sedan skidded, nearly going to the wrong side, buying Aria a few more seconds.

She was farther outside town now, the roads getting narrower and more twisted. Trees pressed in closely.

The sedan emerged in the mirror, inching its way back into view. Aria guided the Jag effortlessly through the curves, but the sedan had to slam on its brakes, giving her a bit more breathing room.

Just a little farther, she urged herself. Then she could shake the tail for good.

As if reading her thoughts, the sedan suddenly peeled off down a side road. Aria's eyes narrowed, suspicious it meant to cut her off somewhere ahead. These winding back roads had multiple connections, many of which were still unknown to her three years after moving to the area.

She eased off the gas. The sedan's disappearance left the woods hushed. She rolled down a window, listening. Somewhere nearby, the sea crashed in endless rhythm.

Then she heard the sedan's telltale engine roar. It tore out of a hidden road just ahead, swerving to block her way. But Aria was ready, braking hard.

At the last instant, she cranked the wheel right and stomped the gas, shooting the gap between two trees onto an unpaved track. Branches scraped the underside of the Jag.

But she'd slipped past the trap.

In her rearview, she saw no sign of the sedan.

Aria allowed herself a grin.

CHAPTER TWENTY-NINE

THE BMW TORE down Oakdale Lane, weaving through the sparse traffic. Silence kept his gaze fixed ahead, mentally tracking their route.

Nearly there.

He didn't remember the names of the streets, but a childhood map of the town was burned permanently into his visually oriented mind. He took a sharp left, screeching within a foot of a slow-moving van, then swiftly veered right onto a side street, the tires squealing in protest.

Bryan sat in the passenger seat, his knuckles turning white as he gripped the door handle tightly. His jaw was tense with stress, every muscle in his face strained.

Tires squealing, they rounded the last corner, and the dilapidated two-story building appeared. The cracked paint. The rust stains. Silence hardly braked before throwing the car into park. They were out and moving in seconds.

They sprinted to the building, retracing their earlier path to apartment 130. Silence pounded on the door.

"*Shawn!*"

No response.

He hammered again, harder.

Still nothing.

Exchanging a tense look with Bryan, Silence stepped back and kicked. The door let out a loud, hollow creak as the force of Silence's blow shattered its weakened frame, sending shards of wood flying and clattering to the floor. As it banged open, a figure charged out of the dim interior.

"Whoa, easy!" Bryan yelled, raising his hands.

There was a tone of familiarity to Bryan's cry.

Silence, too, recognized the young man attacking them.

But the stout silhouette of a man didn't heed the call. Armed with a rolling pin, Malik just continued swinging left and right, advancing at Bryan, who managed to evade the attacks by swiftly ducking out of harm's way at the last moment.

Silence smoothly intervened, deflecting a blow and applying gentle pressure to the teen's wrist until he released the makeshift weapon with a yelp. The rolling pin clattered on the concrete just outside the door. A quick sweep brought Malik's arm behind his back. He yelped again, and Silence clamped a hand over his mouth, checking on either side to see if any neighbors had come out to check the disturbance.

None had.

He pushed Malik into the apartment, which looked disheveled and different than it had earlier. Bryan followed and closed the door behind them. Silence flipped on the lights and released Malik, giving him a gentle shove to put some space between them.

Malik trembled in front of them, rubbing his wrist, cowering. His face was sweaty. He was wearing a *Top Gun* T-shirt.

Bryan stepped forward. "Take it easy, Malik. We're looking for Shawn. Where is he?"

"You guys ... you're not with them?"

Silence shook his head. "Told you earlier..." he said and swallowed. "We're the good guys."

This mollified Malik a bit. His shoulders relaxed.

"Sorry, guys," he said, looking from Silence to Bryan. "I thought you were with them, that they'd come back for *me* this time. Shawn's gone. Some guys came and grabbed him."

Silence surveyed the disheveled apartment, taking in the upended furniture and strewn belongings. There was a plate-sized hole in the drywall.

And a splatter of blood on the kitchen linoleum.

His shoulders tensed.

"When did this happen?" he said and swallowed. "Who were the guys?"

Malik shook his head. "Like an hour ago. I didn't get a good look at them. Three big dudes, military-lookin' guys. Shawn yelled at me to stay in my room when they burst in here." His eyes dropped, expression pained. "I should've come out and helped or something..."

"Any idea where they took him?" Bryan said.

Malik shrugged helplessly. "I heard the conversation before the fight. They wanted to know the same things you guys did—about Mr. Jennings and whatever Shawn knew about his investigation. Shawn said he didn't know anything. I guess they didn't like that answer."

Silence scanned the room for anything the intruders may have left behind. But the ransacking had been thorough. These operatives were careful, leaving few traces.

Aside from the blood...

He remembered what the big guy in the red flannel shirt had said out in the trees—that Shawn was to be the bait to draw out Matt Jennings.

With Matt dead, they must have taken Shawn as bait to draw out someone else...

...Silence.

He met Bryan's worried gaze, seeing the same thought reflected there. Whoever had taken Shawn acted quickly, leaving no evidence behind. Professionals. They'd known Bryan and Silence were closing in.

Now Silence and Bryan's only lead was missing, and Aria was still unaccounted for.

They were running out of options.

And time.

Silence stepped away and quickly searched the hall, more to buy a moment to think than expecting to find anything. He inhaled slowly, re-centering himself. There was always a way forward.

The key was maintaining focus.

That's right, love, C.C. said. *Focus. Find a path forward.*

But there's never been *a path in this mission!* Silence's internal voice replied, frustration mounting. *Every turn has put me at a dead-end.*

Then you're going to need some luck. And how does one acquire luck?

Silence thought for a moment, searching his internal database of C.C.-isms.

Luck directly correlates to taking action, he replied, quoting her.

That's right, C.C. said and left.

He returned to find Bryan helping Malik right some furniture.

"We need to move," Silence said.

Bryan nodded. "Right."

Silence then turned to Malik. "You have..." he said and swallowed. "Somewhere you can go?"

Malik looked confused for a moment, then, "You mean, some place safe? Yeah. My folks."

"Go there."

Malik eyed them both uncertainly. "But what about Shawn? You gonna find him or what? That's my friend, bro!"

Silence was about to reply, but Bryan stepped forward and clamped Malik's shoulder, fixing him with an earnest stare. "We'll find him."

Silence grinned. Impressive. Bryan was winning him over more and more.

Malik searched Bryan's face, then finally bobbed his head. "Yeah ... yeah, okay."

―――

Two minutes later, they were back in the car. Malik had left in an old S-10, headed for his parents. Silence put the BMW into gear.

Bryan scrubbed a hand down his face and exhaled loudly. "Now what? With Shawn and Aria gone, we've got nothing."

Silence paused, considering their options, remembering his mental conversation with C.C.

"Now we take action." Another pause, and then he growled, "*Righteous* action."

CHAPTER THIRTY

To Silence, Detective Rasnick's office felt even more cramped than before, walls lined with files and the weight of unresolved cases. Along with Bryan, he was back in the pair of chairs facing the detective's desk, with Rasnick on the other side. Silence and Rasnick were watching Bryan, who was using his cellular phone, his back turned, his voice a low, urgent murmur.

As Bryan ended the call, he turned, his expression shifting from intense focus to immense relief.

"Aria's safe," he said, his voice carrying a hint of disbelief, as if he hadn't dared to hope for such good news. "She made it to the Due North office. She's digging for intel."

Silence nodded and considered Aria's choice of hideouts.

Shrewd. Intelligent.

"Safest place..." he said and swallowed. "For her right now."

He noted the tension draining from Bryan's shoulders, a physical uncoiling that mirrored the slight easing of the atmosphere in the room.

"Black Thorn Society," Silence said to Rasnick, steering

the conversation back to the heart of the investigation. "Matt found that Gray's Machine Shop..." He swallowed. "Was part of it. Making weapons."

Rasnick took a moment to think, his gaze darting to a locked file cabinet before returning to Silence and Bryan.

"Fine..." he said on a sigh.

With a reluctant expression, the detective stood, reaching into his pocket for a key to unlock the cabinet. He pulled out a stack of overstuffed manila folders.

"These are Matt's files," Rasnick said, his voice low. "I guess you've earned a look."

He handed the folders to Silence, who took them with a nod, his fingers brushing over the worn edges.

Finally.

The nuts and bolts of the happenings in Fort Bragg. The intel that Rasnick had been gatekeeping.

The files were dense, Matt's handwriting cramped and urgent. As Silence flipped through them, a picture emerged, a narrative built from countless hours of research and surveillance and deduction. Matt had been onto something big, something dangerous.

Silence sifted through the material, his eyes catching on three cases dismissed as unfortunate accidents. Matt, however, had suspected something far more sinister.

The first case involved a man who had supposedly fallen off a three-story balcony. The official report chalked it up to an unfortunate slip after one too many drinks at an after-work get-together. But Matt had been suspicious of the absence witnesses and the victim's uncharacteristic overindulgence in booze.

...and the fact that the man had once worked at Gray's Machine Shop.

The second case regarded a woman who had allegedly tripped on her cat and tumbled down the stairs of her apartment building, resulting in fatal injuries. Matt found it odd that the woman, known for her meticulous nature, would, on a seemingly random evening, let her strictly indoor pet roam freely around such a dangerous area.

She'd been an office assistant at Noyo Harbor, dealing primarily with records.

The final report described an alleged boating incident in which a young man capsized during a violent storm. The officials swiftly attributed it to a turbulent sea and careless navigation. Nevertheless, Matt couldn't dismiss his discomfort over the absence of distress signals.

The man was never identified. No one in Fort Bragg was familiar with him. The only bit of potentially identifying evidence was the man's necklace, which bore a pendant of Eastern European design.

Silence flipped faster, examining Matt's overarching investigation notes, which pointed to Curtis Hyer. According to Matt, Hyer was using Gray's Machine Shop to manufacture something far more sinister than car parts and industrial modules—components that could be pieced together with other components made at other seemingly innocuous machine shops to form untraceable weapons.

As Silence delved deeper into the files, a single word leaped out at him, one that had already been trailing him the entire time he'd been in Fort Bragg: *ANCHOR*. It was circled and underlined, the scribbles around it a frenetic web of connections. Matt had linked *ANCHOR* directly to the manufacture of untraceable weapons at Gray's. Custom-built, no serial numbers, no trace—a ghost arsenal for the Black Thorn Society.

But Matt seemed to have never figured out what exactly *ANCHOR* was.

Neither had Silence.

Not *yet*, anyway.

Silence looked up from the files, his mind racing. The pieces were falling into place, a jigsaw puzzle of crime and conspiracy that was slowly forming a coherent picture. But there were gaps, missing pieces that eluded him, shadows in the corners of the narrative Matt had been chasing.

And he realized he hadn't seen *EXECUTOR* in Matt's notes.

He started flipping again. Page after page, until—

There!

There it was—*EXECUTOR.*

It was listed under a dated entry at the back.

The day before Matt died...

Silence read the entry.

Another term came up today while questioning Anonymous Source 32: EXECUTOR. *32 says that* EXECUTOR *isn't advanced weapons tech like* ANCHOR. *It's a person. The leader. Hyer's boss. Dozens of* ANCHOR *units will be moved next week.*

Silence turned on Bryan, spun the file in his direction, and stabbed a finger first at *weapons tech* then at *Hyer's boss.*

Bryan looked up, mouth falling.

Rasnick leaned forward, the springs in his chair squeaking. "What'd you find, fellas?"

But before Silence could respond, the door opened, and a uniformed officer poked his head in. "Sir, Tamson needs you up front for a moment."

Rasnick stood. "Be right back," he said, stepping out and leaving Silence and Bryan alone.

"Holy shit!" Bryan said the moment the door closed behind Rasnick. "Holy shit, man! Hyer isn't the boss? Then who the hell is? *And weapons tech?* I thought we were dealing with, you know, like, pistols with no serial numbers or something. If advanced weapons technologies are being assembled in Fort Bragg, and that tech is being moved tonight, that means—"

"That the Black Thorns..." Silence said, finishing Bryan's thought. He swallowed. "Are in town."

"Holy shit! *Holy shit!*"

Suddenly, Silence needed to recalibrate. It was bad enough when he thought that mere parts of illegal weapons were being manufactured in the town. But with shipments of advanced weapons technology being moved...

His thought trailed off into nothingness.

Because he'd spotted something when his eyes drifted with those thoughts. The drawer from which Rasnick had retrieved Matt's files was still open. Among the clutter, a notepad caught Silence's attention. The word *EXECUTOR* was written at the top in bold strokes. Below *EXECUTOR* was a list of traits:

male
speaks little
shadowy
mysterious
commanding
deep, strange voice

The last one snagged Silence's attention: *deep, strange voice.* Silence shifted in his chair.

And a chill flashed over his skin.

deep, strange voice...

That was him! That was Silence.

Did Rasnick suspect Silence of being the Executor? Was the detective's apparent newfound cooperation a carefully orchestrated trap?

The room suddenly felt even smaller, the walls inching closer.

He looked at the other traits on the list.

male
speaks little

Oh, shit...

As he grappled with this revelation, his gaze briefly met Bryan's. The relief from the phone call with Aria still lingered on Bryan's face, contrasting the turmoil churning in Silence's mind. Bryan was looking at something. Silence followed his sightline.

He was looking at the liquor bottles displayed behind Rasnick's desk. The sight was fleeting, but it spoke volumes.

Because there was a strange look on Bryan's face, almost reminiscent, but also dark.

Had Bryan lied about alcohol's influence?

If so, had he lied about Aria? Had he been an angry, violent drunk?

Or were Silence's internal alarms causing him paranoia?

He had to focus.

Focus.

His eyes found the note in the drawer again.

speaks little

deep, strange voice

He turned to Brian again. "We gotta go!" He swallowed. "Rasnick thinks I'm—"

A shrill ringing interrupted him.

His cellular phone.

He pulled it from his pocket. The multiplex displayed the most recent number he'd added to the contacts list.

It was Juliette.

He flipped the phone open. "Yes?"

"Drew, it's ... uh, it's Juliette. From the yoga thing?" Her voice was urgent, laced with a tremor of fear. "You said I could reach out. Can you come back to the retreat, um, now? It's urgent! I'm outside the camp right now, and—" *A burst of static.* "—losing reception, I think. I—" *Static.*

"Juliette!" Silence shouted, sending a jolt of pain down his throat. He swallowed. "Don't move. Tell me..." Another swallow. "What happened."

"—and if he comes back—" *Static.* "—haven't found Yura, so—" *Static.* "—afraid—"

The line went dead...

...leaving Silence with a phone in his hand and a surge of adrenaline in his veins.

He looked at Bryan, then sprinted out of the office.

CHAPTER THIRTY-ONE

ARIA SETTLED into a chair behind one of three mismatched desks in a rented office space nestled inconspicuously, almost invisibly, in the heart of Fort Bragg's quaint downtown, right there on Main Street, Highway 1.

This was the Due North headquarters, where beneficence thrived beneath the constant buzzing of aging fluorescent lights. Along one wall stood old filing cabinets, while a giant corkboard adorned the opposite wall. It was covered with photos, inspirational quotes, and other bits and pieces pinned up as reminders of the organization's purpose: guiding young people who needed direction. This mission was reflected in the organization's logo, a ship's wheel stenciled large on the wall in the back.

Aria's fingers hovered over the mouse, hesitating. This was the right thing to do—she knew that. Bryan and his friend Drew needed her help, and the stakes were too high to let personal history get in the way. And yet, her hand trembled slightly at the thought of assisting Bryan *again* after what he'd done to her.

Aria closed her eyes briefly, letting out a slow breath. The memory still stung, even after all this time. The anger and betrayal she'd felt when she discovered Bryan had revealed her secret struggle with alcoholism to others.

Back in Los Angeles, after the accident—after losing her dream career in an instant—she'd been temporarily crippled and emotionally broken. Her prescription painkillers had taken care of her knee. But not her soul. She'd turned to the bottle. Before that, Aria had never had a problem with alcohol. She couldn't have imagined she'd get addicted.

But she'd worked so hard to get sober since then, to claw her way back from rock bottom through sheer force of will. Only her closest friends and family knew the depths to which alcohol had dragged her. It was a private battle, and she'd intended to keep it that way.

But Bryan, in a moment of spite during one of their heated arguments, had blurted out her alcoholism to a mutual friend. Just like that, Aria's carefully guarded secret was out there for everyone to know—everyone in this tiny, peaceful city where she'd moved to escape the ruin of her once dreamed-for life, the place she'd gone to start over.

The shame and humiliation had been overwhelming at first, made even worse by having to face those who now saw her differently, as the small-town drunk who'd thrown away a Hollywood career.

She'd cut off all contact with Bryan after that, no matter how many apologetic calls he made. As much as she still loved him, his lack of ability to control his temper had finally become too destructive a force in her life. All his promises to get help for his anger issues, all the counseling sessions he swore he'd attend "someday"—it hadn't made a difference in the end. One lapse in judgment was all it took to shatter the foundation of trust between them.

Aria's eyes opened, refocusing on the present. Bryan needed her again now, just as he always did when his impulsiveness landed him in trouble. This time, though, his impulsiveness was righteous. Brave, even. Her feelings toward him were still a tangled mess of residual affection battling resentment. But she couldn't let that cloud her judgment. Not when Shawn Corzo's safety might be at stake.

She didn't know Shawn. She'd never met the kid.

But that didn't matter.

Shawn, she'd discovered, had been a Due North mentee of Matt Jennings, just like Bryan had been when he was young. Aria knew the positive impact a role model could have on a young life. That's why she volunteered at Due North.

If helping Bryan was the only way to protect Shawn, so be it. She owed Matt Jennings's memory that much. She and Matt hadn't been close, but *everyone* in the Due North program had some level of friendship with Matt, as did most of Fort Bragg. He'd been a damn good man.

With a final exhale, Aria set her mind to the task. Her personal grievances would have to be set aside.

She grasped the mouse and clicked to open the hard drive.

CHAPTER THIRTY-TWO

Hyer was back at the damn foundry—again!—back in the moldy office, sitting in the dry-rotted chair. The landline phone was on the desktop before him, and he had the receiver to his ear. The Executor had insisted they use the secure line again.

"...a problem that needs resolving," the Executor was saying, the encrypted voice crackling in Hyer's ear. "Your man's incompetence allowed Aria Foster to escape."

Hyer's jaw tightened. "It was an unavoidable setback in the field, sir. I've already disciplined Sanderson accordingly."

"You should have eliminated Sanderson, not merely reprimanded." The words were clipped, free of inflection. "Displays of weakness breed further failure."

"Consider it done," Hyer said. "And rest assured, we'll have the Bryan Holifield situation handled soon."

A scoffing exhale filtered through the line. "Your words mean little after this latest disappointment, Mr. Hyer. Perhaps your usefulness has run its course."

Hyer stiffened, face flushing.

His skin flushed, too—with perspiration—at the mere

thought of what the man on the other end of the line could do to him.

A rumor flashed through his mind...

He'd once heard that the Executor had burned a man alive, someone who'd failed him.

This individual had been Hyer's predecessor; he'd held the position Hyer currently occupied.

Hyer swallowed.

"Don't be rash, Executor. I'll get it handled—I'll bring Holifield in myself if need be."

"Bryan Holifield is irrelevant now. The man helping him presents the true threat."

Hyer frowned. "The private eye?"

"Yes, fool. The 'private eye'..." There was a pause, whether for effect or consideration, Hyer couldn't tell. "You idiot. He's not a private investigator. He's ... some sort of pro. A fed would be my guess. Eliminate him."

Hyer had already reached the same conclusion—that Bryan Holifield's private eye was some sort of professional.

But he wasn't going to correct the Executor.

Not with the panic sweat skill wet on Hyer's skin.

Not with thoughts of being burned alive.

The command hung in the air—a death order: kill the professional. Hyer's hand instinctively slipped under his jacket, fingers brushing the comforting weight of his Colt 1903 Hammerless.

"Consider it done," he said, feigning steadiness and confidence. "I'll handle the situation personally this time."

"See that you do. If you hurry, you'll find them both at the police station—Holifield and the professional."

There was a rattle.

And the line went dead, leaving Hyer staring into the mildew-stained wall on the opposite side of the room. Slowly, he lowered the receiver to the cradle.

Hyer inhaled. The air was damp and moldy with the history of the horrible place. His mind flashed to the thought of fire, of being consumed by it. The idea sent a shiver over his clammy flesh.

But not him. There wouldn't be any fire. That wouldn't be his story.

He'd take out the operator first. Make sure of it.

He stood and rushed out of the room.

The Executor had said Hyer would need to hurry to catch Holifield and the professional at the police station.

The Executor had been correct.

Just as Hyer pulled to the end of the block facing the new police facility—with its modern lines and sparkling glass—the professional's black BMW was pulling out of the parking lot, going fast.

Whatever the guy was doing, it must have been crazy urgent. It takes some balls to go speeding away from a bunch of cops.

Hyer averted his face as the BMW zipped past, stealing a glance. He saw the professional's severe visage behind the wheel, eyes cold and focused. Holifield was in the passenger seat.

Hitting the gas pedal, Hyer swung his car around in the intersection and took off after them. At the next intersection, he pulled hard to the left. Slammed the gas pedal. Then, a screeching right. More gas. And another right.

Hyer's hand slid underneath his jacket, hovering over the Colt's grip.

He'd made a large loop. With any luck, he would cut them off at the next intersection.

That is, if he hurried. When he'd last seen it, the BMW had been barreling.

Hyer buried the gas pedal. The engine roared.

The intersection was just ahead. To his right, Hyer saw the BMW zooming toward him, seemingly oblivious. Hyer's finger caressed the trigger guard. He barreled into the intersection, angling to cut off the other car's approach.

At the last instant, the BMW's brakes screeched. It shuddered to a halt mere yards from Hyer's sedan, which also slowed rapidly, its tires smoking, screaming, coming to a stop in the middle of the street, blocking both lanes.

The BMW's windshield was only yards away, right there to the side, just past Hyer's passenger window. He saw them both—Holifield and the professional. Holifield's mouth hung open; his hands were planted upward against the BMW's roof, bracing himself.

But the professional looked unaffected.

He just stared forward.

At Hyer. Locking eyes with him.

Dark, brown eyes.

For a moment, the hushed intersection was frozen in tension, this strange Mexican standoff. Behind, a pair of vehicles crept forward, keeping a cautious distance and, in the process, closing off the escape.

Holifield and the professional were trapped.

The BMW's driver-side door kicked open, and a massive figure emerged.

Hyer felt a surge of vicious satisfaction swell in his chest. This was the man who'd caused so much trouble, so much precious time and resources wasted.

And Hyer was about to bring him down.

Hyer shoved open his own door, stepping fully into the open in one fluid motion. His jacket parted just enough to reveal the dull gleam of his Colt's barrel where it cleared the holster.

"Well now," he called out. "We almost had us a fender-bender."

"What do you want?" The demand was wary yet aggressive.

Damn! The guy's voice. It was ... hideous. Even more bizarre than the Executor's electronically manipulated growl.

It made Hyer freeze for a moment.

Readjusting, Hyer offered a wolfish grin, all teeth. "Just a friendly chat is all. Man to man."

He stared into the professional, and the guy met the stare levelly, weight balanced on the balls of his feet in a textbook fighting stance. Behind, Holifield remained frozen in the passenger seat of the BMW.

Hyer felt a muscle twitch in his jaw as understanding dawned—the professional wasn't trying to avoid a fight; *he was preparing for one.*

Hyer's hand inched toward his Colt. The pro had just elevated this from a tidy execution to something a whole lot messier.

The pro's fists clenched, forearm muscles going taut. Behind him, Holifield wavered, clearly torn over whether to bolt or stay in the car.

Hyer couldn't back down.

Burned alive! he reminded himself.

No, he couldn't back down. He had to eliminate the professional. He moved.

Hyer's boots crunched on the pavement as he advanced.

This was about to get interesting.

CHAPTER THIRTY-THREE

EVEN IN THE tension of this moment, a bit of surrealism played through Silence's mind.

Because there, right in front of him, was Curtis Hyer.

The schoolyard bully. The one who tried to rough up a younger kid, Archie.

There he was. In the present moment. Six feet tall. Broad shoulders. Shaved head. Trim beard over a muscular jaw. A tough-looking dude. Years ago, he'd been a tough-looking kid.

Some things never changes.

Still a ruffian. Still a bully. But now, somehow tied to an international illegal arms manufacturer.

Silence watched Hyer's hand twitching toward the gun holstered beneath his jacket. Silence had noticed that the handle was hammerless and pegged the pistol as a Colt 1903 or 1908. Either was a badass weapon, but he hated giving Hyer any credit, even in terms of taste.

Silence's own gun, his Beretta, was also holstered, also half-hidden beneath his jacket, also itching to be drawn. But Silence wouldn't take it out. Not here in the downtown area with pedestrians everywhere. Not yet.

In one fluid motion, Hyer drew his Colt pistol and lunged forward like a coiled spring unfurling. He held his pistol up with his right hand, attempting to create an opening by distracting Silence's guard.

But Silence was prepared. Using one of C.C.'s techniques, he allowed his mind to merge with the present moment, slowing down his perception of time. His senses sharpened as he honed in on the figure before him and the surrounding terrain, relying on his instincts to guide him.

As Hyer closed the gap, Silence shifted his weight in a slight pivot. Hyer threw a clumsy hook, and Silence effortlessly avoided it by tilting his head to the side. Instantly, he grabbed onto Hyer's wrist with his left hand as part of the same motion.

Hyer snarled, struggling to break free from Silence's grip. But Silence held on tighter and stepped forward, his strong arm pressing against Hyer's now-stiff limb. Their bodies were intertwined for a moment before Silence swiftly turned his hips.

The grip of Silence's armlock contorted Hyer's limb into unnatural angles, causing him to let out a pained scream. His joints protested against the strain as he fell to a knee. The Colt slipped from his grasp, clattered on the pavement.

With a violent shake, Hyer broke the armlock's tentative grip and launched himself forward in a brutish tackle. His bulky mass crashed into Silence like a battering ram, forcing them both staggering back.

Silence smothered the instinct to grapple and instead channeled the momentum into an arching pivot. As Hyer's weight drove them in a staggered circle, Silence lashed out with a spin kick. The *mawashi geri* cracked against Hyer's hip in an impact that echoed through the intersection.

Shock registered on Hyer's face for just a moment before a grimace twisted his features. With a rough shove, he propelled them apart into dual retreating staggers. Distance temporarily established, Silence settled once more into a ready stance.

His mind raced, analyzing the scraps of data compiled so far. Hyer was powerful but lacked technique, overcompensating with brute force and size. Worrying yet manageable if Silence patiently created angles and capitalized on proper leverage. But things could get ugly fast if the burly man managed to smother him in uncomfortably tight quarters. He needed to—

A voice cracked through Silence's honed focus.

"You son of a bitch!"

It was Bryan.

He was running in their direction.

With a rasping growl, Hyer rounded on the outburst, one hand pawing for the discarded pistol. That's when Bryan jumped at him with all the grace of a runaway freight train.

Silence gaped as Bryan threw himself into Hyer just as the bigger man regained his feet. They went down in a sprawl of tangled limbs, grunts of exertion mingling with Hyer's curses. But the advantage of surprise was short-lived—Hyer rolled with the collision and quickly reversed course, one meaty hand now wrapped around Bryan's throat.

Silence sprang forward in a sprint, left arm swinging in a backhand. The strike caught Hyer squarely on the jaw. He slumped sideways, blinking stupidly as Bryan rolled free, wheezing in ragged gulps of air.

Silence hauled the sputtering man upright, propelling Bryan away to temporary safety behind the BMW.

Now that it was just the two of them again, Hyer was already rebounding with burning eyes. Silence steadied his footwork, widening his stance in anticipation of further assault.

Hyer came barreling forward in a clumsy bull rush. Silence

slipped the initial grabbing hands and drove a pinpoint knee into Hyer's chest. The solid hit folded Hyer in half with a guttural wheeze. Silence whipped his elbow down, driving it against the base of Hyer's skull.

Hyer crumpled. He sprawled face-down, unconscious.

The next few moments passed in weighted quiet as Silence powered the BMW through farther up the street. During the scuffle, the cars behind them had cleared, leaving an opening for departure.

Of course, something in Silence had wanted to eliminate Curtis Hyer before they took off. But he had no solid proof that Hyer was a killer, that he was tied to the Black Thorn Society, that he was working for the mysterious Executor. He had no proof of anything.

And since Watchers executions were extra-judicial and illegal, a target was never killed until the organization was "three hundred percent" certain of guilt, as they colloquially liked to say.

Besides, time was short. Silence needed every spare second.

The phone reception-distorted phone call kept playing through his mind.

Juliette's voice.

—and if he comes back— Static. *—haven't found Yura, so—* Static. *—afraid—*

Bryan spoke up. "So...that was...intense."

Silence glanced at the passenger seat. Bryan was still wide-eyed, still taking big panic breaths.

"Yes," Silence said as he turned back to face the road.

"I thought I could help back there," Bryan said.

"Appreciated," Silence said and swallowed. "But you could've..." Another swallow. "Gotten killed."

From the corner of his eye, he saw Bryan bob his head in a jerky nod, chastened.

A few moments passed, and Silence noticed he was gripping the steering wheel tightly, not out of the tension of getting to Juliette.

...but something else.

He needed to add something to what he'd just said to Bryan. He needed to give something else to this imperfect man who'd been impressing Silence more and more, a guy on a path of self-improvement.

A guy who'd once been a kid mentored by a man named Matt Jennings.

"You did well," Silence said and swallowed. "Didn't run from the threat." Another swallow. "Matt would be proud."

Bryan shot him a sidelong look, throat working soundlessly for a moment. When he finally spoke, his tone held a raw edge.

"Thanks, man." A beat passed. "How ... where did you learn to do all that, I guess, martial arts? Those moves! Shit..."

Silence allowed himself the faintest hint of a grin. "Here and there," he said mildly.

He slowed, pulling up to the curb in front of a line of block buildings as quintessentially Americana as the rest of downtown Fort Bragg. A simple sign with a ship's wheel logo announced *Due North*. There was a *Closed* sign on the door. Looking through the display window, Silence noticed a barely visible figure working at a computer on a desk in the back.

After placing the BMW in park, he rested his forearm on the steering wheel and turned fully toward his passenger for the first time.

"Get inside. Stay with..." he said and swallowed. "Aria. I have to go..." Another swallow. "To the park."

Bryan looked out the passenger window and remained frozen for an extended beat before giving a small, resolute nod. Silence returned it.

"I see her in there," Bryan said, still looking out the window.

Silence looked over Bryan's shoulder and saw her too—the figure at the computer in the back.

"I haven't faced her in over a year," Bryan continued. He turned and looked at Silence. "I'm ... scared, dude."

A moment of frustration flushed over Silence. He *needed* to get to Juliette, and he'd just been a good cheerleader for this guy a moment earlier, a guy who'd just bolted into a gunfight unarmed but now didn't have the balls to face his exgirlfriend.

So Silence didn't respond.

As Bryan exhaled heavily and fumbled open the door, C.C. spoke up.

Love, she said. *Don't be a prick. You know what to do.*

Yes, he did.

He called out to Bryan. "Hey."

Bryan was halfway out the door. He turned around and stooped over to look back at Silence.

"Good luck," Silence said.

That seemed to resonate. Bryan gave a thankful nod and shut the door.

And Silence reminded himself again of Juliette's panicked voice, the phone call playing in his head again.

He peeled off.

CHAPTER THIRTY-FOUR

THE WINDING ROAD blurred past in a mosaic of greens and browns, all those giant redwoods melting into one, as Silence pushed the BMW to its limits. The engine's growl seemed to match his own rising sense of urgency, an undercurrent of something primal driving him forward.

Just get there.

His phone trilled from the center console, the ringtone cutting through even the thrum of the BMW's acceleration. A glance at the multiplex showed Falcon's number glaring back.

Of course his boss would be checking in.

Right now.

At this moment.

Of course he would.

If the bastard had only waited a few more moments, Silence would be in an area of sketchy reception, a good excuse to "miss" the call.

Silence flipped open the phone, admitting the call with a resigned exhale. "Sir?"

The rebuke was immediate. "You keep going back to Fort

Bragg, Suppressor. Leaving the yoga retreat. Now you're speeding away from Fort Bragg to the yoga retreat! You're up to something, just like you were in Mobile. You're defying me again already! Suppressor, I demand to know—"

Silence collapsed the phone, terminating the call.

He shouldn't have answered it in the first place. Now, he'd avoid all calls from the Watchers until all of this was over.

There would be ramifications. Undoubtedly. And those ramifications would be a lot worse than another unannounced visit from Doc Hazel.

But he would face those ramifications when they came.

Matt Jennings and, now, Juliette. Two separate and concurrent violations of Falcon's *No involvement in local matters* imperative.

Oooooh, yes. There would be ramifications.

Thankfully, Silence was about to solve one of the two problems. He pictured Vinnie in his mind—the cold eyes, the flushed, angry skin—and imagined himself beating some manners into the man.

Any moment now.

But even when he solved that problem, there was everything else back in Fort Bragg.

Ever since stumbling onto Matt Jennings's unfinished investigation in Fort Bragg, Silence had been chasing ghosts. First the deaths, then the shadowed links to international crime, each uncovered piece of evidence blurring into the next.

His exhale rasped out in the cab. For the first time in longer than he could remember, Silence was floundering. Usually his objectives were surgically defined, sanctioned, contingencies calculated down to the percentile. But here, everything was a mess. And he was alone. He was freewheeling down an unsecured path, operating on instinct and half-glimpsed clues.

That'll happen when you go rogue on a self-imposed mission...

What am I doing here?

In response, his mind flashed an image.

A face.

Matt's face—the young Matt, the one Silence remembered. The quirked half-smile. The casually tousled hair. The warmth of a kid who was so clearly living childhood to its fullest. It was an expression that cut through decades of distance, catapulting Silence's mind back in time to the schoolyard as he and Matt approached Hyer and his two goons intimidating the younger Archie...

Jake strode over, his steps firm and sure. He stopped a yard short of Curtis Hyer, face to face. Their eyes locked in a silent challenge.

"Leave him alone," Jake said. "Give Archie his book back."

Hyer, with a sneer, pushed Jake, trying to show off. But Jake was quicker, turning fast enough that Hyer's hands only grazed his side, sending Hyers stumbling forward.

Jake snatched Hyer's arm, twisting it just enough to be uncomfortable. With his other hand, he plucked the book from Hyer's grasp. Giving the arm a pulse—which made Hyer yell out, much to the astonishment of his two goons—Jake released. Hyer windmilled forward, almost fell.

Stepping in front of Archie, blocking the path, Jake's stance was a clear dare for the thugs to try again. The two henchmen looked at each other before tentatively, half-heartedly advancing.

Matt, watching this, had a surge of courage. He rushed over, attempting to pull Dribble-Nose away. His grip, however, was hesitant, uncertain. Dribble-Nose easily shrugged him off, leaving Matt stumbling awkwardly to the side.

Jake, though, was a picture of controlled strength. As Freckles moved to join in, Jake's hand shot out, pushing him back with just enough force to send him to his butt. Dribble-Nose tried too and had the same result.

And Hyer just stayed where he was, behind his goons, glowering at Jake as he rubbed his wrist.

"You're lucky you're moving out of state, Rowe," Hyer growled. Then he looked at his hangers-on as they pulled themselves off the ground. "Hurry up!"

The trio left.

And Jake handed the book back to Archie.

―――

The BMW came to a crunching stop in the gravel parking area. Silence threw open the door, scrambled outside. He scanned the scattered collection of vehicles, searching for any hint of the sleek Mercedes sedan of Vinnie's.

Nothing.

He looked across to the opposite parking area.

No Mercedes.

With a stabbing sense of disappointment, Silence killed the ignition and climbed free of the driver's seat. All that urgency for nothing.

Wait!

There she was. Juliette. At the edge of the clearing.

He sprinted over to her, but she seemed miles away.

"Juliette?" he called out.

She wouldn't meet his gaze, her eyes darting.

He stepped in front of her. She came to a stop.

"Hey," he tried again, softer this time. "Are you okay?" He swallowed. "Did Vinnie hurt you?"

The moment the name slipped from his lips, her posture turned rigid. "I'm fine," she muttered, her eyes darting anywhere but Silence's face.

Silence studied her, reading the turmoil beneath her forced calmness. He could see it—the raw pain of past abuses that she was trying so hard to bury deep within herself. It was written in her eyes.

And the dark bruise on her right cheek.

That one hadn't been there before.

"Hey ... I'm sorry for calling," she said. "I ... I was being dramatic. Nothing to worry about."

She took off, moving quickly, wrapping her arms around herself.

"Juliette, wait!"

She didn't turn around.

He watched her leave.

As he stood there, he saw two people looking at him from across the clearing: Doris and Kofi. He approached them. They were dour, an unfitting look for this couple.

"She doesn't usually accept help," Doris said in a hushed voice, glancing back toward Juliette's retreating figure. "I guess we should've mentioned that before."

"It's like she's stuck in a loop," Kofi added. "Rejecting the abuse one moment, then denying everything and defending Vinnie the next."

Silence nodded, understanding dawning on him. It was a pattern he'd seen before —denial and defense for an abuser— and one he'd hoped to break with Juliette.

Feeling like a failure, he turned away, his thoughts heavy. He reflected on Vinnie's alcoholism, an issue that resonated too closely. Of course, this brought back those memories of Mrs. Enfield again, the woman who had guided him away from a similar path years ago.

Now she was sick—coughing in Pensacola—and Silence was here on the other side of the country, unable to help her, unable to help Juliette, failing in Fort Bragg.

Mrs. Enfield was sick...

And Mrs. Enfield had told him a story the last time he saw her, when they were discussing the notion of people having disproportionate impacts on each other's lives. She'd said that a friend of hers had died before she'd had a chance to thank the friend.

He pictured the old woman in that creepy house of hers. Coughing.

Alone.

...except for Baxter, cat-smiling at her, drooling on the floor.

Damn Baxter.

A moment to reconsider...

Nah. Truthfully, Baxter was all right. He was a good boy. He took care of Mrs. Enfield.

Even when she was alone and coughing.

Silence pulled out his phone. Checked the signal. None. He nodded his goodbye to Doris and Kofi, then paced to the edge of the clearing, watching the signal-indicator.

No signal.

No signal.

One bar.

He stopped. Dialed Mrs. Enfield.

Two rings, then Mrs. Enfield's voice fluttered through the receiver, brittle as an autumn leaf, "Silence?"

"Yes, ma'am," he started. "I ... I just wanted to say..." He trailed off, swallowed. "You've done a lot for me, and..." He swallowed. A pause lingered then, heavy. "And, I..." Faltering, he trailed off again.

Ugh.

He felt pathetic.

Why wasn't he been able to offer a *true* thank you?

Mrs. Enfield gave a merciful chuckle from the other end of the line, the other end of the country.

"Oh, Si," she said. "What's this all about, huh? I know you

appreciate me. And you know you don't ever have to say nothin'."

But even as she accepted his quasi-thank you, a note of concern had threaded its way into her tone.

"Something doesn't seem right with you, boy," she said. "You sound troubled." Her intuition was sharp despite their distance. Of course it was. "Everything okay?"

"I ... I've been failing a lot," Silence said.

The sigh that followed was not one of disappointment but one filled with empathy and understanding.

"My dear," Mrs. Enfield said softly, "life's all about failure. No one ever did good for themselves without failing. Successful folks fail the *most* often. Hasn't anyone ever told you that?"

Yes, someone had told him that. Years ago.

C.C.

"Yes, ma'am," Silence said.

"Good. Now get back to work. Goodbye, Si."

"Bye."

Beep.

The call ended.

Immediately, the phone buzzed with an incoming call. The multiplex showed Bryan's number. Silence's heart thundered with anticipation, expecting something big, something that would change the tide of misfortune. He held perfectly still to maintain his single bar of cellular reception. He flipped open the phone.

"Yes?"

"Things aren't looking good," Bryan said. "Aria, um ... well, she isn't talking to me, but she gave me her notes."

"And?"

"There's nothing conclusive here. Nothing we can use."

Silence sighed, feeling that sense of failure creep back in only moments after Mrs. Enfield had helped to soothe it.

"Get through to her," Silence said and swallowed. "We need intel. Badly."

"You got it."

Beep.

Yura bounded up. "Drew! So glad you made another session! You're getting better with that. Why don't you..."

She trailed off.

Because Silence was already walking away from her, going back to his BMW, the weight of his failures settling on his shoulders.

CHAPTER THIRTY-FIVE

Bryan stood stiffly in the cramped office of the Due North center, eyes fixed on the slender figure across from him. Aria sat in the chair behind the desk, her back turned, arms crossed tightly over her chest. The afternoon light filtering through the blinds cast bars of shadow across her frame, oddly fitting for the rigid tension radiating from her.

She was there. Right in front of him. All these months later. Dark hair cascading in waves. Angular features, softened by the curves of her cheek and chin. Deep brown eyes. She embodied a kind of easy elegance. Dressed was dressed simply—a light sweater and jeans.

Several stretched-out minutes had passed since Bryan entered, the quiet weighted and complete aside from the low drone of a box fan in the corner. He'd breached the divide with halting words at first, voice faltering in the void.

There'd been no response. Aria had just pointed to a notebook, which Bryan had taken, finding her notes, which were scant. After several minutes of searching through the filing cabinets, comparing what he found to the notes Aria had taken from her computer research, he'd found nothing conclusive. He'd reported the lack of development to Drew. Now, for the last several minutes, he'd been trying to work up the nerve to talk to Aria again.

Clearing his throat roughly, Bryan tried once more. "Aria, I ... again, I owe you an explanation. For back then, what I did."

She remained motionless at the desk, revealing nothing. Bryan wet his lips with a slow exhalation then pressed on. "I know I said it already, but I got to say it again face-to-face. I'm sorry for hurting you like that. For letting my temper get away from me so bad."

He scuffed a hand through already disheveled hair, gaze dropping.

"I never meant to tell Lois about ... you know, the drinking. Your personal stuff. I was just so pissed in the moment and trying to get back at you." His shoulders slumped. "Immature and spiteful. I know that's not close to good enough, but I need you to hear it straight from me."

When the continued quiet stretched unbroken, Bryan risked a hesitant half-step closer across the faded hardwood floor.

"We always brought out big feelings in each other, the good ones and bad. I know I had issues keeping my cool when we fought." He winced at the feeble understatement. "I'm working on it now, I swear, taking an anger-management course. *Tame the Beast*. Back when we were together, the way I loved wasn't exactly ... healthy, I guess."

He swallowed.

"Point is, what happened back then don't erase the real connection we shared too. We had something special once upon a time, before I wrecked it being stupid." His next words emerged hoarse with regret. "Maybe someday we find a way to move past it. But I got to ask if you can forgive me, Aria. I just want to hear I didn't screw this up beyond fixing."

Quiet swept in once more, marked only by the fan's hypnotic susurration and the distant chirping of birds outside. Bryan shifted his weight between feet, then exhaled softly.

"I guess that's all I have to say. The apology's long overdue, but you deserve it all the same."

He looked toward the closed door at the front of the space. It looked inviting. It was an escape.

No!

No more cowardice.

With a shake of his head Bryan started to pivot back, startling when he found Aria finally facing him.

Her features were creased with lingering pain, old scars long buried now exposed to the purplish light of early dusk coming in the picture windows at the front of the space. But she held his gaze unflinchingly, something stoic yet vulnerable in her stance.

When she spoke at last, her voice was low and steady. "I believe you're sorry. But trust..." Aria's delicate jaw flexed, manicured nails pressing tiny crescents into the soft flesh of her folded arms. "Trust isn't easy to rebuild once broken. I can't just pretend it didn't happen."

The charged moment lingered...

...then snapped.

Whack!

The door flew open, flooding the space with more purple glow. Both Bryan and Aria jolted in surprise as Drew barreled inside, movements taut with controlled urgency.

"Matt," Drew said without preamble, his wicked voice booing through the room. "Matt's the key."

Bryan stepped toward him. "*What?* What happened at the retreat?"

"Not the retreat..." Drew said and swallowed. "Driving gave me time..." Another swallow. "To think."

Aria stepped closer. "Um, hi. I'm Aria."

Drew nodded, but didn't break his train of thought. "Gray, *Executor*, Black Thorn, *Anchor*," he said and swallowed. "We've explored everything..." Another swallow. "Except Matt."

"Wait!" Bryan said. "Are you saying ... are you saying Matt could be crooked? Or ... or that *Matt* is the Executor?"

He threw his hands up, incredulous, staring at Drew.

In response, Drew just stared back, cold, calculating.

"*Matt's dead!*" Bryan said.

"Did you see..." Drew said and swallowed. "The body?"

The question hit like a punch. An honest-to-God punch. Bryan instantly felt nauseated.

"I ... well, no, but—"

Drew whipped on Aria. "Where's your intel..." He swallowed. "On Matt?"

Aria faltered for a moment, then stepped back to the desk and grabbed a stack of computer-printed paper, handed it to Drew.

"Now we go..." Drew said and swallowed. "To Gray's. You two are coming..." Another swallow. "With me."

Bryan stepped over. "But you said this is the safest place for us."

Drew shook his head. "Due North was..." He swallowed. "Matt's domain." Another swallow. "You're not safe here."

CHAPTER THIRTY-SIX

The dormant equipment of Gray's Machine Shop was bathed in shadows, barely alight in the dying sunlight coming in through the windows. Silence moved through the space, with Bryan and Aria trailing behind him, their footsteps echoing as they ventured into the dimly lit expanse.

Silence swept a gaze across the space, senses primed for residual threats lurking in the stillness. The last time he'd been here, there'd been muscle. There could be again.

But his focus pulled inward, drawn to the stack of documents cradled in his grip. Gray's files, the ones he'd grabbed the last time he was here. Shipping logs, inventory, email chains—the records containing oblique references to "special order items." There had to be something in the morass to drag the Black Thorn syndicate's true motives into the light.

He hadn't grabbed everything the first time, only what he could carry, what he deemed necessary.

And the first time, he hadn't been looking for documents linked to a specific individual.

Matt Jennings.

Silence's mind churned, wrestling with the idea that he'd

been hesitant to cast a shadow of doubt on Matt. The concept of Matt potentially being the Executor was a harsh truth he'd stubbornly rejected. A twinge of remorse gnawed at his moral core, but it was swiftly snubbed out by the cold practicality that came with his role as a vigilante investigator. He had to remain detached when examining every possible clue.

Silence was an Asset. A Watcher. Impartiality was par for the course.

It was only during the quick road trip back from Navarro River Redwoods State Park that it dawned on Silence that Matt remained an unexplored component in this twisted labyrinth, a puzzle piece whose shape and boundaries he hadn't fully traced yet. And when Silence stepped back to survey the grand scheme, he couldn't dispel the unsettling revelation—Matt wasn't just any piece of this puzzle; he might be the only one that slotted flawlessly into position.

Silence led the other two through the doorway into the foreman's glassed-in office. He splayed the papers across the cramped desk, mixing them with other documents he yanked from the shelf, flipping through personnel reports and time cards. Bit players, useless minutiae, pointless details. He discarded each sheet lacking immediate relevance, slowly winnowing toward potentially critical information.

Then...

Something significant.

A shipping document. The header labeled it simply "ANCHOR SHIPMENT."

Eyes widening, Silence skimmed the short manifest: a list of serial numbers, a quantity of fifty units, scheduled for imminent transportation to the nearby Jackson Demonstration State Forest.

A notation in compact script along the margin caught Silence's attention next:

Ensure shipment readied on time, 2100, the day in question. Absolutely critical these pieces reach Black Thorn reps. (FR)

Another sheet detailed the manufacture of assemblies with special upgraded capability in the prior month. Below it, a release order authorizing the delivery of *ANCHOR* weapon bipods.

Attached to this, technical schematics.

"Son of a bitch," Silence uttered.

Bryan and Aria moved closer. With a quizzical tilt of her head, Aria said, "What is it, Drew?"

"*Anchor* is a high-tech..." he said and swallowed as he looked at the schematics, which showed miniaturized motors and hydraulics—like tiny sets of automotive suspensions. "Bipod stabilization." He swallowed and looked up at the others. "For sniper rifles."

Bryan and Aria glanced at each other before Bryan turned back to Silence and said, "Okay, but what about Matt?"

Silence shook his head, returning to the materials.

What about Matt, indeed?

Silence shuffled to the other side of the desk, pulled Gray's computer monitor closer. His fingers flew across soiled keys to access the aging desktop's files. He pulled up cached records still lingering from Gray's usage despite attempts at erasure, cross-referencing dates and entries between digital artifacts and the paper documents.

Finally, he found what he'd been looking for: Matt's name. It was in an email correspondence. Gray was the recipient; Matt was the sender.

Subject: (No Subject)

From: Jennings, Matt

To: Gray, Daniel

Gray,

You don't have to pretend anymore. I know about the Executor's threats and your forced role in making the ANCHOR components.

I've got a personal angle on the Executor, and I'm working to get him to confess before making a move, considering the international stakes. It's a complex situation, but I'm on it.

Hang in there. It's only a matter of days now. I understand the pressure you're under, and I'm doing everything to end this nightmare soon. Your safety is my priority. Expect more updates from me. Stay strong.

Detective Jennings

Relief surged through Silence, a cleansing tide.

He'd doubted Matt, cast him in the Executor's role. But now, having read the email, he understood Matt couldn't possibly be the Executor. Matt was indeed the honorable cop Silence had hoped.

Good ol' Matt.

Bryan and Aria had stationed themselves behind Silence. Apparently, they'd read the email as well because dual sighs of relief escaped their lips.

For Silence, things began to fall into place. He spun the chair around, faced the other two, and started to explain, "The Executor is the..." he said and swallowed. "Link to—"

Aria smiled and put her hand on his shoulder. "Save your voice, Drew. I got this." She squinted at the screen, rereading a part of the email before she continued. "The Executor is the local connection to the Black Thorn Society, and he'd been blackmailing Gray—through threat of death—to make illegal parts in his machine shop."

She paused again to flip through the materials Silence had

dropped on the desk, the ones he'd nabbed the first time he was there.

"From the sounds of it, this had been going on for years. The latest parts are components of ANCHOR self-correcting bipod systems for sniper rifles, with a shipment being moved tonight. And it looks like..."

She trailed off to flip through the pages some more.

"The Executor is going to personally escort the units to a fire road off a highway in Jackson Demonstration State Forest." She paused. "He's selling that shit in the middle of our damn redwoods!"

Bryan leaned closer, looking at the notes and nodding, "But now that we know Matt isn't the Executor ... who is?"

Silence looked at them both in turn, then spun the chair back around to face the desk. He considered the email system glowing on the screen before him, searching for keywords...

...but he stopped himself.

Because he remembered a detail that had stood out earlier, one he'd filed away in the back of his mind. A pair of letters.

He flipped through the papers rapidly, like a person possessed, until he found the shipping information again.

Ensure shipment readied on time, 2100, day in question. Absolutely critical these pieces reach Black Thorn reps. (FR)

FR....

A few moments earlier, Silence had assumed the letters were a code.

Now, he recognized them as initials.

Matt had said he knew the Executor personally...

F.R.

Before his mind could spin too far into an analytical maelstrom, Silence pulled his PenPal notebook from his pocket and scrawled out the name for the other two to see.

He held it up.

Detective Faron Rasnick.

Bryan and Aria both took in a breath.

It was almost too perfect in retrospect. A ranking officer inside Fort Bragg PD would have access to tap phones, monitor secure databases, and manipulate any inquiries into syndicate activities. The ideal embedded operative to feed intelligence and stymie investigations.

Silence thought of the scribbled *EXECUTOR* profile in Rasnick's office. He'd thought it was describing Silence himself—*speaks little; deep, strange voice*—but these were clearly just character traits Rasnick adopted as the Executor persona.

Audacious. Maddeningly simple.

Bold.

Rasnick had marshaled men like Curtis Hyer and Daniel Gray, profiting immensely while they assumed the operational risks. And now, the detective sought to expand the trafficked arsenal with a massive infusion of untraceable ANCHOR hardware.

Rasnick had Matt's blood on his hands. Gray's, too. And three other people's.

At least.

Probably many more.

Now, fifty high-tech sniper rifle platforms would soon be in the hands of an international arms syndicate. It didn't take much imagination to project the fallout across Fort Bragg.

And the United States.

And the international community.

No wonder Rasnick insisted the units ship today, no matter the exposure risk.

Silence became aware he had crushed the manifest page. Smoothing it flat, he weighed potential countermoves on an accelerating timeline. Silence looked at his watch: only an hour to go.

The first step was ensuring those bipods never reached their intended recipients. Contact the authorities? No, as a police officer, Rasnick surely had contingencies against premature disruption thwarting his operations.

This called for something far less elegant.

Silence was going to cut off the shipment.

He shoved the shipping paper into his pocket.

Suddenly, a new notion materialized, making him angry at himself for not considering it earlier.

He looked at the other two. "We still don't know..." he said and swallowed. "Where to find Shawn." He pointed at the computer. "Dig deep. Find out where he is." Another swallow. "And save him."

He shot out of the chair.

Behind him, Aria shouted, "But where are you going?"

Silence called out over his shoulder. "To say hi to the Executor."

CHAPTER THIRTY-SEVEN

THE ABANDONED FOUNDRY WAS like an old friend to Detective Faron Rasnick.

Naturally, this would seem an odd place to elicit such nostalgia from a cop.

That is, a *good* cop...

Momentarily, Rasnick found himself lost in recollection—old times when he and his buddies would drag suspects to this forsaken place to extract confessions.

It had been a while since he'd been back, and as he looked around at the stark, crumbling walls, he could practically *hear* those bygone screams echoing off the cinderblock.

Hell, if he looked hard enough, he could probably find some blood stains.

Ah, memories.

The air was thick with the scent of rusted metal and damp concrete. Rasnick reveled in the atmosphere, the tapping of his oxfords ringing off the walls.

Turning the corner, he found the man he was to meet staring back at him with wide eyes.

Curtis Hyer.

The man who, for several months, had been Rasnick's right-hand man ... from a distance. They'd only ever communicated by phone.

Hyer's mouth hung open.

"*You're* the Executor?" he said in a hoarse whisper.

Rasnick grinned. "That's right, Curtis. You and Daniel Gray never had a clue. The voice modulator was a nice touch, don't you think?"

He'd used the modulator device every time he contacted Hyer, a purposeful yet delightfully theatrical touch.

Hyer stared at him, mouth opening and closing. Rasnick could practically see the gears turning in the man's head, the pieces falling into place.

It was no wonder Hyer was so stunned. Hyer knew he was working for an intermediary for an international arms outfit. He'd probably thought the "Executor" was a sophisticated out-of-towner, not a Fort Bragg public figure, a face known to most people in town.

Who would have thought someone like Rasnick would become a top operative for the Black Thorn Society?

It had started years ago when Rasnick was a rising star in the department, a young detective with a nose for the truth. He had stumbled upon the Black Thorns almost by accident —a case out of Noyo Harbor—a chance encounter that had changed the course of his life.

He'd investigated, going to the feds and even INTERPOL intel. Rasnick had recoiled at the Black Thorns' brutality at first—such ruthlessness was alien to him. However, over time, the practical side of survival in a cutthroat world wormed its way into his conscience. It wasn't so much the shitload of money they offered him that made him do a complete ethical one-eighty, but the grim recognition of necessity that nudged him to reluctantly accept their offer.

At least, that's what he'd convinced himself.

Maybe it *was* the money...

Over the years, his involvement had grown from a silent partner to a key player. He had used his position on the force to shield their activities, to steer investigations away from their door. And, of course, to commandeer Gray's Machine Shop. All the while, he'd been building his own empire, a network of informants and enforcers that answered only to him.

Hyer's voice snapped Rasnick back to the present. "What about the professional? Drew? He's getting close. He's... figuring it all out."

Rasnick nodded. "I know he is, dipshit. But he's not as smart as he thinks. All we have to do is stay one step ahead."

"Does he know about the shipment? About Jackson Demonstration State Forest?"

"It's possible," Rasnick allowed. "But it doesn't matter. Because tonight's the night, and I'm handling the shipment personally. You have another job."

He turned and strode across the foundry floor. Hyer followed. They went deep into the facility's shadows, shoes clanging against the steel-grated floors, weaving their way through hallways and tangles of rusted machinery, skirting around heaps of scrap metal.

Finally, a humming sound and a light announced they'd reached their destination. They stepped into a room with a generator in the back powering a single light via an orange extension cord. In the center of the room was a cylindrical chamber, its clear plexiglass structure gleaming in the light.

Inside, standing, looking scared as shit, was a figure.

Shawn Corzo stared out at them, his eyes wide with fear. Rasnick stepped forward and tapped on the plexiglass with a finger.

"Comfortable, Shawn? I hope you appreciate the amenities. This little setup is courtesy of my employers, the Black Thorn Society. They have a knack for sourcing specialty items from around the world."

Shawn's mouth moved, but no sound escaped the chamber.

"You were my insurance plan, should things get too messy with your old daddy figure, Matt," Rasnick continued. "But turns out, Matt fell right into my trap at the harbor, my guys beat him to death, and Hyer had those machine shop clowns rig up a gas pedal setup for his car. Got him goin' real fast on the highway, and *crash!*, down into the drink he went."

Inside the tube, Shawn thrashed, his mouth spitting soundless curses.

Rasnick chuckled. "Of course, I own the coroner. He'll do pretty much anything to keep his wife safe ... *and* his daughter. But, hey, I had him say that Matt's death was a heart attack. I could've had Matt Jennings die as a drunk driver." He shrugged. "I owed better than that to Matt, a fellow detective, a..." He paused for dramatic effect, giving Shawn a wink. "Friend."

From behind, Hyer gave a slow clap. Rasnick gave an equally snide bow.

"I ended up not needing you as bait for Matt," Rasnick continued, stepping closer to the tube. "But this professional, Drew, operates at another level. So I want to thank you for remaining so obliviously stagnant in that shithole apartment of yours."

Rasnick turned to Hyer.

"Watch over him. Make sure he doesn't go anywhere."

Rasnick chuckled again as he said it. *Someone* needed to be here, but it was impossible for Shawn Corzo to "go anywhere." The tube was impregnable.

Hyer nodded.

And Rasnick turned to leave. He had an appointment to make.

It was time to sell some weapons.

CHAPTER THIRTY-EIGHT

BRYAN AND ARIA were a team again.

Sort of.

Drew had made them a team, commanding them before his abrupt departure to scour Gray's records, find a link to Shawn Corzo, and then find Shawn himself.

Unlike back at the Due North office when she wouldn't even talk to Bryan, this time Aria had simply taken to their urgent task, circling around the desk as soon as Drew had left and telling Bryan to, "Come on!"

Honorable, purposeful, and decisive.

So Aria.

There'd been no awkward moment. There'd been no chit-chat.

There was no time for that, not with Shawn being held hostage somewhere unknown.

For the last ten minutes, the two accountants had been scouring every piece of information they could find. Daniel Gray's office was a maze of paperwork and old computer data, a reflection of what had been the old salt's world-weary approach to life. Bryan and Aria sifted through the papers, clicked through files.

"Here!" Aria said suddenly. She held up a ledger, her finger tracing a series of numbers. "These shipments, they don't add up. There's a discrepancy here, and here..." Her voice trailed off as she immersed herself in the figures.

Bryan leaned over her shoulder...

...so close that he felt her body heat.

He shook it off, refocused, and tried to make sense of the numbers. "You're right. These are dummy transactions! They're meant to cover something up."

"Cover what?" Aria said.

Bryan shook his head.

He considered for a moment the system Matt had used—overcharging amounts to leave a code system. He doubted Daniel Gray was clever enough to use a similar system, but, of course, this was likely not the work of Gray himself...

...but of the man's handlers.

Bryan and Aria worked quietly, their minds piecing together the puzzle that someone had left behind in Gray's records. It was like before—when they were together, when she would lend a hand to his forensic accounting investigations. A twinge of yearning swelled within Bryan.

"The location," Aria murmured, breaking his thoughts. "It's coded. These numbers here, they correspond to coordinates."

Bryan's heart raced as he followed her train of thought. "Coordinates to where?"

Aria's fingers flew over the calculator, her brow knitted in concentration. She spun the chair around so suddenly that Bryan had to jump out of the way.

"Got it!" she shouted.

She grabbed a notebook, scribbled out the digits. Bryan

recognized the style. GPS coordinates. Longitude and latitude.

"I saw a map earlier," Bryan said, rummaging through the papers on the desk, throwing them to the floor until he found it.

Aria used her palms to flatten out the wrinkled map. She traced a finger along it. "It's right ... riiiiight ... there! It's an old foundry, on the outskirts of the city. *That's* where Rasnick must be keeping Shawn."

Bryan's mind raced. He knew the spot—a dilapidated building hidden in plain sight, the perfect place to hide someone.

"We gotta go. *Now,*" Bryan said and reached for her hand.

He hadn't planned on doing it.

It had been instinct.

Muscle memory.

Aria hesitated for a fraction of a second before placing her hand in his.

The contact sent a jolt through Bryan.

They rushed out of the machine shop, turning down the shadowy halls. As they moved, Bryan's mind was a whirlwind of emotions. The thrill of the investigation, the concern for Shawn...

...and the undercurrent of something deeper with Aria.

Because Bryan and Aria were a team again.

CHAPTER THIRTY-NINE

THE TWO-LANE BLACKTOP unspooled through the towering redwood forest. Under a blazing moon, colossal cinnamon-colored trunks crowded the road, trunks as thick as subway tunnels throwing bars of shadow on the highway.

Rasnick's Mazda was in the lead, guiding a convoy of four pickups through the forest. His eyes kept going to the rearview, checking to ensure the cargo remained secured and battened down tight in the trucks' beds.

This cargo was two dozen wooden crates, dimensioned to military spec and heavily reinforced, packed to the gills with Anchor units. State-of-the-art offensive tech worth millions, concealed behind innocent slats and shiny nails. Rasnick's extremely illicit delivery was bound for the most notorious illegal arms dealer in the world, the Black Thorn Society. This was a sobering thought if he dwelled on the implications.

So he wouldn't.

Those paranoid Romanian nutcases didn't feel comfortable making the handoff anywhere even remotely populated. They had a special kind of bunker mentality, convinced the U.S. federal boogeyman had infiltrated every town and city.

For a moment, Rasnick's mind flashed on the professional, Drew.

Well ... maybe the Black Thorns' paranoia wasn't *that* far off-base.

At any rate, they'd wanted a local yet isolated rendezvous point for the clandestine exchange. Luckily, the Fort Bragg area had no shortage of wilderness, so Rasnick had scouted an abandoned logging road in Jackson Demonstration State Forest. The plan was to peel off the highway onto the dirt road, following it three miles until it dead-ended at a clearing far from prying eyes.

Rasnick's lips cracked into a smirk as he pictured the scene awaiting him. The Black Thorns had told him they'd also be arriving in trucks—brand-new full-sized Chevies. Black in color, naturally. Rasnick pictured them in fruity European clothes—probably dressed head-to-toe in black—looking awkward behind the steering wheels of the giant American trucks.

This made him chuckle.

So far, everything was proceeding precisely according to his year's worth of intricate preparation. Once those fanatical lunatics took possession of the Anchors, the real fun would begin.

The Black Thorns had big plans for the merchandise. They informed Rasnick that among their clientele, one buyer was exceedingly eager to take possession of the units. Rasnick didn't know the buyer's identity, nor did he care.

His chest swelled with dark excitement. After so much risk, so many sacrifices and betrayals, the endgame was finally within reach. As the highway started climbing over a forested crest, the trees parted to reveal five blacked-out Chevy Silverados waiting just off the opposite shoulder. The Black Thorns had beaten them to the rendezvous point.

Perfect.

But then something stole Rasnick's attention. A flash in his rearview mirror. He checked it. A low-slung metallic shape blazed into view. A black BMW sedan far down the highway but closing distance at an alarming rate.

Rasnick's grin turned to a knot of dread.

He knew that car's driver.

"Drew..." he growled through gritted teeth.

CHAPTER FORTY

Tires screaming, the Jaguar plunged into the curve's apex at ridiculous speed.

Aria heard heavy breathing coming from the passenger seat, and despite the tension of the moment, she had to suppress a grin. Bryan was trying to act tough, like a big man, but she could see in the corner of her eye how he was holding on for dear life despite knowing the driver was a professional.

Bathed in the silver glow of a blazing moon, trails of oncoming headlights streaked past. Aria's gaze was locked-in, scanning for hazards...

...and speed traps.

Truthfully, despite her background, she almost always drove the speed limit. Now, though, there was an emergency. For the second time that day, she had to dust off her old skill set.

Even if her knee was starting to ache.

Bryan momentarily released his grip on the passenger seat to reference the map on his lap, the one they'd taken from the machine shop. He squinted at it, then looked through the windshield.

He'd done a great job of navigating despite his white knuckles.

And, Aria had to admit, she liked having him back in the Jag with her.

"Turn left here," Bryan said.

The Jag slewed onto an older side road, suspension protesting. Aria eased them into a sweeping turn.

Bullheaded Bryan. Always steeped in his investigations, never relenting until they were complete. This time, that bullheadedness had manifested as a form of physical bravery. Whatever else she felt toward the man, seeing that gallantry cemented trust that they would find Shawn Corzo. Together.

"There!" Bryan shouted over the roaring V12. The third dirt road."

He pointed toward a rutted path peering from the woods. Aria instantly spotted it and killed the headlights. With measured steering inputs, she angled them onto the rough tract, twigs scraping loudly as the path swallowed them into darkness. She winced, praying the Jag's antique paint was unmarred.

"Should be just over this rise," Bryan said.

They crested an angled berm, chassis nearly airborne. All at once, diffuse light spilled across their path from a low structure just visible downslope. Aria locked the Jag into a controlled skid. Bryan smacked his hands into the dash with a bitten-off curse "Shi—".

And they jolted to a halt.

Ahead, bathed in moonlight, the once-imposing foundry now stood dilapidated. Its enormous steel doors and weathered brick walls were marred by graffiti and overgrown weeds. Broken windows. Strewn metal scraps. Crumbling concrete.

As soon as they were stationary, Bryan bailed out and sprinted for the building.

More of that bullheaded bravery...

Aria threw open the door and hurried to keep up.

Through a gaping hole in the fence.

Through a doorless entry.

And into a maze of metal and cinderblock.

"Shawn!" Bryan shouted, his voice echoing. "You here? It's Bryan!"

A faint hum echoed through the still air, a distant sound that pricked their ears. Aria's eyes lit up with recognition as she identified it.

"Generator!" she called out to Bryan.

They turned down a hallway, tracking the sound, their feet crunching on the rotten concrete and clanging on steel grating. As they journeyed deeper, a soft glow began to pierce the darkness ahead of them.

They followed the light, turned a corner...

...and came face-to-face with Shawn Corzo, standing inside an oversized tube, looking distressed but controlled.

Bryan was already rushing forward—the damn bullheaded fool!—when Aria's stunt-school-honed intuition triggered almost too late. With a choked warning, she made to pull him aside, only for rippling shadows to coalesce behind Shawn's confinement into a familiar brutish form.

"Bryan, down!"

A figure appeared.

Curtis Hyer.

Hyer's first blow went wide right, catching only air as Bryan heeded Aria's scream by instinct. She saw Bryan's eyes flare in startled recognition before narrowing in fury—then he drove a shoulder into Hyer's midsection.

They tumbled sideways in a tangle of thrashing limbs, all technique lost to raw desperation. Aria darted into the brawl, seizing Hyer's wrist just before a piston-like fist connected with Bryan's exposed jaw. She torqued the captured arm back, hearing Hyer grunt in outraged surprise.

Bryan and Hyer scuffled for leverage on the rough floor, exchanging blows intermittently. Aria clung to her quarry's arm as dead weight, throwing the equilibrium off while seeking any opening to assist Bryan, to torque Hyer's arm behind his back.

Hyer was maddened, not incapacitated. His fury seemed to escalate exponentially until, with a beastlike roar, he flung Aria bodily aside.

Aria landed hard.

On her knee.

She screamed.

More pain as she rolled once, twice, gasping—at least one rib was bruised, possibly cracked.

Vision swimming into focus, she saw Bryan launch himself at Hyer once more. Hyer abruptly reared up with another savage bellow and hurled Bryan away like nothing.

Bryan landed next to Aria.

And when he tried to elbow himself up, he collapsed.

Hyer whipped around, glowered at them. Sweat and blood covered his face. He turned and spit a stream of pink saliva on the floor.

With his eyes never leaving them, he strode to the opposite side of the room—past Shawn Corzo in the tube, who was watching everything with his hands plastered to the plexiglass, anger in his eyes, clearly wanting to help—and to a cabinet.

He retrieved a pistol.

And walked back over.

"We were expecting Drew. Hmm. Oh well." Grinning, he looked down at Bryan and Aria. "All right, Mulder and Scully," he said with a dark snicker. "Which one of you wants it first?"

He leveled the pistol.

CHAPTER FORTY-ONE

THE BMW's V8 growled as Silence worked the accelerator, the sedan rapidly devouring miles of the two-lane blacktop. Towering redwoods zipped past the side windows in a kaleidoscopic blur of dappled moonlight.

Up ahead, he could already make out the dual convoys—Rasnick's metallic green Mazda leading four battered pickups, while five shiny black Silverados were parked on the highway's shoulder, facing the opposite direction, waiting.

Silence's eyes narrowed as he willed the BMW faster, rapidly closing the distance. He kept his body poised and ready, but inwardly, his mind was a whirlwind of calculations and scenarios. He could already feel his pulse picking up, the familiar burn of adrenaline seeping into his system...

He tightened the gap.

Closer.

Closer...

As the convoy's taillights rapidly grew in the BMW's windshield, Silence began making minor steering adjustments, lining up a precise angle of approach. At this rate, it looked like he'd plow directly into the back truck's rear quarter panel at over a hundred miles per hour—a catastrophic impact obliterating the luxury sedan's front end in an eruption of crumpling metal and shattering glass.

Maybe that's exactly what Rasnick and his goons were expecting from him—an all-or-nothing suicide run that took them all out in one blazing instance of white-hot violence.

At the last possible second, Silence wrenched the steering wheel hard to the left, the tires screeching as the BMW darted between the convoy's two rearmost trucks. One second, it was shooting straight at them; the next, it was seemingly teleporting diagonally across the double yellow lines.

The trucks had no time to react as the black blur sliced between their sandwiched forms. Two of the trucks clipped each other, trying to swerve clear, their rear fenders deforming with the impact as they careened across the roadway. Another veered into the trees lining the shoulder, exploding in a violent shower of bark and shattered safety glass.

Rasnick's green Mazda twisted left and right. Evasive maneuvers. Silence smashed the gas pedal. He was closing in on the other car when...

...a solid wall of blacked-out pickups suddenly appeared up ahead, Black Thorn's vehicles roaring in from the side of the highway. It was odd that they had jumped into action so quickly, but Silence had always heard they were a paranoid bunch.

That must be how they'd climbed so high in the criminal world.

Before the Black Thorns could open fire or pull any evasive maneuvers, Silence yanked the wheel hard, thundering the BMW into their ranks, clipping a front fender and sending one of the lead pickups into a violent spin that sheared off its rear axle and launched a body tumbling across the tarmac.

Gotta wear your seatbelt.

Gunfire erupted, slugs pounding into the BMW's rear flanks and spider-webbing the windshield. Silence hunched down and cut the wheel, screeching off the highway and onto a narrow dirt road—a derelict logging trail leading into the dense forest, nearly concealed by undergrowth.

Whack!

The BMW had excellent suspension, but it wasn't an off-road machine, and Silence felt the jolt in his bones as the car dropped two feet before the tires found dirt. With most of the dual convoys' vehicles either wrecked across the highway or scrambling to recover—and only a couple of them in pursuit—he may have just bought himself a few precious moments.

Or not.

Headlights flashed in his rearview as one of the Silverados flew off the highway right behind him.

The trail was a minefield of ancient roots and fist-sized craters carved out by erosion. The BMW slammed and bucked, Silence fighting the wheel every bone-jarring second as bullets impacted all around him—thumping into the forest floor, cracking into the BMW's sheet metal. A lucky shot pinged off the side mirror, leaving Silence's ears ringing.

Ahead, a blind rise in the trail obscured his view. The BMW crested it at full throttle to find an enormous gaping hole had swallowed the road ahead, a five-foot cavernous void. With no time to brake, Silence wrenched the wheel again.

But the pit was too damn wide.

The BMW hit the edge with both right-side wheels at easily forty miles per hour, instantly ruining them—rubber, metal, and all. The chassis launched into a violent clockwise spin that tore a trench into the soil.

Silence slammed against the door panel, his shoulder shattering the window. A change of direction, and he was thrown back against the center console as the car's nose finished its rotation. A final vicious impact—right into an ancient tree trunk much larger than the BMW itself—deployed the airbags before rocking the car to a standstill.

He turned.

No Silverado.

His pursuers must have had a similar turn of fate farther back on the trail.

Dazed and half-deaf, Silence tasted blood as he pulled himself out through the shattered driver's window. The BMW was canted up on its side at an angle. Destroyed. Already, he could hear more engines revving down the trail, no doubt more of Black Thorn's forces closing in.

Escape and evade, he told himself, tapping into his Watchers on-board training from years before. The trees would be his new battlefield, their density and unpredictability working to his advantage. He drew his Beretta and sprinted toward the nearest cluster of redwood trunks, the needles muffling his footfalls. As the trees swallowed him up, the only sound was his ragged breaths and the pulse pounding in his ears as his hearing returned.

He waited.

Bring it on.

The thick underbrush and twisted redwood limbs afforded ample cover, the dappled patterns of moonlight and shadow continuously shifting with the faintest breeze, altering sight lines. Silence stayed in a low crouch as he scuttled from trunk to trunk, ears pricked for the slightest noise betraying an enemy's approach.

They were out there too, somewhere, squads of the Black

Thorns' highly trained thugs. They'd surely fanned out amid the forest's labyrinth, searching for him.

There was a *crunch* of branches to his three o'clock. Silence froze, Beretta leveled and ready. A dark form pushed through a wall of ferns twenty yards away, AR platform rifle sweeping side to side. Before the man could locate Silence, he fired twice—a double tap to center mass that dropped the shooter in an eruption of blood.

Silence moved on.

Just then, he heard the unmistakable clack of a rifle's bolt being cycled directly behind him. He snapped around, finding the rifle barrel with his Beretta's front sight, then squeezed the trigger twice before the gunman could fire. As his target crumpled backward, Silence was already spinning back to face his original direction, advancing quickly to find better cover among the massive trunks.

Movement ahead. He could make out the tell-tale glint of moonlight reflecting off exposed skin. A sniper team, one spotter paired up with a shooter deploying a heavy rig complete with bipod legs.

He recognized the weapon. It was a Barrett M82A1. An absolute beast of a gun.

And then he realized…

…he recognized the bipod as well. His eyes focused on the distinctive feature—miniature hydraulics, one on each leg.

Icy realization flooded through Silence's body.

That was no ordinary rifle bipod.

It was an Anchor.

CHAPTER FORTY-TWO

Bryan's heart pounded as he stared down the barrel of Hyer's gun, the steel glinting in the dim light. Beside him, Aria was struggling to rise, her face tight with pain, clutching her bad knee.

The odds weren't in their favor.

But Bryan wasn't the same man he'd been when this all started. He'd learned a thing or two about facing fear head-on.

Drew had influenced him.

No ... *Jake Rowe* had influenced him. The same person who'd had an impact on Matt.

...who, in turn, had impacted Bryan.

Sometimes, things come full circle.

In a flash, Bryan kicked out, his foot connecting with Hyer's wrist. The gun went flying, clattering across the concrete floor. Hyer roared in fury, lunging for the weapon, but Bryan was already moving.

He smashed into Hyer, their bodies tangling. They grappled, trading blows like they had moments earlier, each trying to gain the upper hand. Hyer was a strong son of bitch.

But Bryan knew he had the advantage of grit.

Movement to his left. He looked. Hobbling on one knee, screaming in agony, Aria lunged into the fray, her movements impressively precise and calculated despite her injury.

That's stunt school for ya.

They worked in tandem, anticipating each other's actions, a well-oiled machine, closing in on Hyer from both sides.

Bryan's mind flashed on the search for clues at the machine shop, remembering how they'd puzzled out the foundry's location together. They'd always made a great team.

Bryan and Aria were a team again.

Refocusing, Bryan tried for Hyer's shoulder but instead took a glancing blow to the jaw, tasting blood. He shook it off.

Together, he and Aria drove Hyer back, their combined assault wearing him down. They maneuvered the man toward a small room off the main floor, its door hanging crookedly on rusted hinges.

With a final, coordinated effort, they shoved Hyer inside. He stumbled, off balance, fell to his ass, and Bryan slammed the door shut, throwing the deadbolt. Through the small, grimy window set into the door, he could see Hyer on the floor of the dusty room, his face twisted with rage.

Bryan turned to Aria, chest heaving. She had a hand on the wall, taking the pressure off her knee. She met his gaze, her own breathing ragged. Something passed between them for a moment, a flicker of the old connection, the shared adrenaline of victory.

But there was still work to be done.

Bryan broke their stare, and together, they hurried over to Shawn's prison, examining the high-tech tubing for a release mechanism. Shawn watched them anxiously.

"Hang on, buddy," Bryan murmured, his fingers searching for a latch, a button, anything. "We'll get you out in no time."

Aria joined him, her own hands skating over the smooth surface. They worked quietly; the only sounds were their harsh breaths and the distant pounding of Hyer's fists against the locked door.

Finally, Bryan found a hidden catch. With a hiss of released pressure, the front of the tube swung open. Shawn practically fell into their arms, his legs wobbly from confinement.

"Thanks," he said in a small, hoarse voice.

Bryan clapped him on the back, relief washing over him in a wave. "We've got you, Shawn. It's over."

But even as he said the words, he knew it wasn't entirely true. There were still questions to be answered, loose ends to be tied up.

...and a vicious man locked in a room.

And then there was the matter of Aria and whatever this thing was between them.

But for now, they had Shawn. They had each other. And that was enough.

Bryan glanced at the room in the back. The pounding had stopped, but there was Hyer's face in the window, glowering, drenched in sweat and blood.

Pulling his cellular phone from his pocket, Bryan checked the multiplex. "No signal in here," he told Aria. "I'll go outside and call Drew."

She nodded.

"We make a pretty good team," he said.

Aria's lips quirked in a small smile. "We always did."

Bryan smiled. And left.

Yes, Bryan and Aria were a team again.

CHAPTER FORTY-THREE

RASNICK USED binoculars to peer through the shattered rear window of his Mazda, scanning the forest's edge near the rutted fire road where Drew had vanished in his BMW, followed moments later by one of the Black Thorn trucks. A glint of reflected moonlight on metal gave away the Black Thorn shooter's position.

The sniper was prone in the underbrush with a Barrett sniper rifle shouldered, its Anchor bipod legs splayed for stability. Of course, Rasnick couldn't see minute details from this distance, but he knew that at that very moment, the Anchor unit would be reading digital input from the scope, as well as information the sniper entered manually, its motors whirring, adjusting the tiny pneumatics in real time to align the perfect shot.

It was like autopilot for a shooter.

Rasnick chuckled at Drew's fate. The irony of that self-righteous prick being cut down by the very technology he'd hunted down—flying in like a wrecking ball here in the redwoods and nearly destroying Rasnick's entire operation—was just too rich.

He turned to survey the rest of the battlefield. Ruined trucks everywhere—upturned, broken, wrapped around colossal tree trunks. Metal creaking. Fires crackling. Smoke and flames.

All of Rasnick's vehicles were incapacitated. All his men, dead. Only one of the Black Thorns's Silverados remained. The idling diesel's headlights probed the darkness as a pair of the Romanians carefully loaded the crated Anchor units from the remains of one of Rasnick's trucks.

Minutes earlier, witnessing the carnage, Rasnick had felt a spike of dread, knowing what the Black Thorns could and *would* do to him. But then, as he watched the crates being loaded into the Silverado, his mouth spread into a smile as the realization dawned—this wouldn't be a total disaster after all.

Sure, Black Thorn wouldn't receive the full payload they'd been promised. But they were still getting their hands on the core Anchor tech, and this blueprint that would allow them to reproduce the platforms en masse across their entire network of seemingly innocuous machine shops. They'd find a new equivalent to Daniel Gray's shop in some other Fort Bragg-esque shithole, and they could proceed as planned. And once they'd secured a distributed supply chain and manufacturing chain, they could seed the augmented weaponry across the globe to any rogue regime or anti-government element willing to meet their price.

Maybe, just maybe, Rasnick could still end up in their good graces after this fiasco. At the very least, he'd avoid their kill list and be able to pursue opportunities elsewhere when the dust settled.

Yes. Yes, this would still work out just fine in the end.

But a little insurance wouldn't hurt.

He opened his door and stepped outside, going to the nearest immobilized truck. It was one of his contingent—a rusty twenty-year-old Ford, mangled and hissing. There was the smell of antifreeze. Rasnick tried the tailgate. Wouldn't budge, too bent. So he climbed up and strained to pull one of the heavy crates out of the back and over the edge of the bed.

It landed with a heavy thud on the dirt, and Rasnick took a quick breather before lifting it again with a grunt. After a few moments of toil manipulating it into the Mazda's backseat, he was back behind the steering wheel, panting.

He looked from mirror to mirror and evaluated his potential exits. Ruined trucks and broken crates were blocking off the route they'd entered from. But he saw a bit of breathing room to his rear. If he could weave through the debris minefield to the east flank, there was a narrow corridor between the overturned trucks with enough clearance to punch out onto the empty lane of the highway. From there, it was a straight shot west where he could disappear into the night.

Yes, that could work. Rasnick's grin stretched even wider as he guided the Mazda into reverse, thumping over the twisted wreckage in his path. The tires spun and shrieked, clawing for purchase.

For a moment, he was stuck.

He put the Mazda into drive. Spun the steering wheel. Gave it some gas. And powered past the offending debris—a twisted chrome bumper—as it screeched down the side of his car.

In the rearview mirror, the wreckage looked like an obstacle course.

But he could still see the path he'd laid out in his mind.

His exit.

It was going to take a couple of minutes.

But with Drew in the woods facing an Anchor-equipped Barrett M82A1—probably dead already—Rasnick could spare a bit of time to ensure he made it out safely.

Then all would be good.

His insurance package was on the backseat behind him. Should the Black Thorns get tough with him, he could threaten to sell their tech to another interested organization.

Rasnick was still in the game. And once the dust settled, this disaster in the trees was a setback he was confident he could overcome.

CHAPTER FORTY-FOUR

CRACK!

A round from the Barrett struck the earth a yard and a half to Silence's right, peppering him with dirt and debris.

His jaw clenched as he weighed his severely limited options. Outgunned, out-manned, and rapidly being boxed into a killing floor—this wasn't looking good.

He was crouched behind a redwood stump the size of a Volkswagen. Ahead was a smoking divot where the round had just struck. That was the second shot that had come in that area. Clearly, the sniper thought that was Silence's only path out.

But the man was wrong.

Silence had spotted a narrow gap beneath a fallen branch, which was as large as an entire full-sized tree of non-redwood proportions. If he could keep the sniper team thinking he was going to his right—to the north—then he could dart in the opposite direction and go for the hidden escape he'd spotted.

He put his hands on a boulder beside him. A growl escaped his lips, burning his ruined throat as he strained every sinew in his muscular form to dislodge it from its firm the earth's grip.

Movement.

Breaking free from the soil.

Silence's body shook, teeth grinding.

Finally, the stone broke free of the grip and emerged from the depression. It rolled. Slowly. Then faster. Faster, picking up speed as it journeyed down the gentle slope to his right.

CRACK!

The sniper had taken the bait and fired at the moving target.

Seizing this opportunity, Silence darted in the opposite direction and jumped, rolling under the branch and into safety beyond.

Now, it was time to take care of these guys.

In addition to the sniper team, there were two more with AK-47s roaming to the east.

They'd be first.

Silence went utterly still. He steadied his breathing, using diaphragmatic breaths like C.C. had taught him.

And he listened.

There. Five yards out. Footsteps.

He saw them. The two with AKs.

As the lead man neared Silence's hidden position, he exploded upwards in a whirling dervish of coiled violence. His left hand clamped down on the gunman's weapon while his right snapped up and locked behind the man's skull.

With a torsion of his hips and shoulders, Silence wrenched savagely, the crack of shattering vertebrae loud as a thunderclap. The lifeless body crumpled to the forest floor as Silence pivoted and opened fire on the second shooter, his Beretta barking twice in rapid succession to drop the man where he stood.

Not breaking stride, Silence spun to locate the sniper

team. They were hastily repositioning, the Anchor gunner struggling to make some sort of adjustment to the rifle's Anchor bipod as Silence cut them both down with another double tap each from the Beretta.

Slowing his breathing again, Silence surveyed his surroundings. He detected twin beams of headlights carving through the foliage up on the highway. With the moonlight as bright as it was, he could see it all through the gaps between the giants.

One set of headlights belonged to Rasnick's Mazda, slowly navigating through the debris on the highway.

Heading west.

The second was one of the blacked-out Silverados, its cargo bed stacked with wooden crates.

Heading east.

Silence's mind absorbed the implications as the truck heaved up onto the highway, accelerating in the opposite direction from Rasnick. Even if the Black Thorns missed out on their complete payload, that single truckload of Anchor units was more than enough for them to reverse-engineer the work done in Fort Bragg and manufacture more across their global network.

Yet, there went Rasnick, the shithead who was behind everything in Fort Bragg.

The man who'd killed Matt.

Going in the opposite direction.

Having only seconds to decide, Silence made his choice: the Silverado.

Silence couldn't allow the Black Thorns to escape with even one Anchor unit— the risk was far too catastrophic.

Rasnick would have to wait.

Besides, Rasnick wasn't going anywhere just yet. He was still navigating the wreckage on the highway, and by the looks of it, he'd gotten stuck again.

Silence took off at a loping jog toward the edge of the forest and the highway beyond, where he saw a crumpled but still intact Dodge Ram waiting, beckoning him.

He sprinted down the fire road, dodging branches and ruts in the dirt, and made it to the truck. He wrenched open the door, and a bloody body in a trucker jacket fell halfway out, face split wide open. Silence undid the seatbelt, and the body collapsed onto the roadside.

He climbed in. The engine was running. Silence could see the Silverado's taillights receding along the empty highway that stretched eastward into the moonlight. He threw the gear selector into drive and mashed the accelerator, the big V8's roar echoing off the redwood trunks as the truck clambered up the embankment and onto the road surface.

One second, he was stationary; the next, he was already hitting seventy, the big knobby tires finding incredible purchase as he set off in pursuit.

He tightened his grip on the steering wheel, which was wet with the previous driver's blood, still warm but coagulating into a sticky mess.

Up ahead, the fleeing truck was already a half-mile gone, the gap seeming to grow. But Silence kept the pedal planted, exhaust roaring furiously.

Silence's commandeered truck ate up the distance, its powerful engine snarling as he pushed it to the limit. But the Black Thorn driver was no amateur, weaving and dodging with practiced skill to keep the Silverado's bumper maddeningly out of reach.

Silence gritted his teeth. The gap narrowed inch by hard-fought inch, his training and instincts guiding him as he stayed right on the Silverado's bumper.

Closing in.

The other driver grew desperate, attempting increasingly reckless maneuvers to shake his dogged pursuer.

But Silence had a career's worth of hard-earned experience behind the wheel. With a deft flick of the wrist, he feinted left, then right, herding the Silverado toward the shoulder.

The Black Thorn truck swerved, tires scrabbling for purchase on the loose gravel. Silence seized his chance, ramming the other vehicle's rear quarter panel in a PIT maneuver with a sickening crunch of metal on metal.

The Silverado fishtailed wildly, its driver struggling to regain control. Tires screeching, smoking, nearly holding on...

...but it was too late.

The truck careened off the road in a plume of dust and debris, plowing through the underbrush before slamming into a redwood with a deafening crash.

Silence brought his own truck to a skidding halt, the acrid stench of burned rubber filling his nostrils. He threw open the door, jumped out, and approached the wreck cautiously, Beretta drawn.

The Black Thorn driver lay slumped over the steering wheel, blood trickling from a deep gash on his cheek. But his chest still rose and fell in ragged gasps. Alive.

For now.

The passenger was already dead, a tangled mess on the Silverado's dash.

Silence reached through the shattered window, pressing the muzzle of his gun to the driver's temple. The driver's eyes fluttered open, unfocused and glassy with pain. His lips moved soundlessly, a wordless plea for mercy.

Silence fired. Two pulls of the trigger.

Crack! Crack!

A slight adjustment.

Crack! Crack!

A double tap for the presumed-dead passenger.

Presumed.

Silence didn't take chances.

He turned away from the scene, looked in the opposite direction.

There was the Mazda in the distance. Rasnick was still navigating the wreckage.

But he was almost clear of it, yards away from bursting free onto open highway.

Silence sprinted back to the Ram.

CHAPTER FORTY-FIVE

Rasnick's Mazda devoured the moonlit blacktop, mile after mile. The engine snarled as he jammed the accelerator to the floor. He was almost back to Fort Bragg. He saw lights ahead.

In the rearview mirror, the wreckage was nowhere to be seen, far back there in the distance. All he could see was a massive plume of black smoke twisting up over the tree line, contrasted against the blazing moonlight.

He grinned. He'd slipped the noose and even salvaged a fraction of his operation. The crate of ANCHOR tech sliding around the backseat was his saving grace.

A flash caught his attention, and he looked at the mirror again. A set of headlights. Ballooning larger, closing the gap at an alarming rate. He saw the battered chrome grill of a Dodge Ram.

Squinting, he leaned closer to the mirror...

...and could just discern a maddeningly familiar figure silhouetted behind the wheel.

Drew.

"Shit!"

Rasnick smacked the steering wheel, pressed his foot even harder, feeling it all the way up his calf, coaxing every ounce of speed from his piece of shit Mazda.

To no avail.

That bouncing, beat-up truck behind him was gaining.

And gaining.

And gaining...

In the mirror, Rasnick caught a flash of Drew's face in the moonlight. Blank. Cold. Angular.

Shadow swept over the Ram, washing Drew away, a silhouette once more.

Shit, Rasnick needed an advantage, a way to flip the script. An idea ignited in his mind, and his grin returned, sharper than ever.

He knew just the place.

It was close, really close.

Half a mile.

Quarter mile.

Here!

Rubber screamed against asphalt as Rasnick pulled the Mazda through the curve, the old building appearing ahead in his taillights. He stomped the brakes, skidding to a halt outside the looming husk of the abandoned police station.

Once an Art Deco jewel, the building now sagged in decaying grandeur, windows boarded over, masonry crumbling to dust. Rasnick barely spared it a glance, his hands scrabbling beneath the passenger seat for his twin insurance policies—a Glock 9mm and a sleek pair of tactical glasses.

HORIZON tech, another bleeding-edge gift from his Black Thorn benefactors.

He slipped the glasses over his eyes and thumbed the power switch. The lenses flickered to life, projecting a dizzying tactical HUD across his field of vision. Glowing reticles, range-finding algorithms, ballistic calculators.

A thing of deadly beauty.

He wanted to take the ANCHOR crate with him. Couldn't. Drew would be there any second. The thing was too damn heavy. But Drew wouldn't know it was back there, so Rasnick felt confident in leaving it.

Anyway, Drew would have to contend with Rasnick's HORIZON-equipped sidearm first. Rasnick allowed himself a moment of smug satisfaction. Drew didn't stand a snowball's chance in Hell.

The Ram's headlights knifed through the gloom as Rasnick sprinted for the station's gaping maw of an entrance. He plunged into the murk of the interior, the HORIZON HUD automatically adjusting to the low-light conditions, dimming its display. The fetid stench of mold and rat droppings assaulted Rasnick's nostrils.

But it was familiar territory all the same.

He moved swiftly through the derelict halls as memories of his time in uniform guiding him to the ideal choke point. Footsteps echoed from the darkness behind.

Drew had entered.

The footsteps got louder, inexorably closer. The guy was good. A true pro.

But he still had no idea what awaited him.

Rasnick called out, his voice dripping with taunting condescension.

"I know every inch of this place, Drew. Worked here for years. And I've got another ace up my sleeve." He ran a finger along the glasses. They even felt expensive and high-tech. "Turns out Black Thorn's just full of fun surprises. They let me test-run something far more advanced than ANCHOR. It's called HORIZON. These little beauties make targeting child's play. You're walking face-first into a slaughterhouse, buddy."

The footsteps faltered, then resumed at a warier pace. Drew was shrewd enough to know Rasnick wasn't bluffing.

Yes, a true professional.

"After I killed your buddy Matt, I did the same to ol' Daniel Gray," Rasnick said. "The poor sap had himself an accident, just like all the rest of them. It bothered me a bit; not gonna lie. I always liked that old shit. But he got sloppy, so what're you gonna do?"

Rasnick turned a corner.

And waited.

He reached up to the glasses, pressed a rocker button a few times. His smile grew as he watched the HUD paint his approaching quarry in lurid shades of infrared.

Big ol' Drew.

Moving in Rasnick's direction.

And not even knowing it.

The reticle settled over the biometric center mass, the Glock automatically syncing targeting data with the glasses. Like shooting fish in a barrel.

If only there wasn't a pair of walls between them.

Rasnick moved on. He slipped through mildewed corridors and crumbling offices, an apex predator guided by bleeding-edge tech.

A reverberating crash echoed from somewhere deep in the building. Engrained memory told him the exact location of the disturbance.

The old records room.

Engrained memory also told him that the records room was a dead-end.

He grinned.

Rasnick zeroed in on the noise, the HUD sketching a vivid outline of a male figure crouched behind a bank of decrepit file cabinets. Trapped like a rat.

Rasnick's pistol barked once, twice, three times, the

muzzle flash strobing like a camera in the fetid gloom. Chunks of the concrete wall exploded mere inches from Drew's position, clouds of choking dust billowing outward.

A strangled grunt of pain. The HUD pinpointed the heat signature of fresh blood droplets, painting the floor in glowing spatters of yellow.

Rasnick hadn't tried to shoot Drew.

He'd aimed for the wall beside the guy, spraying concrete shrapnel on him

Like a bank shot.

That's the sort of taunting tomfoolery one could indulge in with HORIZON.

The tech was that good.

"Might as well give it up, Drew," Rasnick called out in a singsong voice, inching ever forward. "Can't hide from HORIZON. I seeeeee you."

No response from the shadows.

No problem.

Rasnick advanced down the hallway, Glock at the ready, finger hovering over the trigger. The door to the records room yawned ahead, Drew cornered within like an animal, right around the corner.

In the room ahead, moonlight speared through narrow gaps in the boarded-over windows, throwing splinters of illumination across mildewed shelves sagging under the weight of decaying files and black-mold-encrusted furniture.

There he was—more of that yellow-glowing blood and a giant mass of heat right around the corner. The HUD reticle pulled to the right and began flashing. Right on center mass.

Rasnick's feral grin widened, his heart beating a staccato rhythm.

Time to finish off this stranger who came close to ruining everything.

"End of the line, dickhead!" Rasnick screamed.

The file cabinets loomed. Drew's heat signature glowed.

One step.

Two.

Three...

CHAPTER FORTY-SIX

PAIN BLAZED along Silence's ribs where concrete shrapnel had raked across him moments earlier.

Crack! Crack! Crack!

More pain along his left flank.

More dust. He coughed as he squeezed tighter against the upturned desk that lay just around the open doorframe.

Rasnick screamed out to him. "I'm coming, Drew!"

Focus, he told himself. *Study the moment.*

It was a C.C.-ism. Mindfulness. Situational awareness.

Jaw set, Silence analyzed the situation.

It was a records room, evidenced by the massive filing cabinets and a mound of shattered computer monitors.

It was also a dead-end. That's why Rasnick had corralled him there.

A turncoat detective ready to seal his deception among the ghosts of *good* cops' work. There was something sick about that.

Silence stole a glance around the corner, getting a quick flash of Rasnick. He saw yellow-tinted wraparound lenses over the man's manic eyes—the HORIZON tech Rasnick had described, advanced gear, some proto-military system with uncanny targeting.

In that fraction of a second, he also saw a Glock.

And a slash of feral teeth in a cruel sneer.

Silence jumped back behind his cover.

Crack! Crack!

More debris rained down on him.

"I still see you, big boy!" Rasnick yelled.

Silence grimaced. The shrapnel wounds on his left ribs were worse than he'd thought. He glanced down. Blood was seeping into his shirt, several dark blotches on the gray seersucker fabric. Fiery pain shot up his side.

He tuned out Rasnick's rasping diatribe.

And tried harder to focus.

Focus!

With adrenaline turning his vision crystalline, Silence noted the parallel rows of ceiling-high steel cabinets, which once would have been racked heavily with decaying manila folders, all empty.

Now, they stood starkly bare, a ghostly echo of the archive records of thousands of cases and convictions that had once defined the diligent detective work within these very walls.

The shelves may have been empty of any police records.

But they still looked sturdy, solid...

...and heavy as all hell.

Don't build 'em like they used to.

Plus, with a bit of real-world geometry, Silence saw that they were positioned just right...

Biting back a grimace, Silence braced one shoulder against straining steel. A guttural cry burst past clenched teeth with the effort as he shoved with manic urgency.

Metal groaned and screeched. And moved. Slowly.

An inch.

Two.

Footsteps.

Rasnick: "Oh, there you are!"

Three inches...

...and the cabinets came tumbling over.

Silence jumped to the side. With rapidly gathering momentum, the cases tipped and crashed over.

That real-world geometry came into play, and the cabinets barreled down right where Silence had anticipated: into the open doorway.

At that exact moment, Rasnick appeared in the same doorway.

Pity.

Rasnick had time only for a choked half-turn toward the noise before a couple hundred pounds of old-school steel fell directly on him.

He was vertical one moment, prone the next.

There was a wet thud punctuated by two distinct sets of cracking noises: floor tile...

...and bone.

Silence staggered slightly, coming to his full height from his slumped position. When he was confident his feet would support him reliably, he stepped over to Rasnick.

Rasnick's head, right arm, and left hand were visible beneath the cabinets. And that was it; everything else was crushed.

His eyes were closed. He was moaning. His right arm twitched, the Glock bouncing in his loose grip. Silence kicked the gun away.

The detective looked up at Silence. The glasses were askew on his face, one lense shattered. An odd clicking noise came from the unit.

The guy was dying. Yet he still clung to wild hope, eyes smoldering beneath ruined yellow lenses. One bloody hand seized Silence's ankle.

"You ... you gotta pull me out..." Pain and desperation had completely overtaken Rasnick's bravado. "Ah, shit, it hurts, man. I'll split the take from ... from the Black Thorns with you. Swear to Christ! Just ... just get me out!"

Disgusting.

As a vigilante assassin, Silence had witnessed serial killers and wife-murderers display more courage when facing the inevitable.

Silence raised his Beretta.

"No!" Rasnick said. "No, please! I—"

Crack! Crack!

Two rounds to the head.

A double tap. Silence's preferred method. No chances.

Rasnick had said it hurt. Silence put the guy out of his misery.

Silence was a big Boy Scout like that.

The tight pairing of holes spouted blood just beneath where Rasnick's right eye used to be. Silence had positioned the shots carefully.

To preserve the tech.

He bent over, removed the glasses from Rasnick's face, pocketed them.

Standing again, he looked down at the body.

Bryan had told Silence that the building was due for demolition next week.

How fortunate.

This was a fitting grave for a supposed cop.

―――

Pain shot up Silence's side as he dropped the wooden crate on the Ram's passenger seat. The thing was damn heavy. It had been a bitch to move.

But now it was his.

And soon, it would be in the hands of Watchers Specialists.

He circled around the hood and dropped into the driver's seat. Panting, he took a half second to catch his breath, then stowed the half-destroyed HORIZON unit in the glove compartment. It would also be with Specialists soon.

The ANCHOR units and the mangled HORIZON would go a long way toward tracking down the Black Thorns Society.

Silence checked his watch.

He had just enough time to get there.

...if he hurried.

But...

He checked his cellular phone—four missed calls from Bryan. He flipped the phone open, called him back.

Two rings, then, "Drew! Thank God you called right now when I'm outside with reception. I was just about to call *you*. We got him!"

"Hyer?"

"Yeah. Got him locked up. You gotta get back here and—"

"Locked up good?" Silence said.

A pause, then, "Yeah..."

"Can you keep him..." Silence said and swallowed. "Secure for a bit longer?"

Another pause. "Sure, but—"

"Good. See you soon."

Silence flipped the phone shut, dropped it in his pocket, checked his watch again.

To make it there, he'd have to leave *right now*.

He threw the Ram into gear and peeled out, spraying chunks of rotten asphalt from the tires.

CHAPTER FORTY-SEVEN

The Ram's tires bit into the gravel parking lot in a spray of loose stones as Silence slammed the brakes.

He stomped out into the towering redwoods that encircled the clearing, which glowed warmly in the night with its smattering of tiki torches. Yogis unfolded their mats and chatted while sipping on mugs of tea. Some sat cross-legged in preparation for meditation. The air was filled with a gentle hum of voices and the pleasant scent of burning incense.

Silence hated to disturb the peace of the place.

But violence was sometimes necessary. Even in tranquility.

He scanned the lot surrounding him for the Mercedes. It wasn't there.

He looked through the trees, past the clearing, to the opposite parking area.

No.

No.

Yes! There it was. The Mercedes.

And there was Vinnie.

...with Juliette.

Their silhouetted figures were in obvious confrontation.

Juliette was looking down, arms wrapped around herself, as per standard. Vinnie was speaking to her, crowding her, fists clenched at his side.

Silence strode directly across the grounds toward them. As he passed the clearing, Doris and Kofi rose from their mats and approached him, all smiles, each holding a steaming mug of tea.

But Silence didn't so much as glance their way, just picked up the pace.

His eyes were locked on Juliette and Vinnie.

As Silence closed at a loping jog, Vinnie's voice rang out in an angry bark. "Who the hell are you?"

Silence stopped a foot in front of Vinnie, who narrowed his eyes, stuck out his jaw ... and took a step back.

Juliette looked up, then quickly back down. Silence fixed unblinkingly on the lurid contusions on her face. He glared at Vinnie.

"You do this to her?"

The man brayed out a snorting half-laugh and stuck his jaw out a bit farther as he stabbed a finger into Silence's pec. "So what if I did?"

With a blur of movement, Silence grabbed the finger poking his chest.

And broke it.

Snap!

The sound was disproportionately loud as it echoed off the surrounding redwoods.

The bully's furious bravado shattered like thin ice, his mouth frozen wide around a shrill howl of shock and agony that rippled back across the yoga group, eliciting murmurs and gasps.

Silence instantly clamped down on the man's wrist and twisted, hauling him stumbling behind a massive redwood trunk. Alone now, hidden from the yogis' view, he spun Vinnie around, slammed him into the tree.

"637 Pine Ridge Road, Sacramento," Silence said. He swallowed. "Sound familiar?"

Silence had made a call just before heading back to the park—another information request, this time regarding one Vinnie Morrison. The Specialist who'd taken the call had been kind enough to oblige...

...despite the request being non-mission-related.

Eyes streaming with tears, Vinnie could only nod weakly amid panicked gasps as his broken finger spasmed.

"UC Berkeley, class of..." Silence said, swallowed. "'89. Business administration."

"That's..." Vinnie said, groaning. "My degree."

"Stephanie and Robert Morrison," Silence said, swallowed. "Parents. Michael Taylor, best friend." He paused. "Get the picture?"

Naturally, Silence would never lay a finger on innocents. But this was far from a promise; it was a threat, intimidation.

After several hoarse breaths, Vinnie finally managed to rasp out a hoarse acknowledgment. "Yeah, you ... you know everything about me ... What, are you, like, a hitman or something?"

Silence ignored the question, allowing Vinnie's imagination to do the work. "Don't go near Juliette again. Or...?"

He left it open for Vinnie to finish.

Panic flooded the bully's already bloodless features.

"You'll ... hunt me. Track me down ... and..." His voice drained away into a thin squeak of terror. "Oh shit..."

Silence simply nodded.

"Okay, man, okay! I won't ever talk to her again, I swear! Just let me go, I'm leaving right now!"

Silence grinned. "Oh, no, you're not." He swallowed. "Not yet."

After Silence made Vinnie's face match Juliette's and sent the piece of shit packing in the Mercedes, he emerged from behind the redwoods' concealing flanks, walking with Juliette. They hugged, and she drifted off to get a mat.

They'd exchanged a few words after Vinnie left. Silence didn't get to know her well, but he could tell Juliette was a good soul.

C.C. had always told him he was good at reading people.

Doris and Kofi moved to intercept him, questions forming on their lips, but Silence cut them off.

"Can't talk about it," he said.

They both glanced at blood on the side of Silence's shirt, where he'd been struck by the concrete shrapnel, and exchanged a look. Then, in unison, they turned back to Silence. They were both smart enough to not press the issue.

...though they probably assumed the blood was Vinnie's.

Perhaps some of it was.

Doris said, "Are you staying for the evening session, Drew?" And when Silence started to protest, she added, "Come on! This one's only half an hour."

Silence was tired and hurting and mentally exhausted. And, likely, he wasn't entirely done—there was still Curtis Hyer to contend with. He'd killed several people that night. He'd stopped illegal arms from getting into the hands of terrorists. He'd slapped the shit out of an abuser...

...oh, and broken the guy's finger as well.

Silence wasn't feeling like yoga tonight.

But when he looked down at Doris and Kofi—their mismatched love, their pure smiles, their steamy mugs of tea—he just said, "Wouldn't miss it."

CHAPTER FORTY-EIGHT

Aria felt trapped in the dimly lit room at the back of the foundry. The weight of the past few hours was starting to get reeeeeeally heavy.

Shawn was spent, too, sitting in the far corner, butt on the floor, head between his knees, arms draped languidly.

Next to Aria, Bryan provided a strong and steady presence. He'd taken it upon himself to rally everyone's spirits. He'd also left intermittently to make more attempts at reaching Drew via his cellular phone.

"Are you sure Drew will know what to do?" Aria said.

Bryan nodded. "Yeah, Drew will know. I don't know exactly who he works for or what he does, but I'm pretty sure he's some kind of fed. Sort of a cop, I guess. Like Matt. He'll make sure Hyer faces justice."

Aria opened her mouth to respond, but a sudden movement to her right made her gasp. She whirled around, heart pounding, only to find Drew standing in the doorway, his expression unreadable.

For a moment, Aria couldn't breathe. How had Drew

managed to enter so silently, so stealthily? The man was *huge*. But apparently, he could move like a ghost.

Bryan seemed less surprised. "What took ya so long?"

"Yoga," Drew replied, his tone flat.

"*Yoga?*"

Bryan's eyebrows shot up, but Drew didn't elaborate. Instead, he looked to the back of the room, nodded at Shawn, and then turned his intense gaze to Aria.

There was were large patches of blood on his shirt.

"Drew!" Aria said. "What happened?"

He ignored the question. "You have him…" he said and swallowed. "Trapped?"

Aria nodded, finding her voice. "Yes. Back here."

Bryan glanced at Drew, a hint of anticipation in his eyes. "Justice time, right?"

Drew's answer was a curt nod. Aria led the way to the back room, Bryan and Drew following close behind. With a deep breath, she pulled back the deadbolt and swung the door open.

Drew entered while Bryan and Aria stayed back.

Hyer was waiting, standing in the center of the room, his face twisted into a sneer. He looked like a caged animal, all wound-up anger and bared teeth.

Drew continued inside and stopped. He met Hyer's gaze without flinching.

"You killed people?" Drew said.

Hyer's sneer widened. "You bet I did."

What happened next seemed to unfold in slow motion. Drew reached under his jacket and came out with a gun, which he leveled at Hyer. Two shots rang out, deafening in the enclosed space.

Aria watched, frozen, as Hyer's head snapped back, blood splattering the wall behind him. His body crumpled, dead before he hit the floor.

Beside her, Bryan was equally still, his face a mask of shock.

Aria's mind reeled, trying to process what she'd just witnessed. She'd never seen anything like it, never been so close to such ruthless violence.

She'd seen plenty of fake blood in stunt school.

But that abstract art splash of crimson dripping down the wall was different. It was real.

And it was full of bone shards and...

...and...

...brain.

Drew just shrugged, his expression never changing. "Justice."

He walked past them, jerking his head toward the door. "Come on."

CHAPTER FORTY-NINE

Bryan's eyes fluttered open as the morning sunlight slanted across his face. For a moment, he lay disoriented, blinking against the brightness, wondering where the hell he had just awoken.

Then he remembered.

He was at Aria's place.

The familiar contours of Aria's living room came into focus around him, and memory came flooding back. The previous night's events still hung over him like a shroud—the tension, the revelations, the sudden violence of Drew's extrajudicial execution.

After witnessing Hyer's abrupt end, Aria had invited Bryan back to her place so they could both decompress. They'd talked for hours, the conversation leaving the night's events and roaming across their shared history and the still-raw wounds of their past relationship.

But despite the charged intimacy, they hadn't entirely succumbed to old comforts. They hadn't slept together.

Aria slept in her bed.

Bryan slept on the sofa.

And Bryan was genuinely okay with that.

As he sat up, stretching the kinks from his back, he took in the details of Aria's space with fresh eyes. The bookshelf overflowing with well-thumbed paperbacks, the framed prints on the walls—splashes of vibrant color against the crisp white paint. It felt warm. Lived-in. A real home, not just a place to survive.

A smile tugged at Bryan's lips as a tingle of hopefulness bloomed in his chest. After everything he and Aria weathered together yesterday, and with the long conversation they'd had last night, there was a chance now for them to start over. To build something new from the ashes of their shared past.

As if conjured by his musings, the bedroom door swung open. Aria emerged, wrapped in a fluffy blue robe, her brown hair delightfully mussed. Bryan's heart clenched at the sight, a flood of memory threatening to overwhelm him. How many mornings had he seen her just like this, soft and rumpled and achingly beautiful in the gentle light? It was a small detail but one he hadn't realized he'd missed until that moment.

"Morning," Aria said, padding with a limp across the carpet toward him. "How'd you sleep?"

Bryan gave a nonchalant shrug. "Can't complain. Your couch beats the hell out of my sad excuse for a mattress."

Aria's laugh was like music. "Hungry? I can whip up some breakfast."

He followed her into the kitchen as she began puttering about with bowls and spoons. The space was compact but efficient, a tidy expanse of butcher-block counters and gleaming appliances. The window overlooked the glistening cove.

"So, I was thinking," Bryan said, leaning against the wall. "We talked for hours, but it still felt like there was more to say, so many things to catch up on. Maybe we could talk more over coffee?"

Aria paused, a box of cereal hovering over the bowl. When she turned to face him, her expression was soft. Sad.

"Bryan..." she began, then trailed off. The unspoken rejection hung between them.

"I know," he sighed, the hopefulness in his chest already dimming. "Too much, too soon."

"It's not that." Aria set the box down, her gaze steady on his. "I care about you. I always will. But we're not getting back together. No matter how intense these past couple of days have been."

Bryan opened his mouth to argue, then thought better of it. He couldn't force Aria to want the same things he did. If there was one thing his self-help journey had taught him, it was the importance of accepting hard truths.

"I get it," he said instead. And he meant it.

He saw his portable CD behind her—on the counter where he'd left it last night. There were still two more discs left in the *Tame the Beast* Program. He'd been listening to it for Aria's sake, to improve for her, but he wasn't going to stop now. In fact, he wasn't going to stop his *overall* self-improvement journey.

In a moment of clarity, he realized Aria had returned to his life not just to freshen the fantastic memories of their time together but for another reason—to show him the man he could become. The path forward wouldn't be easy, but it was one he was finally ready to walk.

And he had Aria to thank for that.

CHAPTER FIFTY

SUNLIGHT BATHED THE HEADSTONE, casting a long shadow across the manicured lawn and sparkling the granite in the freshly cut lettering that spelled out *MATTHEW DELVIN JENNINGS*.

Silence stood before the grave with his cell phone pressed to his ear. Beside him, Bryan waited quietly, hands shoved deep in his pockets.

"Black Thorn operation in..." Silence said to Falcon on the other end of the line. He swallowed. "Fort Bragg dismantled." Another swallow. "Anchor and Horizon tech secured."

Falcon's reply was curt. "The Watchers are already tracing the origins of both projects, Suppressor. And Specialists retrieved the remaining Anchor units from the *war zone* you left behind on the highway." A pause. "But it sounds like..." He trailed off. Then, a long sigh that bordered on a growl. Then, "Sounds like you did good work out there, even if it was off the books."

Silence allowed himself a slight grin. Falcon usually came around to seeing things Silence's way.

Smart man.

"Yes, sir."

"But let's be clear," Falcon said, his tone sharpening. "This doesn't change the rules. No involvement in local matters. *Period!*"

"Yes, sir," Silence said. But Falcon had already hung up.

Pocketing the phone, Silence looked down at the faded photograph in his hand. In it, two young boys grinned up at the camera, their arms slung around each other's shoulders in front of an old red brick schoolhouse. Innocent. Carefree. A lifetime ago.

Jake and Matt.

For a moment, Silence was back at the schoolyard. He let his mind finish the memory he'd been chewing on for days.

Jake approached Archie, holding out the battered book. "Here," he said, handing it over with a smile. "I think this belongs to you."

Archie took the book with trembling hands, his eyes wide behind his oversized glasses. "Thanks, Jake," he mumbled, pride and humility battling it out. "For everything."

Jake just shrugged, his gaze flicking over to where Matt stood nursing his split lip. The other boy met his eyes. Something like reverence mingled with the pain on his face.

Jake nodded.

Matt did the same.

Turning back to Archie, Jake said, "You gonna be okay?"

The smaller boy managed a shaky nod. "Yeah. I'll be fine." With a final grateful look, he turned and hurried away across the schoolyard.

Jake watched him go, then ambled over to Matt, still leaning against the brick wall, dabbing at his lip. "How about you? You all right, man?"

Matt took his fingers away from his lip, examined the blood. "I guess. Feel kind of stupid, though. Not being able to help more, I mean."

"You did plenty," Jake said. "Standing up to those jerks? That took guts."

"Not as much guts as you," Matt said, a hint of admiration creeping into his voice, matching that look of reverence he'd shown a moment earlier.

Jake just shook his head. "It's not about guts. It's about doing what's right, even when it's hard." He reached out and clapped Matt on the shoulder. "And you did that today."

A slow smile spread across Matt's face, transforming his bruised features into something warm and bright. "Yeah," he said softly. "I guess I did."

Side by side, the two boys set off across the schoolyard under the warm afternoon sun.

Silence blinked, the memory fading as the graveyard came back into focus around him. Beside him, Bryan was watching with a questioning look.

"None of this would..." Silence began and swallowed. "Have been possible..." Another swallow. "Without your mentor's work." He gestured to the headstone. "He was a good man."

Bryan nodded. "Yes, he was."

Silence crouched down, retrieving two bottles of Heineken from the six-pack nestled in the grass by his feet. He retrieved the opener he'd slid into the case and popped both caps—*hiss, hiss.* Standing back up, he handed a bottle to Bryan, then raised his own in a toast.

"To Matt," he said.

"To Matt."

They clinked the bottles together. As they each took a

long pull of the cold beer, Silence felt a weight lift from his shoulders.

He hadn't realized the weight was there.

But he recognized then that coming into Fort Bragg, his frustration had been centered on the fact that he hadn't known the adult Matt, only the kid from the schoolyard memory.

Now, somehow, he felt like he'd gotten to know the man.

Maybe Doc Hazel had been onto something after all.

CHAPTER FIFTY-ONE

BAXTER STARED UP AT SILENCE, his golden eyes unblinking, a string of drool dangling from his whiskered chin. The cat's expression was one of pure adoration, bordering on worship.

It made Silence grumble.

He returned to the task at hand: repairing the broken leg of Mrs. Enfield's antique end table. He was back in her living room, back in the gloom, surrounded by creepy old knick-knacks and faded photographs, the air heavy with the scent of mothballs and lemon furniture polish.

Silence's hand slipped, and his finger shot forward, a splinter of wood piercing his skin. He flinched.

"Ow! Shit!"

There was an immediate rebuke from a withered voice. "Language! Watch how you're talkin' around an old lady, Silence baby."

Mrs. Enfield scowled at him from her perch on the armchair.

"Sorry, ma'am."

Silence was no stranger to fixing things, but the splintered wood seemed determined to thwart his efforts. He growled under his breath as the leg refused to align properly.

"You'll get it, Si," Mrs. Enfield said. "Don't worry."

Her encouragement only compounded his frustration. He glanced at her, taking in her dark, papery skin and milky eyes.

She coughed.

But it was a gentle cough. Less crackling than it had sounded before Silence had left. Less phlegmy. Mrs. Enfield's head cold had passed, leaving only a faint rasp to her breathing.

But the close call had shaken Silence more than he cared to admit.

Last night in California, when he called her, he thanked her. But he hadn't *really* thanked her.

She'd been so important to him for so long. A guiding light. A caring soul.

And she'd been the one, all those years ago, to steer him away from self-pity, from the bottle, from becoming another carbon copy of his old man, a person who'd effectively died shortly after moving across the country to Pensacola, leaving the memory of his real self back in Fort Bragg.

"I want to..." he said, setting the table leg aside. "Thank you for all..." He swallowed. "You've done—

She waved a hand, cutting him off. "I know, Si. You already thanked me last night."

"But—"

"*Shh*. You stop this."

"But I want to say it."

Mrs. Enfield smiled. And sighed. "Well, go on, then."

"Thank you."

"I'm here for you," she said simply. A beat passed, then, "Now fix my table."

"Yes, ma'am."

He went back to work.

As he twisted a loose shard of wood away from the break, he considered what Mrs. Enfield had said before he left for Fort Bragg—that it's okay for two individuals to care about each other in unequal measure.

Maybe she would never know how much she meant to him.

Or maybe it was the other way around.

He felt eyes upon him. Turned.

Baxter had moved in the last minute or so, unbeknownst to Silence. Now, he was seated a few feet behind Silence. Purring. Cat-smiling. Drooling on the hardwood.

Certainly, Baxter was more attached to Silence than vice versa.

But ... perhaps the connection wasn't *that* lopsided. Even with the ghastly drooling, Baxter was a good boy.

That's how connections form. That was the way of things. Different levels of feeling, all tangled up together.

In the end, maybe that was okay.

ALSO BY ERIK CARTER

Ty Draker Action Thrillers Series
Coming soon.

Silence Jones Action Thrillers Series
Novels:
- *The Suppressor*
- *Hush Hush*
- *Tight-Lipped*
- *Before the Storm*
- *Dead Air*
- *Speechless*
- *Quiet as the Grave*
- *Don't Speak*
- *A Strangled Cry*
- *Muted*
- *In the Dead of Night*
- *Tell No Tales*
- *Unspoken*
- *Dying Breath*

Novella:
- *Deadly Silence*

Dale Conley Action Thrillers Series
Novels:
- *Stone Groove*

Dream On

The Lowdown

Get Real

Talkin' Jive

Be Still

Jump Back

The Skinny

No Fake

Novella:

Get Down

ACKNOWLEDGMENTS

For their involvement with *Tell No Tales*, I would like to give a sincere thank you to:

My ARC readers, for providing reviews and catching typos. Thanks!

Printed in Great Britain
by Amazon